LONG TIME COMING

AN EASTERN SHORE MYSTERY

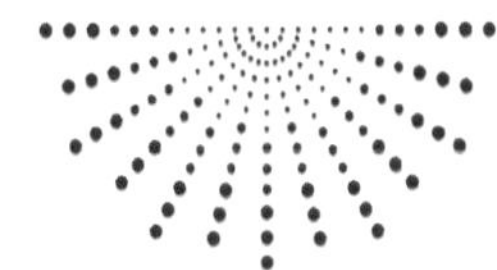

CHERIL THOMAS

A mysterious fire, a dead man, and a hurricane on the way.

When an abandoned church goes up in flames in the middle of the night, attorney Grace Reagan assumes it's an accident—until a body is found in the ruins and her trusted assistant, paralegal Lily Travers, becomes the prime suspect.

The only witness is Irene Jensen, a sharp-tongued neighbor with a grudge—and a shaky grasp on reality. Her wild accusations trigger an investigation that unearths a shocking link to Lily's past and disturbing questions about the victim's identity. And when a charming Baltimore police detective arrives, the mystery—and the danger—only deepen.

With Hurricane Florian bearing down on the Eastern Shore, Grace and Lily stumble into a deadly trap. A rescue mission turns into a nightmare as they're targeted by a killer with nothing to lose —and every reason to silence them.

Long Time Coming **is a gripping, twisty tale of loyalty, long shadows, and the desperate choices that come back to haunt us.**

The eighth installment in the beloved Eastern Shore Mysteries is perfect for readers new to the series as well as longtime fans.

The Eastern Shore Mysteries

Grace Reagan Novels

Squatter's Rights

A Commission on Murder

Bad Intent

Death and Consequences

Twisted Karma

In the Absence of Truth

Tangled Webs

Long Time Coming

The Eastern Shore Mysteries Box Set, Books 1-3

The Eastern Shore Mysteries Box Set, Books 4-6

A Little Christmas War (A Grace Reagan Short Mystery)

Borrowed Trouble (A Grace Reagan Novella)

Ellender York Novels

The Nineteenth Gift (An Ellender York Short Mystery)

The Correction Agency (A Grace Reagan and Ellender York Novella)

Want a **FREE** copy of **BORROWED TROUBLE**?** Sign up for my monthly newsletter! https://www.CherilThomas.com.

Thank you for reading!

*For Cynthia Haddaway, Judith Hohman, Tarah Kleinert,
and Roxanne Tury.*

"To be wronged is nothing unless you continue to remember it."

— CONFUCIUS

"Guilt doesn't die with the one who earned it."

— MARJORIE BATTSLEY

CHAPTER ONE

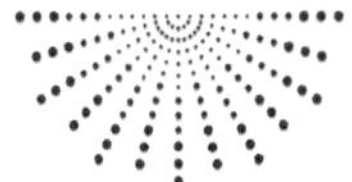

WEDNESDAY, SEPTEMBER 12

IRENE

"Doctor!" The old woman on the stretcher was frail, her hands shaking so hard the sheet was wadded into a ball, but her voice was clear when she repeated her demand for a lawyer.

Dr. Orlando Linbow glanced at the chart that held little information for a patient delivered to the hospital with a police escort. "Let me check with—"

"My lawyer," Irene Jensen snapped, sounding less like an octogenarian and more like someone who could reach up and smack him if he gave her grief. "Don't know which last name she uses now, but her first name is Grace. Works over in Mallard Bay."

The ER doctor checked the patient's chart again. Mrs. Jensen looked old enough to match her birthdate, but her deep-set brown eyes were sharp, and they were focused on him. When she addressed him as "doctor," her tone suggested she doubted his qualifications.

"No ma'am. I don't know your attorney, but there's a sheriff's deputy in the waiting room. Do you want me to—"

"I *want* . . ." Irene sat up suddenly, startling the doctor, who jerked backward.

"Your attorney," he said hastily, moving to open the cubicle's glass door. Privacy no longer seemed prudent. "Let me see what I can do."

In the hallway, he saw only fellow employees plodding through the last half of the midnight-to-eight shift.

He could feel the woman's eyes on him as he fumbled his phone out of his jacket pocket and called his mother. If he had to wake someone at this hour, it might as well be someone useful. His parents lived in Denton, but municipal boundaries were just lines on a map to Eastern Shore natives. Within five minutes, he had the number for Reagan and Mosley, Attorneys at Law.

He tried to speak with authority as he left a voicemail for Grace Reagan, but lost credibility when Mrs. Jensen added to the background noise, yelling, "Are you playin' on that phone? I thought you were gettin' me a painkiller!"

He wrapped up his voice message with, "Just come as soon as you can," and hung up as his patient started yelling for a bedpan.

It was going to be a long three hours until his shift ended.

CHAPTER TWO

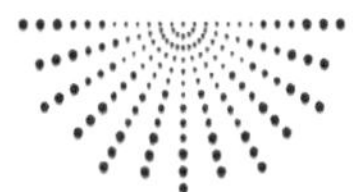

It was never good when mornings started before sunrise with a call from the Kingston County Sheriff. Grace Reagan watched her husband pulling clothes out of the closet while holding his phone between his shoulder and ear. His side of the conversation consisted of "Where," and "when," and ended with, "I'm on my way."

Grace had been the wife of Mallard Bay's police chief for only a couple of years, but she knew whatever had happened wasn't good.

Mac sat beside her. "I don't have much in the way of details, but Lily is at the scene of a fire out at Twin Corners—that abandoned church is burning. She called 911, and the responding sheriff's deputy called me."

Lily Travers, who practically ran Grace's law firm single-hand-edly, was one of the smartest people she knew. Why was she out in the middle of nowhere in the wee hours of the morning? "Wait, that's where the Jensen family lives. Irene used to be a client of mine." Grace paused as another thought struck her. "Why did the deputy contact you? Twin Corners isn't your jurisdiction."

"Irene asked them to. I've—"

"Known her for years," Grace finished for him, frowning as she sat up. If she lived in Mallard Bay for the rest of her life, she'd still be a 'come here.' Mac would always outrank her on the trust meter with his fellow locals.

"Try to get a little more sleep, honey," Mac said. "The sheriff is in charge at the scene. I'll just stop by there and see if they need anything, then I'll go to the hospital and check on Irene. Apparently, her granddaughter is out of town and Irene was alone at the house. I'll call you if she needs you. And I'll make sure Lily's okay." His phone rang again, and he smiled at Grace. "Avril. I guess she's heard about the fire, too. She'll be calling you next, you know."

"That's what friends do—share the panic." Grace blew him a kiss as she watched him leave.

They'd left the windows open the night before, and the air smelled faintly of creek mud and the brackish tang of the Little Wye River. Storms were moving in—too late to stop a fire, though. She remembered the heavily wooded area around the Jensen home and the abandoned church next door. Grace had always thought it was a creepy setting and couldn't imagine how frightened Irene must have been.

When she heard the front door close, she grabbed her phone and found Irene's number. Not surprisingly, her call went to voicemail, and she left a message. Sometimes it seemed that her work for clients was part legal maneuvering and part minding other people's business.

Her phone rang just as coffee began dripping into the pot. Avril Oxley's voice filled the kitchen. Grace's best friend was an institution in Mallard Bay and a force to be reckoned with. Twice Grace's age, most days Avril also had twice her energy. She had gotten all the information Mac had, and now she needed a sympathetic ear.

While packing lunch and preparing breakfast for her children and their springer spaniel, Rocky, Grace listened to Avril lament the loss of the eighteenth-century church, which was slated to be renovated by a local historic preservation society. "The fire didn't damage Irene's produce stand, at least that's something," she said. "But there's so much damage to the church, the county may condemn the entire property, which would mean customers won't be able to use the parking lot over there anymore."

That would spell disaster for Irene's little business but Grace didn't add that gloomy thought to Avril's worries. Soon the urgent demands of three-year-old Fiona and eighteen-month-old Sonny freed her from the call.

She kept checking for messages throughout the morning routine, but nothing came from Mac. Local news channels were focused on a tropical storm that was threatening the mid-Atlantic seaboard. The thought of shortages—toilet paper, eggs, milk—at the mere suggestion of a potential hurricane made her groan. But there were immediate problems to handle, and she needed to get to work.

As the managing attorney for her law firm, Grace liked to be the first to arrive at the office. It seldom happened, though, and this morning was no exception.

"Have you heard the news?" Marjorie Battsley asked as soon as Grace walked through the back door of the stately old Victorian that housed the firm.

"You mean your cousin is finally going to fix the air conditioning?" Marjorie was talking about the fire at Twin Corners but Grace wanted her to focus on her job and not local gossip. The building's aging HVAC system labored against the humidity, making the air inside feel only marginally cooler than outside.

"I told you the boy will be here when the parts he needs come in." Diplomacy and deference weren't Marjorie's strong suits. "I'm talking about the old church out next to the Jensen place."

Well, she'd wanted information on the fire, Grace thought. This was a fast way to get it. Her partner's longtime secretary, not-too-affectionately known as The Bat, kept a finger in every pot in the county. If Marjorie wasn't connected to someone who'd been present at a disaster, she was consumed with tracking down the details. Her reports were usually exaggerated but always contained a nugget of truth.

"Mac's out at Twin Corners, but I haven't heard from him," Grace said, taking the path of least resistance. "What about you? Any information about how it happened?"

Marjorie actually smiled, a rare occurrence this early in the day —especially if Grace was present—but being first with fresh gossip was her everything. "No. But that's not the big news. I got the latest from Lee a little while ago. I'm sure he let you sleep right through everything."

As Mac's former sister-in-law, Marjorie took every opportunity to reinforce her status by using his formal first name. Mac said every time she did it, he felt like he was ten and about to be punished.

Grace made herself let it all slide. The longer she talked with Marjorie, the longer she went without coffee. "Okay," she said with a forced smile. "What did my husband say?"

"That he needed to cancel lunch with you. A body was found in the church, and the arson investigation is focused on that. He called because he knows old Irene Jensen has been a client of ours."

Grace was so shocked she said the first words that came to her. "Are you sure? I mean about there being a body in the church."

"Well, I'm not making it up!"

Jeff Carone, the firm's administrative assistant, poked his head around the doorway to the outer office. "Not that I'm eavesdropping," he winked at Marjorie, who gave him a thumbs-up, "but I heard one of the other customers talking about Twin Corners while I was in line at Three Pigs. Marjorie's right. They said the police don't know who the dead guy is, but he looks like he just went to sleep." He waved a white bag in front of them. "Feels crass to mention food after that, but there was a special on bacon croissants. I got four."

Not taking her eyes off the delectable smelling pastry Jeff placed on the counter next to her, Grace called Mac, only to be immediately shuttled to his voicemail.

"Lee said he'd be unavailable for a while." Marjorie delicately touched the corners of her mouth with an embroidered hanky. Half her croissant was gone, and she was eyeing Grace's.

Snatching it up, Grace thanked Jeff profusely and without looking at Marjorie, said, "Maybe Lily will have more details."

As she headed toward her office, Marjorie called out, "I'm sure she will, but you'll have to wait to hear them. Word is, Lily's going to be arrested."

CHAPTER THREE

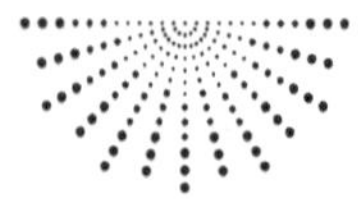

"I got a phone call from Irene Jensen." Lily looked as neat and efficient as always, but her face told the story of her long night. "I hadn't talked to her in ages. Her granddaughter, Dove, is a friend of mine. I'd agreed to be an emergency contact for Irene while Dove delivered her five-year-old daughter, Brooklyn, to her ex in Los Angeles for court-ordered visitation. I never expected Irene to contact me—she's never liked me."

"Doesn't like me either, remember?" Grace smiled sympathetically. "She fired us."

"Yeah. Anyway, Dove can back me up on this. She told me her grandmother has night terrors that have been getting worse. Apparently, they're bad enough that Irene agreed to stay with her sister and Dove left thinking everything was handled. She wasn't in the air an hour before Irene made her sister Mimi take her home."

"Sounds about right. As I recall, those two are like oil and water."

"More like gasoline and a match." Lily broke into nervous laughter. "Jeez, it was a long night. That was a terrible thing to say."

Grace refilled their coffee cups while Lily got herself together.

"When Irene called me about three o'clock, she was crying and talking about noises at the church next door. When I realized she was at home alone, I suggested calling the police, but she said she was more afraid of them than intruders." Lily's cheeks flushed pink. "I swear, Grace, if I thought there was real danger, I would've called Trey."

Despite the tense atmosphere, Grace grinned. Lily's relationship with Tremaine Harper, Mac's backup on the Mallard Bay police force, was the worst-kept secret in town, but Lily never mentioned it.

"Trey had to be on patrol early this morning and I didn't want to wake him. I thought I knew what I was dealing with when Irene asked me to come out. I must have been half asleep because I felt relieved that she wanted help and wasn't being rude."

"So, what happened when you got there?"

"Irene's house was dark, and she wouldn't answer my knocking. That's when I saw flames coming from the church. I called 911 and kept pounding on her door until the fire trucks arrived."

"Was she okay?"

"Appeared to be. Once the firefighters showed up, she came out in her robe and pajamas, demanding to know what was happening. When she saw the church, she started yelling." Lily's voice turned bitter. "And after *that* she said, 'Lily Travers, why did you set that fire?'"

They heard a snort from the outer office. Lily shrugged, raised her voice and said, "Marjorie, come on in. You may as well hear it all from me. I'm sure we'll all be dealing with the fallout from last night for a long time."

"In short," Lily said, "it was chaos. A sheriff's deputy arrived during Irene's tirade, and then a firefighter found an unconscious person in the coat closet of the church."

"That much is already making the rounds," Marjorie said. "Do you know who it is? What happened to them?"

Lily looked more upset with each question. "It was crazy for a while, especially when we heard the person was dead. Someone let it slip that the deceased was a man, and that was enough to set Irene off. She switched to saying I'd killed him. I might've been in real trouble, except that right after that, she announced that I was working for Avril."

"Avril?" Grace said. "That's crazy."

"Glad you think so."

They all turned as Avril walked in.

Grace got up and dragged another chair over to the table. "Mac would have called me if you needed legal representation. Come sit down and tell us what's happening."

"I was bringing everyone up to speed," Lily added. "I just got here myself, and now you and I can compare notes."

"Oh, good," Avril said sarcastically. "Then perhaps we can get a group rate from our favorite attorney."

Grace, Lily, and Marjorie exchanged glances. Whatever differences they had in the office, they were united in their friendship with Avril.

Lily spoke up first. "I'm sure neither of us is under serious consideration for anything that happened out at Twin Corners. Irene acted irrationally, but that might have been the shock of seeing the fire. Besides, she's never liked me, and there I was standing in her yard."

"But she called you and asked you to come," Grace said.

"Which she denied before 'remembering' it." Lily said. "She was all over the place, jumping back and forth between things Dove and I had done as kids and her disapproval of my current lifestyle.

She's still mad at you, boss. And somehow, she knew about Trey and me."

"I knew it!" Marjorie sat back in her chair with a satisfied smile. "You two aren't fooling anyone, you know."

Lily ignored her. "Irene really sounded unhinged once she got started on you, Avril. Which is a good thing for us, I guess. She said you sent me to burn the church down because she wouldn't let you develop the property."

"She's certainly been hostile in her protests against the Preservation Society's plans to save the building and sell it, but that's insane," Avril said.

"I tried to reassure her, but she fell apart, saying there were already too many strangers and people watching her. She cried until she got sick. Eventually, a deputy called an ambulance for her. After that, she demanded to see Mac."

"Anyone mention questioning you further?" Grace asked.

"When Mac showed up, he sort of organized everything with the sheriff's deputy who was in charge by that time. The deputy told me that Avril and I will have an interview with Sheriff Carlisle later today. Hopefully, they'll have some information about the poor person in the church soon."

"Are you okay?" Marjorie asked Avril. "You look tired. Let me get you some coffee and something to eat."

"I don't want anything but answers," Avril said. "I have to say that I've been worried about Irene for a while. We've known each other all our lives. Not close friends, but still. She's not been looking good. I wish I could help her."

Grace tried to imagine Avril and Irene as kids. Of course, they'd been young once, but both were formidable women in their eighties, and that was the only way she had ever known them.

Lily said, "I've talked to Mimi. She's at the hospital now, and promises not let Irene out of her sight until Dove gets home."

Grace's cell phone lit up with her home number. "Oh, good," she said, reaching to take the call. "I was worried I wouldn't have any more problems today."

CHAPTER FOUR

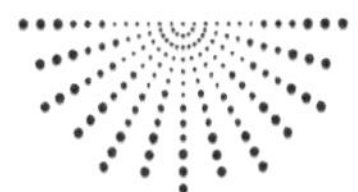

"Your sister arrived a half hour ago," Hallie Overton said, her irritation coming through clearly, even though she was whispering into her phone.

Grace winced. Their nanny was the only reason she and Mac could keep up their demanding work schedules, and if Hallie decided to move on to a less chaotic household—well, Grace never let her thoughts wander into that territory. "I promise this is news to me. Stephanie didn't tell me she was coming. Did she say how long she's staying?"

Sounding somewhat mollified, Hallie said, "No. She also said not to call you because she's giving you a surprise party. There are four suitcases and about a dozen shopping bags in the hall, and the kids are going through piles of candy and toys. She's given me the afternoon off because she's going to take care of her niece and nephew."

"No, no, no. I'm so sorry, Hallie. No, I don't want you to leave her there alone with the children." Grace stopped abruptly, surprised at the vehemence she felt behind her own words. Stephanie was family, after all. A half-sister Grace had only known less than a year, but still, why shouldn't she be left alone with Fiona and Sonny? She shut down the internal argument and apologized again to Hallie. "It's not your job to deal with my crazy sister. Get the children's lunch ready. They probably won't want it now, but they'll go for a picnic in the backyard. Meantime, I'll call Stephanie."

And, as usual, that turned out to be easier said than done.

"That little tattletale!" Stephanie sputtered. "She's ruined my surprise. I was going to have a nice dinner on the table and the children all played out and ready for bed when you got home. I thought that would be a nice change for you, seeing as how this place is usually a wreck. Honestly, that girl really needs to do better at keeping the place clean."

"That girl," Grace said with exaggerated patience, "is a professional child caregiver, not a maid. She doesn't clean houses. We've talked about this before, Stephanie. Both kids have issues with sugar. Please tell me you haven't let them eat candy."

"Don't be silly. I've raised two healthy girls, you know, and I always let them have a little candy. Life is too short, Grace, and you should see the smiles on their faces." Grace heard the phone drop, and then bits and pieces of disjointed conversations, and a child crying. When Stephanie came back to the phone, her tone was brisk. "Everything is okay. All kids throw up when they eat too fast, but I cleaned it up."

"Which one?" Grace asked and wasn't surprised to hear that it was Sonny who had lost his breakfast.

"Well," Stephanie sighed, "what are we going to do? I'm out in the kitchen, leaving Miss Thang to take care of her charges. Honestly, Grace, I only meant to give all of you a nice surprise. I also want to make it up to Mac for the last visit when I never got around to making my special paella. That poor man had to cook every dinner while I was here, and I wanted to show him how much I appreciated it."

Grace hung onto her temper as her sister managed to insult her cooking, choice of caregivers, housekeeping, and henpecked husband, all in a non-apology. This wasn't a conversation to have at the office. She lured Stephanie out of the house with an offer of lunch at Adelaide's Garden, hoping that in a neutral setting, she could make her sister understand her visits needed non-negotiable boundaries.

But for the moment, she still had her paying job to handle. She went out to Lily's desk to rearrange the afternoon schedule, wrapping her instructions up with, "Call me if anything else happens about the fire. I can be back here in a flash."

"Sure," Lily said, but she didn't look up from her computer screen. "I'll move some stuff around, but before you go, take a look at the transcriptions of our voicemail messages." She waved Grace around to her side and pointed at the screen.

"We missed calls?" Grace frowned. "When? Jeff's been right by the phone."

"Five ten this morning. Another at five thirty and the last one at six fifteen. I guess Marjorie decided not to check because, technically, that's my job and I came in late."

They both aimed glares in the general direction of Marjorie's office on Cyrus Mosley's side of the building.

"Anything urgent?" Grace said. "Other than my desire to fire someone?"

"Hard to say." Lily leaned in to read the screen. "The first one is from a Doctor Linbow at Easton Hospital asking you to come to the ER as soon as possible. Irene Jensen was asking for you." She looked up at Grace and added, "That must have been where the EMTs took her this morning."

"But she—"

"Fired you last year. Yeah, apparently, she remembered that because someone else in the ER called twenty minutes later and said they'd reached Irene's sister, and you didn't need to come. I listened to the recording, and you can hear Irene demanding breakfast."

"You recognized her voice?"

"Known her all my life, remember?" Lily said. "The last message is from Irene herself." She opened the message and hit the Play arrow.

"Sorry for the trouble, Grace." Irene Jensen's words had a quiver but were easy to understand. "I forgot I fired you, but I'm okay now. Talking to Mac made me feel better. You're still fired, so never mind." The loud click of the landline phone ended the brief message.

"Goodbye to you, too, Irene," Grace said, but she was smiling in relief.

"Pretty much the way she fired us last time," Lily said. "Only then she wasn't accusing me of arson."

Grace sighed. "You know the drill. Preserve the messages so no one accidentally deletes them. Send me copies of everything. We may need to interview the doctor and staff later."

"Got it. Enjoy your lunch with Stephanie."

"Very funny. If I'm not back by two, call me with a crisis that can't wait."

"Will do," Lily said. "There ought to be several to choose from by then."

CHAPTER FIVE

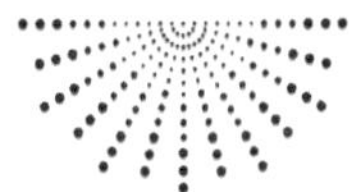

Over crab bisque and a fruit salad, Stephanie gradually came through with the real reason she'd shown up with no warning.

"I'm in shock and had to get away from home for a while," she said. "Jerry is selling our house out from under me. He wanted me to be there today to meet with the real estate agent and her appraiser, but I couldn't make myself do it. I know it's inevitable, though. He talked me into signing for a second mortgage six months ago, then he spent all of our equity." She downed half a glass of wine in two gulps and ran a finger carefully under her wet lower eyelashes. "And that's not all. Three weeks ago, the firm he worked for decided Jerry was a liability and cut him loose."

"What?" Grace reached across the table and took Stephanie's hand. The last time she and Mac had been with Stephanie's stockbroker husband, all Jerry could talk about was his clients' successes. He'd offered to set up a portfolio for them "with a heavy family discount." Mac told Grace later that he could understand why Jerry was so successful, but there was no way he was getting his hands on their money.

"A *liability*," Stephanie repeated. "That's their term for sleeping with a client's wife, skimming money from the client's accounts, and using insider knowledge to build a new portfolio for his girlfriend."

Grace was speechless. All she could come up with was, "Oh, Stephanie."

"Yep. Last year's little hairstylist wasn't his first dalliance. He wasn't discreet with his new illegal hobby, or the married woman he was cheating with. They were caught in bed by her husband, who fired Jerry, then audited his portfolio and sued the firm. Cuffer, Swaine, and Ruddle paid out a huge hunk of money to make everything go away. Money they want Jerry to pay back."

Grace thought about good, solid, *boring* Jerry. She couldn't match her memory of him to the story Stephanie was telling. "So, he isn't facing any criminal charges for embezzlement, or anything?"

"Not as long as he stays out of the industry and doesn't contact or have anything to do with the firm. In short, he can flip hamburgers or sell cars, but his career in the financial world is over."

Grace just waited, speechless with pity, while her sister sipped more wine and calmed down. She couldn't imagine being in such a situation. In the first awkward months of her relationship with Stephanie, Jerry had been gracious to Grace. He appeared to support Stephanie, and, as far as she could see, had been kind to their father. But all of that changed after Jonathan's death in early February. Whatever tie had bound him to Stephanie and their marriage seemed to vanish almost overnight.

"You'll get through this, Steph," she tried, inwardly cringing at the banality of her words. "And you'll be happy again."

"Well, that will be a neat trick. Happiness means money, Grace. And Jerry spent all of ours." She sat up straight and added, "But I'm not helpless, or stupid, and I'll make Jerry sorry that he ever thought I was."

CHAPTER SIX

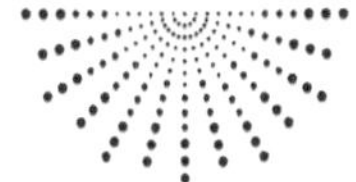

THURSDAY, SEPTEMBER 13

Mac left early again the next morning, but not before they had coffee on the patio. The overnight rain had left everything with a glistening sheen, though the moisture was already evaporating in the morning warmth.

Grace wanted to think of it as a romantic connection, but she knew Mac just wanted to talk outside in case their conversation woke Stephanie. She'd skipped dinner last night and stayed in her room, but Mac had heard her leave at eleven.

"Your sister didn't come in until nearly five this morning. I don't like this, Grace."

She didn't like it either, but she knew Stephanie often went driving when she was upset, and right now, there was plenty to be upset about. Still—six hours? There was nothing to be done about it now, though.

She changed the subject to the Twin Corners fire.

"No new developments that I know of." He drained his cup and stood up to leave. "Try not to worry. Just because I can't talk about it doesn't mean things are worse for Lily."

He wasn't budging off the position he'd held the night

before. He hadn't shared any information she wouldn't hear at the bank or market. Or through the grapevine at the office. He'd even been short with her in describing his conversation with Irene Jensen at the hospital, saying only that Irene insisted on going back home alone instead of to her sister's house.

"That's it?" Grace protested. "That's all you're going to tell me?" She didn't want to start an argument before he left, but before she could think of another way to get the information she wanted, he grinned at her and gave her a sound kiss.

"Let's make a deal," he said, still holding her close. "You stop looking so tense and I promise I'll give you all the best gossip before I tell Margie."

"But you aren't telling me anything!" She swatted his arm, he tickled her, and with another kiss, he was gone.

As she watched him drive away, noise from the nursery pulled her back to reality on the home front. She called Hallie, who was delighted with the suggestion of taking the kids to Giggle and Romp, a new activity center for preschoolers on Kent Island.

"I'll drop them off with you on my way into work," Grace said. She wasn't taking any chances of Stephanie and Hallie meeting up today. Her family sorted for the moment, she got the kids and herself ready, refusing to worry anymore about her sister until she absolutely had to.

"Mac called," Lily said as she walked into the office.

Grace checked her phone. No missed calls or messages. Why had he tried to reach her on the office line? She had her answer when he picked up her return call and she heard his professional tone. This was business. No teasing or affection, just, "I'm on my way over. I need to talk to Lily."

Not her. Lily. There was trouble, and he brought it to her office five minutes later.

"I need to take Lily's statement about the fire out at Twin Corners," he said when the three of them were seated around the small conference table in Grace's office. He set his phone to record, covered the preliminary details and cautions, and said, "Where were you on the evening of Tuesday, September 11?"

Mac made notes as Lily described coming home from a friend's wedding in Richmond earlier in the day and having a late dinner at her house with Tremaine Harper. He didn't smile or even blink at the mention of his sergeant's name. Grace was sure he'd gotten those details from Trey.

"And in the early morning hours of September 12?"

"I got a call from Irene Jensen saying she needed help. She had promised her sister Mimi that she would call me if she had trouble, because I'm closer to Twin Corners than Mimi is. She lives in Centreville. Irene insisted she didn't want the police. She was just scared. I went to her home, saw the fire and called 911."

Mac said, "The good news is that Dove has confirmed that you were Mimi's backup if she had a problem with Irene. Dove got home late last night, and the sheriff is interviewing her today. The not-so-good news is that you're still a suspect because Irene was emphatic in her statement that you started the fire."

"Oh, how stupid!" Lily looked first at Grace, then Mac. "No one believes that, do they?"

"Sheriff Carlisle doesn't know you like I do," Mac said. "And preliminary reports indicate the deceased person found in the church didn't die of natural causes."

"Whoa," Grace said. "You couldn't have opened with that bombshell?" Mac hadn't read Lily her rights, so she wasn't in eminent danger of being arrested, but Grace still didn't like the way the interview was going. "So, how did this person die?"

"I don't have that information."

Grace's neck tingled as she picked up on what he wasn't saying. "What information do you have? Was it smoke inhalation?"

Mac gave her a level look and ignored her questions. "Strange or not, everything Irene Jensen said has to be investigated." Turning to Lily, he said, "When was the last time you talked to Dove or her ex-husband, Dominic Pontello?"

"I haven't talked to Dom since he left Mallard Bay. Dove called me yesterday before she boarded her flight in Los Angeles." Lily hesitated, then continued. "I told her everything that had happened. She was really upset."

"With you?" Mac asked.

"No!"

"When did you last see Dove and Irene before the night of the fire?"

"I keep in touch with Dove and babysit for Brooklyn fairly often. I saw Dove last week. As for her grandmother, if I see Miss Irene, I avoid her, but I don't think she leaves home much anymore. I saw her in the bank last month, I think."

"Let's try this another way," Mac said. "When was the last time you were at Irene's house?"

Grace was surprised when Lily said, "Last year." She sounded evasive and looked embarrassed but didn't elaborate.

The office's unreliable central air system had given up the fight against the oppressive humidity outside. Patches of condensation fogged the windows and gave the room a claustrophobic feel. Mac took a handkerchief from his pocket and wiped his forehead. "Don't make me pull it out of you, Lily," he said.

Grace nodded when Lily looked at her.

"Last summer, a year ago, in August. The day after I got home from camp."

"That would be the Marine reserve annual training camp?"

"Yes," then after a moment, Lily added, "Dove asked me to come out to their house and help her install new locks on their doors. Irene was upset about hikers and campers in their woods, and Dove had to do something to appease her. When I got there, Irene asked—told—me to go over and have a look at the church. She's been the unofficial caretaker of that property since the last congregation dissolved and walked away years ago, and she thought it might need new locks, too. She was worried about trespassers."

Mac looked surprised. "She didn't mention that."

"As I said, she's strange. Probably thought she'd get blamed for the fire."

"Do you think she set it?"

"I don't know."

Mac waited for more, but when Lily stayed silent, he said, "Did you put new locks on the church?"

"There was nothing wrong with the old ones. We just cleaned them up and oiled them. Irene was happy with that. Well, as happy as she gets when I'm around."

"What was the condition of the church? Did you go inside?"

"Dove and I did, yes. It was older, dirtier, and more cobwebby than when we played in it as kids, but otherwise about the same. It looked as if the last preacher out the door just took the candlesticks and hymnals and left. The pews were still there, and the stained-glass windows were intact. There was a small hole in the ceiling. A few soft spots in the floor."

"Any idea when it was used last?"

"For religious purposes? I don't know. As kids, Dove and I played in there a lot. It had been abandoned for a while even back then. Miss Irene would get really mad if she caught us. Once, she said we were little heathens, and a lightning bolt would hit us." Lily's face lit up at the memory and she lost her defensive posture. "I went home and asked my mom what a heathen was. She made me look it up. Then she said Miss Irene was an ignorant curmudgeon, but that Dove and I were sacrilegious. Then I had to go back to the dictionary to look all that up while I did time out in my room."

"Awesome," Grace said. "I need to take notes from your mother."

"She's a fan of yours too. If you two ever gang up on me, I'll have to reenlist to save myself."

"Can we return to this interview, please?" Mac smiled briefly. "Dove was living with her grandmother back then, right?"

Lily blinked and said, "You know she was, Chief."

"And I am establishing what you know," Mac countered.

After a pause, Lily said, "Dove's mom, Debbie, was never in the picture. She left Dove with her grandparents when she was an infant. Dove doesn't talk about her—ever. Debbie died the summer before second grade from a drug overdose. Then, a couple of years later, Mr. Harvey died." With a glance at Grace, she added. "He was Irene's husband—Dove's granddad. Since then, it's just been Dove and Miss Irene. Dove calls her 'Reenie,' by the way, but I guess you know that."

"Other than the years she was married to Dominic Pontello, has Dove always lived with Irene?"

"Yes, but now that Brooklyn's getting older, she wants to move out of that house. It's not a good place to raise a child."

"So, what do you think?" Grace asked Mac after Lily returned to her office.

"Honey, I really don't know much at this point." He leaned over to whisper in her ear. "Will you do me a favor, anyway?"

"I'm going to take a leap here and guess that you don't mean anything we might both enjoy?"

"We need to talk about your sister."

"Mac, please—"

"Just reminding you we have to make some decisions about her."

When he was gone, she pushed her aggravating home life out of her mind. Lily didn't want to talk about the fire, so for the rest of the day, they dealt with clients' DUIs, neighboring property owner disputes, and broken contracts.

Mac called just as Grace was leaving the office at four o'clock. "Can it wait?" she asked as she opened the rear door of the office. "I'm doing a grocery run before I get the kids from Hallie."

"Sorry." He was back to the formal tone she had heard that morning. "The sheriff wants to talk to Lily."

CHAPTER SEVEN

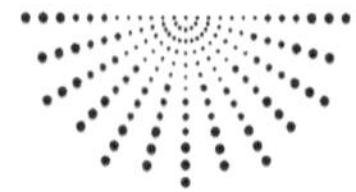

Grace and Lily sat facing Sheriff Grant Carlisle and a baby-faced deputy in an interview room at the Kingston County Sheriff's Office. Mac sat at the end of the metal table, looking uncomfortable. He'd told Grace that Carlisle just wanted to update Lily's statement, but he had seemed worried. Lily was family to them and Grace knew her husband was in a difficult position.

They waited while the sheriff started the recorder and identified each of them, the date and time, and the location. Finally, he read Lily her rights. "I'm recording this conversation and following standard protocol," Carlisle said. "We're investigating a complaint by a citizen, and this conversation is as much a fact-finding mission as anything. The sooner we put rumors to rest, the sooner Kingston County can move on from this tragedy."

The sheriff was a thin man with a beaky nose that gave him a hawk-like appearance. Grace hoped Mac was right about Carlisle being an experienced law enforcement officer. So far, he just sounded like a politician. She said, "You've given my client a Miranda warning for a fact-finding mission?"

"Chief McNamara and I discussed that," Carlisle replied. "With another person of interest and a different attorney, we might've done that. But I'm sure you will appreciate our abundance of caution once we explain what we're here to discuss."

Mac frowned, and Grace thought he wasn't pleased at being included in the Sheriff's dubious explanation.

Carlisle opened a folder and slid a photograph across the table. "As you can see, this was taken today at Twin Corners Church."

Grace picked up the photograph. Only the rear of the building looked damaged.

Carlisle handed her two more photos of the church from different angles. "Three burn barrels of cardboard boxes and paper were lined up against the rear outside wall and set on fire. Fortunately, the fire department arrived in time to save the building, but a lot of damage was done." He paused, then asked Lily if she wanted some water.

"No," Lily replied, then added politely, "Thank you."

"Ms. Travers, I have the statement you gave Chief McNamara, as well as statements taken from Mrs. Irene Jensen. There are some inconsistencies."

In the silence that followed, they could hear bits of conversation from the hallway outside. Grace looked at her watch. "Sheriff Carlisle, neither Ms. Travers nor I will volunteer information without specific questions from you. I'm sure you'll appreciate that this has nothing to do with our lack of respect for you or your office. But if you want to know something, ask your questions. Again, no disrespect, but I'm paying double time for a babysitter, so if we could move this along?"

Sitting military-straight and speaking in a neutral tone, Lily answered questions for the next half hour. Her relationship with each member of the Jensen family was established. Then she briefly described her interactions with Dove since they'd left high school and gave a detailed accounting of the day and evening before the fire.

"So basically," Carlisle said, "you and Dove Jensen are close friends even though you don't visit her home. You babysit for her, but you aren't in each other's company often without her daughter. Is that correct?" He pursed his lips when she agreed. "But it sounds like back when you were kids, you told each other everything. You were BFFs in your teenage years. Would you have told Dove when you did something wrong?"

"Is that a rhetorical question, Sheriff?" Grace asked.

Carlisle took a small recorder from his uniform pocket, laid it on the table between them, and hit *Play*.

The wavering voice of an old woman filled the room, and they listened to Irene Jensen say that fifteen-year-old Lily had defaced the interior of the Twin Corners Church and threatened to burn it down.

Grace shut the questioning down immediately. "Is that recording your evidence, Sheriff? Because I'll—"

"Hold it, hold it." Carlisle held his hands up in mock surrender. "If I put any stock in what Mrs. Jensen said, I would arrest Ms. Travers. But I have to investigate every angle, you know?"

Lily reached out and touched Grace's arm.

"A word with my client in private?" Grace said. "And not in this room." She pointed to the mirror.

"I understand." Carlisle stood and gave her a rueful smile. "You are welcome to adjourn to the ladies' room, unless you think I have someone watching in there, too?"

"Are you serious?"

Carlisle turned to Mac. "Your wife doesn't have much of a sense of humor, Chief."

Mac didn't respond.

After a moment, Carlisle began to backtrack. "My apologies." He waved a hand between Grace and Mac. "Ms. Reagan, you're welcome to use my office."

Grace could see he was losing patience, but it couldn't be

helped. "Thank you, but we'll talk in the parking lot and meet you in your office in ten minutes, if we have any more to tell you."

"If you—" Carlisle stopped and took a breath. "I'm busy this morning. Ten minutes. After that, I'll need to move on."

He didn't say what he would be moving on to and Grace knew she was taking a gamble. Did he have enough to charge Lily with a crime? There was only one way to find out.

"Well?" she said to Lily when they were alone. It was damp and windy outside, causing them to stand close together and raise their voices, stopping whenever anyone passed them.

"You trust him? The sheriff, I mean," Lily asked, looking toward the rear door of the public safety building.

"In this situation? Absolutely not. But he isn't here to be your friend. Now we don't have much time. What did you want to tell me?"

"That incident when we were fifteen was nothing, Grace. Dove will back me up. We used to hide out in the church to get away from Irene. That day we were talking about boys and playing cards. Dove had some cigarettes, and we were smoking. Irene went berserk when she caught us. I never said anything about burning the church down. She's the one who said we could cause a fire. She ordered me to leave, and I had to walk home through the woods. Dove was grounded for a month, and I was too, which is why I remember it at all."

Grace checked the time. "I've pushed Carlisle as far as I'm willing to at this point. There's no sense in provoking him if we don't have to. Let's go see if he'll believe what you just told me."

"I hope he does, because that's all there is."

The sheriff was less than impressed when Lily gave him her

statement but agreed to question Dove. He cautioned Lily not to discuss the details of their conversation.

Once the recorder was turned off, Carlisle said, "I can't control the rumor mill in this county, but I don't spread gossip, either. No need for Mrs. Jensen's accusations to be released at this time."

"We appreciate that," Grace said.

"One more question, off the record?" Carlisle's smile was insincere, but his tone was mild.

Grace said, "You can always ask. She may not answer."

"Of course." Carlisle nodded to Mac. "I've already shared with the chief that I think that crazy old lady, Mrs. Jensen, set the fire. She didn't want neighbors moving next door in her patch of the woods. I don't think she intended to kill anyone, but we might be talking felony murder. I'm still waiting to hear if the deceased died in the fire or before it was set. You got any thoughts on Mrs. Jensen you'd like to share, Miss Travers?"

"I do not," Lily said firmly, which earned her a puzzled look from the sheriff.

"Doesn't make sense for you to protect someone who seems to hate you," he said with a shrug. "But hey, you do you. Just remember this. If you or the Jensen woman are hiding something from me, I'll find out. Think about that."

CHAPTER EIGHT

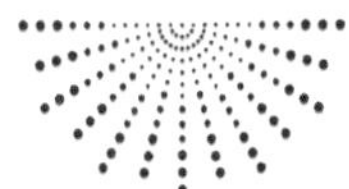

Grace met Hallie and the kids at Avril's and agreed to stay for dinner. Mac was tied up at work, and Stephanie had called to say she'd gone out for a late lunch and needed time alone, which suited Grace just fine. She hoped to pick Avril's brain about Twin Corners and get some background on Irene, but her usually informative friend only wanted to play with Fiona and Sonny.

"What do you think is going on with her?" Hallie asked while they made a salad and burgers. "She should be in here driving us crazy. Every time I brought up the subject of Twin Corners today, she shut me down."

"It is beyond odd," Grace said quietly. "This stoic refusal to discuss what's happened is so unlike her. I'm not sure what to make of it."

Hallie hesitated, then said, "If I didn't know better, I'd think she was scared. She's awfully worried about Mrs. Jensen. Maybe she just can't deal. She seems more sad than anything."

Grace stopped peeling a cucumber and thought about that. As far as they knew, the only personal impact to Avril was the loss of the church and her preservation project. But Hallie was right. Avril seemed to be sad, even depressed. That realization opened new avenues of thought that weren't suitable for dinnertime with toddlers. Adding another topic to her list of procrastinations, Grace focused on getting through the meal and managing the children's mounting fatigue.

By the time she got home, the kitchen was dark, and Mac was already in their bedroom with the door shut. Grace could hear the shower running upstairs and fervently hoped Stephanie wasn't preparing for another late night of driving. There hadn't been time today for them to talk, and Grace didn't have the energy to handle it now.

Once the children were settled, she finally made it to the bedroom where she found Mac reading an old John D. MacDonald mystery. He glanced up at her arrival and gave her a distracted, "Hi. Need help with the kids?"

"They went out like a light. Are you living vicariously through Travis McGee? Or just revisiting *The Busted Flush?*"

"I'm at a good part." He didn't look up from the yellowed pages.

"Enjoy," she said curtly and went to take a bubble bath. If it made Steph run out of hot water, good. If Mac interpreted her tone correctly, even better. They could both just tiptoe around her for a while.

A half hour later she crawled into bed, not relaxed exactly—she'd been the one who'd run out of hot water before the tub was full—but feeling better after a lukewarm soak.

Mac closed the book, turned out the light and said, "Is it too late to talk?"

"I tried that before my bath." But she knew neither one of them would sleep until they cleared the air. She decided to start with the least personal topic and ease into the ones that preoccupied them both. "What do you know about Irene's background? Has she ever done this before—made wild accusations like the one against Lily?"

"Not where I wanted to go, but okay," Mac said. "The Jensen family has operated a produce stand out beside their house for as long as I can remember, but now it's mostly Irene who works it. Over the years, though, she also took on all kinds of other odd jobs to make ends meet. She's observant and not afraid to speak up, so yeah, she calls now and then to report things she sees. But nothing like this. Did you ask Avril?"

"No. But I think she would have said something if she'd ever heard talk of Lily and Irene clashing like that." Grace turned on her bedside lamp and rolled over to face him. Propping herself up on an elbow, she watched him rubbing his face and decided to keep her worries about Avril to herself for now. "Was Irene always so... intense?"

"No." Mac pulled a second pillow under his head, then reached for her hand. "She was different when her husband, Harvey, was alive. Standoffish, yes, but reasonable. Harvey Jensen was her anchor to the community."

"Sort of like you and me, huh?" She leaned over and kissed him. She'd make him pay for choosing Travis McGee over her, but not tonight.

"Not even a little." He gave her a weary smile. "I don't see anything of Irene's personality in you. And Harvey Jensen didn't have a suspicious bone in his body. He'd have made a terrible cop. He was one of those people everyone knew—always chatting with customers at their produce stand, telling jokes, making people feel welcome. Irene's had to downsize the operation a lot since he died."

"I've seen Dove helping her there sometimes."

"Dove takes after Harvey. In looks, I mean. But she has sort of an emotional wall around her, like Irene."

"I never noticed," Grace said. "But I've never spent much time with Dove, either."

"They both put on a good front when it suits them. After Harvey died, it was like the light went out in Irene. But even before that, she could be distant sometimes. Even cold, which isn't surprising given the tales I've heard about her father."

Grace was wide awake now. "Her father? I've never heard anything about her early life."

"Pastor Stoker. He was the last preacher at the old church before it closed. Real fire and brimstone type. The kind who saw sin lurking behind every door and demons in every shadow."

"Demons? For real? Irene talks about devils being in the woods, but back when she was my client, she told me that was what she called the hikers and campers on her property." The ceiling fan turned lazily above them, casting slow-moving shadows across the walls. Grace suppressed a shiver. "You don't think Carlisle believes Irene's wild tales about Lily, do you?"

"I don't know what to think about our sheriff after today."

It wasn't exactly the opening she'd hoped for, but she took it. "There was someone watching our interview, wasn't there? We were in an interview room with a one-way observation mirror."

"All three interview rooms have them, honey, but I got the same feeling. Grant kept glancing at the mirror. He's probably awful at poker. And you really pushed his buttons when you implied he would eavesdrop on your confidential conversation with Lily. He asked me to leave as soon as you two were gone."

She was processing that tidbit when he changed the subject.

"Speaking of people leaving. When is Stephanie going home?"

Grace wanted to say, "I feel your pain," but it would only make matters worse. She'd complained about Stephanie a lot in the beginning of their relationship, never realizing that she was souring any chance of Mac accepting her half-sister as family. "She just got here," she whispered even though she knew Stephanie couldn't hear her from the guest room upstairs.

Mac didn't follow suit but did lower his voice a bit. "Last time she stayed a week—in and out at all hours, sleeping half the day, keeping you on edge the whole time. I don't want that to happen again. What's her plan?"

"That was a month ago and she stayed five days, not a week. I don't know what her plans are, but she and Jerry are finished, and she's devastated." Grace gave him a rushed recap of the misery Stephanie had unloaded on her during their lunch the day before. "I spared you the gory details last night, but I should have told you this morning. I'm sorry."

She hoped he'd ease up after hearing what Jerry had done, but instead he said, "Well, that is awful, but what can you do about it? Will you still be holding her hand this time next week?"

"She's in shock," Grace insisted.

"Honey, Hallie has told you she can't deal with Stephanie. Are you really willing to risk losing our nanny?"

This was a low blow, but Grace knew it was a valid point. Hallie was already enrolled in online classes at the University of Maryland for the fall semester, and Grace constantly worried she'd decide to be a full-time student and live on campus in College Park. Hallie was twenty-one, and if anyone deserved a carefree college experience, it was a young woman who'd never had a real childhood.

"Give me a break, okay?" she said as she turned out the light and rolled away from him. "I'll make all your troubles go away tomorrow if you will just let me sleep tonight."

There was a brief moment of silence, and then he pulled her to him, kissing her hair and wrapping her in his arms. "I'm sorry. But this really does have to stop, and you're the only one who can make it happen. Unless of course, you'd let me get rid of her?"

"Oh, go to sleep."

To her amazement, he did, but it was a long time before she joined him.

CHAPTER NINE

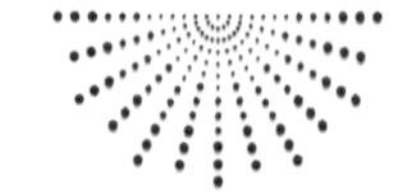

FRIDAY, SEPTEMBER 14

Friday morning's forecast announced that Tropical Storm Florian was now a Category 2 hurricane on a trajectory that could take it up the Chesapeake Bay.

"That's just great," Grace groused to herself as she filled her travel mug with coffee. She wasn't looking forward to another day of borderline hysteria as Mallard Bay prepared for the storm. Then she discovered that she needed milk and several other essentials. She hadn't made it to the market yesterday, and now she'd be stuck in the melee of people shopping as if they'd never see toilet paper again.

She heard tires on the oyster shell driveway and breathed a sigh of relief. Hallie was early, so if she hurried, she could get to Baldy's Market before work and grab enough to keep them fed through the weekend.

"Where is she?" Hallie said as she came into the kitchen with a box of groceries in her arms.

"If you mean Stephanie," Grace said, "she's upstairs, asleep, and will be for a few more hours. But why are you bringing me groceries? Not that I don't appreciate it, but you didn't have—"

"Yes, I did, because I mentioned to Avril that you were out of milk. She added a few more things to the order and said she'd settle up with you later."

"Thank—"

"Hold up on that gratitude. She also came to work with me."

Grace looked out the window to see Avril weeding the geraniums that bordered the walkway.

"I know I need help with the gardening," Grace said dryly, "but seriously?"

"She looked so down this morning, I didn't want to leave her alone. We can take the kids to the park before Stephanie gets up. This is supposed to be the last sunny day for a while." She moved past Grace into the house, where she was greeted with a chorus of happy squeals from the children.

The perfect match—a disaster forecast and Stephanie, Grace thought sourly as she went outside. She couldn't do anything about either one.

"We're changing those geraniums over to winter pansies this weekend," she said as she joined Avril.

"It's early for that. But since you've let them get all leggy and weedy, you may as well. After the hurricane, of course."

"Not you, too!" Grace sighed. "No hurricane talk. Thank you for the groceries. I was going to the market before work, but now you've saved me some time. Want a cup of coffee?"

"Don't let me hold you up," Avril said. "I came to see Stephanie."

"You did?" Grace asked.

"That's right. I want to get to know her better."

"Well, you're going to have a bit of a wait. I heard her come in at some time after three. I'm pretty sure she's not going to be up before eleven."

Avril rolled her eyes. "I was afraid of that. I'll find something to do." She looked around. "There's no shortage of chores around here."

"No," Grace said firmly. "We're going to go walk down to the beach, and you're going to tell me what's going on."

They sat on the stone bench at the edge of the little sandy beach that ran along the rear of Mac and Grace's property. Grace waited, trying to recall how long Avril had been acting this way. Her unusual level of worry and non-communication had been growing for weeks. At first, Grace had put it down to late summer allergies, overexertion in gardening, and overindulgence in volunteer work. But Hallie had nailed the problem when she said Avril seemed sad.

"I had a physical last week," Avril said.

Grace's heart skipped a beat.

"Apparently, I'm in excellent shape for a fossil. Thom Pearson and I went to school together, you know. I told him I could still outrun him, and he had to admit I'm healthier than he is."

Relieved, Grace saved her argument for a new doctor. Preferably someone who'd graduated from medical school in the last forty years. "Did you think he would find something wrong?"

Avril turned and looked at her straight on. "Yes, I did. I'm slowing down."

Grace gave her friend a hug, which, as usual, was not returned. "You haven't changed a bit, just as cuddly as always."

"I don't cuddle," Avril said. "Well, not in a long time."

"We live in hope," Grace teased. "You don't seem relieved that Dr. Pearson says you're fine."

"He meant I was fine compared to everyone else my age. And that's not good enough. It never has been. I don't get sick. I don't take naps. I stay busy. The devil can't catch you if you keep busy."

Grace tried to make sense of that. Despite the fact that she rarely missed the service at Saint Mary's, Avril was not religious. Yet, here she was, talking about devils.

"Oh, don't mind me." Avril sat up a bit straighter. "That's something Irene's father used to say, and that family's been on my mind. Pastor Stoker was a nasty piece of work, if you ask me."

"What's upsetting you?" Grace asked gently. It had to be more than a long dead preacher.

"Same thing that's bothering everyone. I'm off kilter because of the forecast. I'm not afraid of much, but if a Chesapeake Bay hurricane doesn't scare you, you don't have good sense."

"Are they worse than hurricanes in other places?" Grace got a look that stopped her attempt at humor.

"Every hurricane is bad for someone. They usually dissipate or turn before they reach us, so people around here can forget how dangerous they can be and don't prepare properly. That's what happened with Isabel in 2002. I lost half my garden and the roof off the garage. Emma's car was crushed under a tree just minutes after she got out of it."

Grace looked at her in surprise. She'd never heard that story about her grandmother.

"The storm surge came right up through town. No one died, thank goodness, but water was knee-deep on Main Street, and most of the buildings from Memorial Park up to Baldy's Market flooded. All the riverfront homes had standing water in them, and a lot of the watermen lost their boats. Don't get me started on FEMA and insurance companies." She stopped and drew a long breath. "We locals may sound silly to you with our 'sky is falling' behavior, but you haven't been through a storm like that. You don't know."

Before Grace could form a response, a loud voice from behind made them both jump. "Well! I hope you two are having fun. Can't you hear the noise your kids are making?"

They turned to find Stephanie marching towards them, wearing a nightgown and robe, and complaining that Hallie was letting the children run wild.

Grace stood, gently squeezed Avril's shoulder and said, "You came to see her. Here she is. I'm leaving soon if you want a ride."

As she passed her sister, she said, "We need to talk tonight, Steph."

CHAPTER TEN

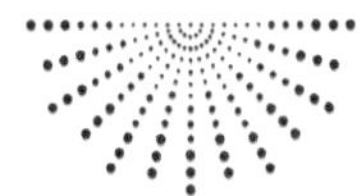

Grace dressed as fast as she could while keeping an eye on the backyard to see what was happening with Avril and Stephanie. When she was ready to leave, Avril waved her away, saying, "I'm staying a while."

Stephanie said nothing but didn't look upset. Grace grabbed her keys and briefcase, determined to leave before whatever they were discussing required her participation.

Hallie met her at the front door and walked her out to her car. "We won't have any problems today," she said quietly. "I am sorry that I've behaved badly with Stephanie. It's not like I don't have experience with her type." Then she sighed. "Sorry, again. That came out wrong."

"No worries," Grace said. "You've only seen the most annoying side of Stephanie. You and Mac didn't see what good care she took of our father. She's had a really hard time since he died, and now there are new problems she's dealing with." She opened the driver's side door of the BMW but didn't get in. "Look, it's going to take a while to straighten everything out with her, but if you can't put up with it, tell me."

"It won't be a problem," Hallie said quickly, then looked away and cleared her throat. "You're helping her, just the way you understood when my life was in turmoil, and you helped me. You didn't judge me. You didn't judge my parents or our lifestyle, either. You just helped us. I'm fine, Grace, and I'm not going anywhere. At least not until January."

Grace chose to ignore that last sentence. "Thank you. Let's take things day by day. The kids come first, and I want their nanny to be happy." As she left, she felt as if she had just dodged a disaster that would eventually find its way back to her.

'Hope for the best,' she told herself as she drove away, but she knew it would be more prudent to plan for the worst.

Several hours later, she sat back in her swivel chair, took off her reading glasses, and rubbed her nose. She'd spent the last hour reviewing all the work she'd done for Irene Jensen up until last year when she'd refused to file a claim of adverse possession of the Twin Corners Church property. She had explained to Irene that she didn't meet the criteria for claiming ownership of the church property, despite having been its caretaker for decades.

Irene's enraged reaction in their last conversation was an unsettling memory.

She recapped the situation for Lily when they broke for lunch.

They had taken their sandwiches outside for a change of scenery, but the darkening skies threatened rain. "I don't see how Irene's recent troubles explain her accusations against me," Lily said. "Have you thought that maybe the reason she's so adamant that I started the fire is because she doesn't want the sheriff to look at her? She's right to be worried too, because if he talks to her sister, he'll hear how she insisted on coming home and being alone the night of the fire."

Grace frowned. "That has worried me. Why would her sister take her home if she knew Irene needed someone with her?"

"Because Irene can pitch an unholy fit like you've never seen. Mimi told me she held firm until Irene started calling around looking for a ride. Mimi packed a bag, intending to stay over in Twin Corners, but Irene wasn't having that, either. They agreed Mimi would check in by phone throughout the evening and if Irene didn't answer, Mimi would call me. When she dropped Irene off, Mimi called to alert me. I'd just gotten in from Richmond."

A fat raindrop splattered on the pavement, but neither of them moved. "You think Irene set the fire?" Grace asked.

Lily didn't hesitate. "Yes, I do. I don't know how she managed it, but if anyone her age could pull it off, it would be Irene. Maybe she got scared when she saw the flames, or maybe she just planned to blame me all along, but she called me and asked me to come over. There's nothing wrong with that old lady's hearing, you know. She called me for help, then refused to come to the door until she had firefighters there to witness her performance."

"But if she burned down the church, the property owners would still have the land to sell. As I recall, a redevelopment firm in the Midwest acquired it. A bulk deal on foreclosed properties."

"Yeah," Lily said. "But you're underestimating Irene. She can't afford to compete with the Preservation Society to purchase the church. The sellers were donating a huge chunk of the purchase price back to the Society for a tax write-off."

"But if there's no church . . ."

"Then the sellers only have the land, and it has a graveyard. You know the restrictions Kingston County puts on those properties with cemeteries. Especially ones that were once public."

Grace did. That had been a headache for Avril's group, too. "I guess that will lower the purchase price of the land significantly."

"Maybe low enough for Irene to manage, but not if she's in prison for arson—or murder. Irene Jensen never liked any of Dove's friends, but she especially didn't like me. I was a ready-made scape-goat for her when I agreed to help out while Dove was gone."

Grace wanted to argue with Lily, but all the pieces fit together so neatly. The memory of Irene holding Sonny, calling him "Little Lee," was fresh in her mind, and it hurt to think of Irene any other way.

"I can see this is hard for you to hear," Lily said. There was a new edginess to her voice. "Imagine being a kid and dealing with her. Now you know why Dove brings Brooklyn to my house when she needs a sitter. Irene loves Dove and Brooklyn, and they love her, but Irene doesn't have the patience to raise another. And Dove doesn't want Brooklyn to be frightened by her grandmother's night-mares and hallucinations."

"Why didn't you tell Carlisle and Mac all of this?"

"I'm hoping everything will clear up without having to drag Irene's dementia, or personality disorder, or whatever it is, out in public. Dove is terrified Brooklyn's father will use it as grounds to gain physical custody. He's taking her back to court as it is."

"Oh, good Lord."

"Yep. Dove needs time and money to get herself and Brooklyn into a new home and Irene into a care facility, so she takes every extra shift she can at the nail salon. She dates a little, now and then, but mostly all she does is work. That's why I keep Brooklyn in the evenings when I can, to give Dove a break. Come to think of it, if Irene gets me convicted, she'll be removing the one person helping Dove build a new life."

Grace had heard enough."You get on the state databases and make an exhaustive list of any legal actions Irene or Dove have ever been involved with. Go back as far as you can search. Keep it all quiet and don't involve anyone else for now. Do as much as you can online for now."

Lily frowned. "Legal actions? I don't think either one of them has ever been arrested."

"I mean arrest records to property purchases. Lawsuits of any kind. Criminal complaints, even if they were dropped." Grace stopped and thought for a moment. "Newspaper articles, too. If Irene's made trouble for people or businesses she doesn't like, we can use that to show a pattern of behavior. We aren't taking any chances. Let's learn as much as we can about Irene and that fire."

CHAPTER ELEVEN

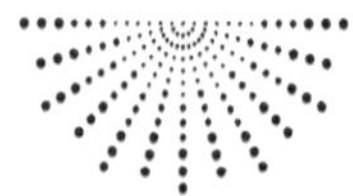

As if they'd heard her, an hour later Mac came into the office with Grant Carlisle.

"To what do we owe this surprise visit?" Grace asked Carlisle, giving her husband a 'what the heck?' look behind the sheriff's back.

Carlisle said, "I've just learned the deceased individual in the Twin Corners fire has been identified. What I'm about to tell you is highly confidential and has to remain that way. I haven't even had a chance to tell the chief."

Mac's expression said he wasn't happy about that, either.

Carlisle handed Lily a photograph. "Do you recognize this person?"

The color drained from Lily's face, and it was a long moment before she answered. When she did, her voice shook with anger. "You obviously know who he is. This is my brother Joshua."

The first thing that registered with Grace was not Lily's reaction, but Carlisle's. The sheriff smiled. "Are you sure?"

"Of course," Lily said flatly. She passed the photograph to Grace, even though the sheriff had his hand out. To Mac she said,

"It's Josh." She turned away from them and put her head in her hands.

Carlisle watched her but said nothing.

"May I?" Mac said, moving to Grace's side to look at the photograph.

"Is it him?" she asked quietly, praying that he would say Lily had been wrong.

"I believe so," Mac said. His voice was harsh, and he was staring at Carlisle.

"What happened to him?" Lily turned back to Carlisle. "How did he get like that? He's barely thirty-six."

Grace viewed the photograph again. The man who lay on a steel table, covered from neck to toe by a white sheet, had matted graying hair and a scruffy beard. Even in death, he looked tired and timeworn.

Lily opened her phone and with a few taps pulled up a snapshot. Showing it to Carlisle, she said, "Second from the left. This is the last family photo. It was taken about a month before I went into the Marine Corps."

"So, it's eleven, twelve years old?" Carlisle said. "When did you see Travers for the last time?"

Lily closed her eyes for a second and said, "Eleven years ago next month. Our father's funeral."

"Did you know about this, Chief?" Carlisle's tone was cool, as was the look he gave Mac.

"That Lily has a half-brother named Joshua? Yes, I know that. But if you had shared that photo with me earlier, I wouldn't have recognized him immediately. Not in that condition." Turning to Lily, he said gently, "I'm so sorry for your loss."

Grace moved to Lily's side, ignoring Carlisle.

He didn't give them long to recover from his devastating news. Pointing to the conference table, he said, "Let's sit down. I might have handled this badly, but we still need to talk."

Lily exploded. "You *might* have handled it badly? We can talk right here. I want some answers from you. My brother is—was a detective with Baltimore PD's homicide squad. How did he end up like that, and why the hell was he in the Twin Corners church?"

"You really have been out of touch a while, haven't you?" Carlisle watched them as if waiting for someone to break. "*Former* Detective Travers was dishonorably discharged from BPD two years ago. He was a drug addict who stole evidence to feed his habit and got caught—"

"That's not true!" Lily yelled.

Carlisle kept going. "So, it's not at all surprising that he ended up homeless and died under suspicious circumstances. The only questions are the how and why of his death. Tell me what you know, and I'll leave you to come to grips with your family's loss."

"I don't know anything," Lily said. "I haven't had any contact with him in years. What do *you* think happened?"

But the sheriff wasn't going to be sidetracked. "You showed up at the exact location where your brother's body was discovered in a burning building. A witness claims you are the arsonist who probably killed him."

Grace objected, but Lily talked over her. "You know Irene Jensen is crazy. You said so yourself!"

Carlisle cocked his head in mock surprise. "What I *know* is that for four years, you were a highly trained officer in the military police, and you should understand what is happening now. Everyone at Twin Corners the night of the fire is a suspect, and the victim's family is always at the top of the list."

"That's enough," Grace said. "We're done here."

Carlisle ignored her. "Poor Mrs. Jensen isn't the only one who's concerned about your involvement, Miss Travers. Your good friend, Dove, agrees with her grandmother. She says you knew Mrs. Jensen was alone and afraid and unlikely to come out of the house to investigate any kind of disturbance. Even a fire next door. I'm not convinced yet, but it was the perfect setup for you to get rid of your brother, wasn't it?"

Lily didn't waste time wringing her hands after Mac and Carlisle left. Over Grace's objections, scalled Dove Jensen. She put the conversation on speaker, and Grace could clearly hear Dove's outraged response to Lily's questions.

"Of course, I didn't say you killed that man!" Dove's voice crackled through the phone. "I told him my grandmother said she'd seen men in the woods behind our house, but I had thought she was imagining things." Her voice grew shakier. "I do believe her now— I mean, there was a dead man in the burned-down building next door, for God's sake."

Lily and Grace exchanged glances. It didn't sound like Dove knew it was Joshua Travers who had died.

"Any idea why the sheriff would lie to me?" Lily asked, her knuckles white against the phone.

"No! I thought he was really nice! I'm stupid, okay?" Dove's voice caught. "And I'm so freaked out I can hardly breathe. I haven't slept in three days."

Grace shook her head and mouthed, "Move on."

Lily clearly didn't appreciate the interruption, but she softened her tone and asked if Dove had heard from Brooklyn.

There were rustling sounds, then Dove said, "Sorry, I needed a tissue. I thought I was cried out, but I guess not." She drew a shuddering breath. "I'm living in a nightmare, Lil. Dominic met us at the airport this time. No nice dinner, none of his smarmy politeness. He had his mother with him, and she took Brooklyn to get something to eat. As soon as they were out of sight, Dom told me he's hired a lawyer to get custody of Brooklyn, and he's not returning her when his visitation time runs out."

Lily's mouth fell open in shock, but she recovered quickly. "Slow down. He can't do that."

"You didn't see him. He was so cold and talked as if it was all finalized and I was the one who'd have to settle for visitation, not him. I've been on the phone every minute I can get away from Reenie, but neither Dom nor his mother will answer my calls. I never should have left California and come back here, but I'm broke. I have to work, but I'm also dealing with this awful fire and the trouble Reenie is causing you."

As Lily talked Dove down, Grace thought of a number of ways Dominic Pontello could keep Brooklyn with him while fighting his way through a court system three thousand miles away. Some were legal, and some weren't, but all of them meant heartbreak for Dove and her little girl.

"I'm so, so sorry you've been dragged into all of this, Lil," Dove said. "You're my best friend, and you're in a mess because of it. I should've put my foot down with Reenie ages ago, and now I have no choice. Aunt Mimi is willing to take her in, and she's just gonna have to accept that arrangement, or share a room in a nursing home or memory care place. After this, I don't think any assisted living facility will take her." She paused, then continued with sudden urgency, "But wait! There really was someone in the woods. Reenie wasn't really lying or hallucinating—except for the part about you, of course."

Grace's heart went out to Lily as Dove's words hit home. Irene was in the grasp of dementia of some sort, or she was a cunning liar —maybe even a murderer. Either way was bad for the Jensen family and Dove's chances of regaining physical custody of her daughter. But if Lily was accused of setting the church on fire with her brother inside, all the Jensens' legal problems went away.

It wasn't hard to guess where Dove's allegiance might lie.

CHAPTER TWELVE

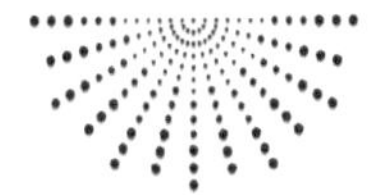

Grace couldn't remember the last time her partner joined her in an active case, much less came into the office on a Friday afternoon, but Cyrus Mosley arrived at three, surprising everyone but his secretary. Marjorie refused his instructions to leave early. She was the one who'd called him with the news of the sheriff's visit and all the yelling she'd heard coming from Grace's office.

Mosley wore his usual Duck Head slacks and a blue button-down oxford cloth shirt. He was sockless in polished Bass Weejuns, and as soon as Grace saw him, she knew he was in warrior mode. Her spirits lifted and she surprised them both by hugging him. This was one time she'd welcome his offer to take over a case if it meant he could clear everything up for Lily with a few phone calls.

When she finished updating him on the identity of the dead man in the Twin Corners fire and Carlisle's treatment of Lily, Mosley was furious, but focused. Dove Pontello's description of Irene's behavior had him shaking his head. He murmured, "So unfortunate," before asking where Lily was.

"Gone home to tell her mother about Josh," Grace said. "I couldn't talk her out of it, and she insists Denise won't spread the news. There's no legal gag order, but Carlisle's already got Lily pegged as the suspect, and I don't want to make him any more antagonistic. Yesterday, he was fixated on Irene. Today he was locked in on Lily and determined to craft a narrative around her involvement."

"It's a clumsy tactic," Mosley said. "It sounds as if Carlisle is fishing and using unseemly behavior to bait Lily into incriminating herself."

Grace thought about that. "He was definitely provoking her from all sides, insulting one minute and outright accusatory the next. And the crazy thing is, I don't think Mac expected any of it. Carlisle hadn't shown him the photograph of Josh or shared his identity."

"Looks like you'll have an interesting dinner conversation tonight, m'dear," Mosley said.

"Yeah, but it won't be about this. Stephanie's here and Mac's not happy about it."

"No need for details," Mosley said quickly. "I'm sure you and your husband will manage just fine. Now, to wrap up office matters. Lily will understandably be pulled away from her duties here a great deal over the next few weeks. According to Marjorie, in addition to our other clients who are coming in on Monday morning—we have the Bakersfield divorce case. I'll take that on. Butch and Martha will be fine with it. They're a nice couple parting amicably. I'll be in early on Monday to prep and handle them. What do you have coming up, Grace? Do you need help while Lily's attention is diverted?"

She looked at her watch. There was plenty to do before she could leave for the day, but setting their professional house in order now would speed things up for next week. "I guess we should bring Marjorie in for this?" she said.

"Right here." The Bat sailed in and joined them at the conference table. "What?" She looked at them innocently. "You left the door open, and I didn't want you to have to repeat everything when you finally realized you needed me."

Mosley gave her a conspiratorial grin, and Grace didn't bother to complain. Right now, she needed all the help she could get.

When they had wrapped up their scheduling assignments, Mosley turned his full attention to Marjorie. "I'm assuming you know the latest developments in the Twin Corners fire?"

Grace filed her partner's clever wording away for future use and enjoyed seeing the uneasy look on Marjorie's face.

"I ran into my nephew this morning."

"The Sheriff's Deputy?" Mosley asked. "Or the handyman who hasn't fixed our air-conditioning yet?"

To Grace's surprise, it was the slow moving, always late handyman who'd told Marjorie that the dead man was Josh Travers. Marjorie hurried to explain that her nephew had been called out to the sheriff's office this morning for an overheated compressor that was adding to the hot air circulating in the building. She paused to let them appreciate her joke, then added, "The mechanical room is next to Grant Carlisle's office, and you know how his voice carries."

"Thank you," Grace managed. "I'll let Lily know."

Mosley jumped in before the unusual cooperative atmosphere deteriorated. "Well, since we don't have to worry about spreading gossip ourselves, Marjorie, could you fill Grace in on Joshua's life growing up here in Mallard Bay?"

"*All* of it? Maybe Lily would be the best person to do that."

"All of it, please," Mosley said. "With the proper decorum, of course."

Grace perked up. If Cyrus was ordering Marjorie to gossip, there must be a good reason.

Marjorie gave them both skeptical looks but started talking. "I may not approve of the personality that Lily projects in the office, but I've always admired her family. Especially her mother. Denise

Travers had a three-year-old, Emily, and was pregnant with Lily's twin sisters when Wayne's mistress showed up at their door with her newborn son. The hussy's name was Sasha Something-or-other, and she had the nerve to name the baby Joshua Wayne Travers, Junior."

This wasn't the type of background Grace wanted to hear, but it might be useful information. Besides, she couldn't stop Marjorie now if she wanted to.

"I guess Denise had the option of throwing Wayne out and raising her girls by herself," Marjorie said. "But instead, she acknowledged what had happened and, from what I could tell, treated the boy as her own whenever his mother would let him visit. As you know, we're no strangers in this area to mixed-up families, but that one was a head-scratcher for a while. Denise insisted on calling the boy by his first name, Joshua, but that Sasha always referred to him as 'Wayne' and sometimes 'Junior.'"

"Sounds awful," Grace said. Lily had never said much about Josh, and what she had shared had been funny, even tender, memories. She'd never mentioned his uncomfortable relationship with her mother.

"You're probably wondering why Lily doesn't talk much about him," Marjorie said. "But why would she? He isn't in her life anymore, or he wasn't until yesterday. Besides, most of the time we're all inundated with your private life and there's not much time to talk about anyone else's."

Grace could hardly protest. It was true, and she saw her partner was having a hard time not laughing.

"Nice," she said to Marjorie, but she chastised herself. *Shut up about personal problems* went to the top of her ongoing mental To Do list. "Is that all the gossip that's circulating right now?"

Marjorie shrugged. "Well, that and the rumors of lawless men living in the woods at Twin Corners and preying on women who live alone. Irene's sister has told everybody who will listen that

Irene's been seeing at least two men out in their woods. Course, any evidence out there will be gone after the hurricane comes through."

"Oh, for heaven's sake! Don't start the hurricane talk. I've got enough to deal with."

"I haven't even started with hurricane talk," Marjorie assured her. "But maybe that excitement will work for us. Sheriff Carlisle's going to be busy with disaster preparations."

"It's an ill wind that doesn't blow some good." Grace smiled at the irony of one of her mother's favorite sayings.

A second later, a thunderclap rattled the windows, and she wanted to take her words back.

CHAPTER THIRTEEN

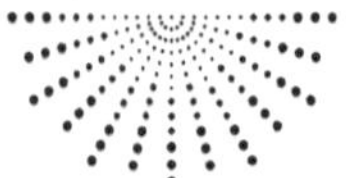

SATURDAY, SEPTEMBER 15

IRENE

It would be winter soon. The thought brought Irene a rare sense of peace, even if frigid weather was hard to imagine when the pre-dawn sky backlit the still lush foliage of her beloved woods.

Most people her age dreaded cold weather, but when the leaves fell and the undergrowth in the woods died back, the view from the back of her house opened up and she could see the small clearing where she and the children had spent so many happy hours.

The loblolly pines in the woods behind her house were tall, their evergreen branches clustered at the top of their spindly trunks to catch the sunlight. Below them, a chaotic mix of oaks, dogwood, and the occasional holly bush battled for space with a tangled mass of vegetation.

Once she and Harvey had maintained the paths to the clearing and on down to the creek, but now there was no one to do the work. She had to wait for the deciduous trees and plants to die back so she could safely make her way to the clearing where she had first taken Debbie, then Dove, to picnic on warm days. This year, she would take Brooklyn, but first, she had to clean it up, and before she could do that, she had to make sure it was safe. Her eyes welled up as she wondered what it looked like now after a summer of neglect.

A glance at her watch told her she'd been lost in thought for nearly twenty minutes. She couldn't afford to waste time. The cold knot in her stomach reminded her that something was wrong, and she needed to fix it.

The men in the woods.

That's what she was supposed to be doing—watching for the men in the woods.

But one of them was dead, wasn't he? Yes! She'd seen him when the EMTs carried him out of the smoking church, but it had been too dark to see his features. Not that she needed to see how he'd ended up. However he'd gone to his judgment day was no concern of hers. Unless she'd sent him there. She couldn't imagine such a thing, but she hadn't checked the inside of that church in ages. Had one of the devils gotten inside before she lit the fires? And what happened to the second one?

She was sure there had been two devils in the woods. Or had she dreamed that?

Stop it! She had to stay focused, and she couldn't talk, or even *think* about devils anymore. That had been father's word for anyone different. She had seen men, not that they were any better. But calling them devils was dangerous. Dove was already worried about leaving her alone, and Irene knew what that could lead to.

If she wasn't careful, she'd end up in a care facility with strangers. Who would tend to the clearing then? Who would keep her family safe? She needed to make herself behave reasonably and appear to be useful to Dove and Mimi. If those two got riled up, her next stop was a nursing home.

Maybe it wouldn't be so bad at Mimi's. She'd have the large, sunny bedroom at the back of the house, overlooking the vegetable garden and soybean fields. It had a private bath, and Mimi claimed to have set it up just for Irene. The campaign for the sisters to live together had begun even before Dove had Brooklyn, but Mimi had stepped up the nagging lately. Irene felt sure it was because Dove was sharing her worries with her great-aunt. The two always had been thick as thieves.

She couldn't blame either one of them, though. She hadn't been truthful with them.

What on earth had possessed her to accuse Lily Travers of setting fire to the church? She supposed that's what a lifetime of deceit could bring a person to—spitting out the first easy lie that comes to mind.

Then she'd repeated that lie to the sheriff and watched his eyes light up. He'd looked just like her father. Both men, strangers to each other, shared a despicable trait. They enjoyed correcting others' transgressions and reveled in dispensing punishment. So, when Sheriff Carlisle had smiled and nodded knowingly, she knew just how to handle him. He *wanted* Lily to be guilty, and he'd made Irene feel special for making it happen.

But now, in the morning light, she knew she'd been wrong, and she had to set things right. She should be brave and finally tell the truth. She pictured the sheriff's face when he heard she set the fires.

Maybe she should tell him the whole story. Confess it all and be done with it. The thought was barely formed before it was rejected. The police would take her away, and she couldn't leave this place. She couldn't leave the woods, or the little grave where Aaron had slept for seventy years.

Aaron. Just saying his name made her smile.

Her father had dug the tiny grave on a sunny Saturday morning a week before her fifteenth birthday. He'd said her boy had never lived, and God would surely punish her for being prideful enough to claim the holy status of motherhood when all she'd done was behave like a Jezebel.

But her baby had lived when he was inside her, kicking and moving, letting her know he was there, and he was hers. She'd also known when he died. The movements slowing, weakening, until they stopped. Seven decades later, she was still his mother as surely as if she'd raised him.

No, she couldn't leave him, and she couldn't let her lie stand.

Somehow, she had to correct what she'd done to Lily, and that wasn't going to happen while she watched the woods like a ninny.

She went into the kitchen and took stock of the day ahead of her. She was clean and dressed and able-bodied. She wasn't forgetful or addlebrained—no matter what anyone said.

When Irene Jensen was landed with a problem, she fixed it.

Hadn't she saved up three months of flammable recycling in the shed just waiting for the chance to be rid of that blighted building once and for all? She rubbed a sore muscle in her back. It wasn't the only reminder of the work she'd done the night of the fire.

If she walked outside, she'd see the three blackened cans and catch the sweet, acrid scent of the partially destroyed church. How could she remember her plan to burn the church so clearly, yet have no memory of lighting the fires in the barrels? Was it just another sign that Dove and Mimi were right? Was she losing her mind?

That didn't sound right. Certainly didn't feel right. Once she'd recovered from the horror of Aaron's birth and his death, she'd handled every other blow fate had thrown at her and come out the other side stronger for it. She wasn't a happy person, but she wasn't crazy, either.

So why couldn't she remember setting the fires?

CHAPTER FOURTEEN

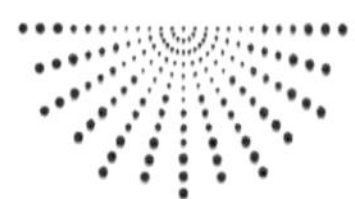

It felt like ages since she had been able to talk freely with Mac, and as Grace pulled into the driveway at their riverfront cottage and saw Stephanie's car, she knew it wouldn't happen over dinner. She braced herself to face her sister, but when she walked inside, she heard laughter coming from the back of the house.

Hallie popped out of the kitchen and gave her a big grin. "Before you ask, it's been a good day. Avril stayed through lunch, and she and Stephanie had a long talk outside. I don't know for sure what's going on, but everybody is in a good mood."

Shedding her boots and raincoat, Grace padded down the hallway to find Stephanie sitting on the floor of the playroom, telling an extremely altered version of Goldilocks and the Three Bears, and acting out all the parts.

"Do 'gin!" Fiona demanded when Stephanie stopped to greet Grace. "Mama watch!"

When Hallie left, Stephanie quickly wrapped up what she insisted was her tenth performance and declared it to be wine time. Together, the sisters got the kids through dinner and a bubble bath without a single tear being shed by anyone.

When Mac arrived tired and out of sorts, Stephanie said good-night, insisting she'd had a late lunch and didn't want dinner. But even then, Mac remained in the monosyllabic mode. He took a bottle of Natty Boh from the fridge and told Rocky to find her ball. The rain had stopped, but Grace knew he'd have gone outside even if it hadn't.

She watched them go, then scrambled around in the kitchen looking for something that resembled an adult meal. Inspiration failed her, so she threw together two cheese sandwiches, pretzels, the remaining half bottle of wine, and grabbed a large plastic table-cloth on her way out to join her husband.

"Let's go," she said as she walked past him and down the path to the river's edge. She ignored his complaints about the damp and the distant rumbles of thunder, and eventually they fell into their usual rhythm and discussed their day.

Mac didn't share any new information about the Twin Corners fire or Lily's brother, but he listened carefully to her recounting of Dove's description of her interview with Carlisle.

It was hard when they had these situations—with him on the side of law enforcement, and her representing a person of interest in a crime—but they had developed a sort of dance that allowed them to communicate without crossing any ethical boundaries. The stretches of silence grew longer, as each of them stopped to gather their thoughts and words.

When Grace double-checked the nursery with her phone's nanny cam app, Mac asked if she was ready to go in.

"In a little while," she said. "Stephanie will probably come down for a snack and catch me. I'm too tired to start a long conversation tonight."

"That's ridiculous," he said flatly. "Just tell her you're tired and do what you want."

She didn't answer him. She had no answers to make him happy, and she wasn't going to argue with him, either. After a moment, she finished her wine and stood up, taking his hand. "Don't you want to take me to your workshop and show me the new game table you're making for the playroom?"

"Not really . . ." Then he saw the way she was smiling. "Yeah," he said, getting up and pulling her into his arms. "That's exactly what I want to do."

The toolshed he'd renovated last year was spotless, as usual, and the old couch he kept in there was big enough for both of them.

For a little while, all their troubles disappeared.

Saturday morning was calm, but the skies were steely, and the air smelled of the storm to come. Mac said he would keep Fiona busy helping him with sandbags and taping up the first-floor windows if Grace would take Sonny with her to the grocery store.

She opened her mouth to say she hadn't planned to go to the grocery store, then remembered that he had warned her the night before that they needed to have enough provisions to get through the end of the next week in case they were caught here if the roads washed out. She hadn't taken him seriously, and she still didn't. But she wasn't going to tell him that.

What was the point of having an argument when she had something she needed to do and now she wouldn't have to explain why she was leaving? She would get the groceries, but it would be her second stop of the morning. First, she was going out to Twin Corners to see the crime scene and, with any luck, talk to Irene Jensen.

Mac wouldn't approve, she knew, but she couldn't see any harm in it. Sonny loved to ride in the car, and Irene Jensen loved Sonny. Or at least she had the last time she'd seen him, which now that Grace thought about it, was quite some time ago. The rambunctious toddler no longer resembled the cuddly infant that Irene had held while they had discussed her determination to stop the renovation of the church and purchase the small strip of land where her produce stand had stood for so many years.

If Mac thought it was odd that Grace gave in so easily and was ready to go so quickly, he didn't say so. Handing her a ridiculously long list, he said, "Get what you can and just leave the non-perishables in your trunk. It'll save time if we have to pack up in a hurry."

"You want to take food with us if we leave? We're going to Avril's, remember. She'll be insulted."

"I assure you, she will not," he said firmly. "Get back as soon as you can and be sure to pay attention to the state of the roads on your way into town and on the way back. If the water level rises in the drainage ditches, even a little, we'll need to get ready to leave. If they're full when the storm hits, we won't have any time." He took in her skeptical look and added, "Sooner or later, if the forecasts are accurate for our area, our driveway will flood down near Killian Road. If we're still here when that happens, this is where we're staying."

Grace heard him but still thought he was overreacting. She took the list, bribed her baby with a cookie and left before his father could remember something else they needed to do before the apocalypse hit.

CHAPTER FIFTEEN

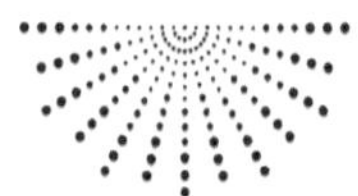

It was only a fifteen-minute drive to Twin Corners. When Grace caught her first glimpse of the old church steeple, she could see that the produce stand was still there. It was half empty, but Irene Jensen sat in a folding chair in front of neatly stacked cartons of sweet potatoes, corn, and squash.

"Morning," Irene said briskly as Grace got out of the BMW and opened the car door to get Sonny. "Before you ask, I don't have much today, an' I'm shuttin' down when this is gone. County says it ain't safe 'cause of the state of the church. Good thing the inspectors don't work on the weekend, though."

Grace hesitated, wondering if Irene recognized her. "Hi, Mrs. Jensen. Remember me? I'm Grace Reagan. I—"

"'Course I know who you are. You used to be my lawyer until I fired you." The words were delivered without heat and ended with a knowing grin.

"Yes, ma'am." Grace returned the smile and tickled Sonny until he laughed, too. "We came out to see how you are. This is my son, Liam. We call him Sonny. The last time you saw him—"

"He was a baby." There was a softening in the elderly woman's features. "Spittin' image of his daddy, that one is. I'm pleased to see him again." She reached into an open basket next to her and held out a cookie. "Made these this morning—oatmeal with a few raisins."

Grace's "thank you" was drowned out by Irene's laughter as Sonny bounced and squealed, reaching for the treat.

"His daddy felt the same way about my cookies," Irene said. "He's a fine man, your husband."

Grace thanked her again, sure that the polite small talk wouldn't last long once she started asking questions. She wiped a trickle of sweat from her temple, marveling at how Irene seemed completely unfazed by the stifling air.

"Stockin' up before the storm?" Irene asked, gesturing vaguely toward the gray horizon. "You'll be on to town next, I bet. Baldy's and Three Pigs is sellin' outta milk and bread like there's another plague comin'. Folks get worked up over nothing these days."

Suddenly Grace wished she could leave Irene on a positive note, but even as she tried to think of something entertaining to say, Irene solved the matter for her. Drawing herself up and squaring her shoulders, she glared at Grace, who instinctively tightened her grip on Sonny.

"As for your question," Irene said, "I'm doing just fine. The doctors at the hospital said I had a UTI and slapped me on antibiotics, so I'm a bit queasy, but other than that, as long as I behave myself and drink enough water, I'll be fine."

"Oh good," Grace said hastily, not wanting to hear any more details about bodily functions.

"Nobody'll be moving in next door now, will they?" Irene said, glancing at the church. "But you're still Avril's friend, right?"

"Well, yes—"

"And that girl, Lily. She still work for you?"

"Yes."

Irene shook her head. "That's too bad. The sheriff said I

shouldn't talk to no one about the other night, so no point in you trying to get me to say what I shouldn't."

"I came—" Grace stopped. Irene was looking steadily at her as if to say, *Go on. Lie.* "I came to see how you were and to see the church." She looked at her son with his crumb covered face and added, "And I'd like to buy the rest of those cookies since the McNamara men are so partial to them."

Sonny lurched forward, arms outstretched toward Irene. A second later her cranky former client was holding him, and Sonny had a cookie in each hand.

Grace was amazed at the transformation in Irene. Years fell away as she laughed at the wriggling child. Then she called him 'Little Lee.'

"Mac said you were old friends, but I didn't realize you knew him as a baby."

"Of course I did. Everyone knew each other back then. Not like today. His parents were nice folks."

Grace thought of the laughing young couple in the photographs that were scattered throughout their house and tried to imagine them being as old as Irene. Hester McNamara had been a tall woman, too, and she wondered if this was how Sonny might have looked in his grandmother's arms.

"You be sure and tell Mac I appreciate that he came out here the other night," Irene said as she patted Sonny's back. "He didn't have to, but I sure felt better when he got here. It was such a shock, and it was good to see someone I trusted, what with Dove gone, and all."

"I'll tell him," Grace said, still smiling from her thoughts.

"If you came to look at the church, there's no one to stop you from going over there. I'm just a neighbor, after all, even though I've taken care of the place for nigh on forty years." The injured tone was back.

Grace took her time shuffling through her bag to find a baby face wipe. She considered repeating what she knew Irene understood: that while Irene had been taking care of the church, she had also been paid in kind, allowed to use the parking lot and church grounds for her produce stand and garden.

But Sonny was getting restless, so she just smiled and said, "Miss Irene, if I can ever do anything for you, give me a call." She took Sonny and cleaned his face. "I still consider myself to be your friend, you know. Mac and I will do whatever we can to help you."

Then, feeling foolish when Irene didn't respond, she paid for the cookies and walked away. As she carried Sonny to the car, his little shirt already damp against her arm in the thick air, she decided there was no point in going over to the church. Any evidence of a crime would have been collected or trampled over by now.

As she turned the car around, she gave Irene a final wave, but Mac's old friend just watched, unsmiling, as she drove away.

CHAPTER SIXTEEN

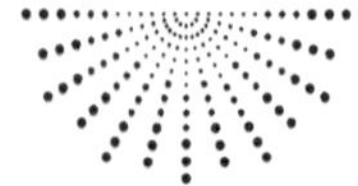

LILY

Lily examined her hands critically. For once she was pleased with the state of her fingernails. They were awful, which served her needs just fine. Dove wasn't answering her calls, but she wouldn't turn away a paying customer at the salon where she worked.

The too-cheerful receptionist at Nail Elegance informed her that Dove was with a client, but if Lily would pick out a color, another tech could work her in.

"Oh, dear." Lily looked around and leaned in closer to the woman. "I'm terrified of clippers and files," she whispered and held out a hand as proof of her lack of grooming. "Dove's a friend of mine. I can't possibly let a stranger work on me. Please let her know I'll wait for her."

Dove interpreted her message correctly. "Seriously?" she said, rolling her eyes as she led Lily to a small workstation at the rear of the salon. "I would have called you back when I could talk."

"We need to talk."

"I have to work," Dove said flatly. "If you want a manicure, sit down." Grabbing one of Lily's hands, she made a sour face. "Oh, forget it. No quick manicure will fix these."

"Then do a long one."

Soon, Lily had run through all the easy small talk in a mostly one-sided conversation. Dove offered nothing useful and kept her head bent over Lily's hands, her mouth in a tight, straight line.

When Dove finished cleaning and filing and pushing at the edges of Lily's untamed cuticles, she brushed a clear liquid on the nail of her left index finger. Lily frowned as Dove dipped the wet nail into a small jar of white powder. When she switched to a jar of gray powder and started the second coat without speaking, Lily gave up trying to wait her out.

"I need to talk to you about what happened Tuesday night. Well, Wednesday morning, really. Irene made some bizarre accusations."

"Later," was all Dove said. She finished another two rounds of the polish and powder dip routine, then attacked her handiwork with an electronic file. The process was repeated, and Lily's fingers were placed under ultraviolet light.

"They're staying this color?" Lily stared at her nails in dismay. Dark gray.

"Fantasy Twilight," Dove said. "It's a popular color. Don't move or you'll ding the finish."

"Who's it popular with?" Lily demanded.

"Everyone with any fashion sense. Besides, you used to rock the goth look in high school. This is an upgrade, girl." Dove sighed and gave Lily a small smile. "Sorry I'm so bitchy. And I'm really sorry Reenie gave you a hard time at the fire."

"Hard time? She told the sheriff that I vandalized the church when we were kids and that I threatened to burn it down! She also accused Avril Oxley and the preservation group of trying to take her land, which was actually good for me, because that was when the police finally realized she was bat sh—hallucinating." It was hard to keep her voice low, but a woman sitting one table away was straining to hear their conversation.

Dove rubbed lotion into Lily's left hand while her right one baked. "I've already told you that Reenie's mind is going. I can't get her to drink enough water, and I can't make her eat the right foods, and I don't know what you expect me to do."

Now they both were getting looks.

"We have to talk," Lily pleaded. "It's worse than you think, Dove. So much worse. Can we go outside?"

The little nail oven beeped. "Take your hand out," Dove said. "You're done."

Lily checked her nails. Still gray. Her fingertips had little helmets.

"Wash your hands if you want to and pay up front," Dove said. "I told them to give you the family discount."

"You have another appointment?"

"Yes. A regular. She doesn't like to wait."

Lily swallowed all the things she wanted to yell at the top of her lungs. "Your customer needs to wait this time. I have to tell you something, and it can't wait."

Dove leaned in so close Lily could smell the coffee she'd been sipping. "Why did you go over there, Lil? You were supposed to call 911 if Reenie was in trouble while I was gone. She'd have been all manic with whoever showed up, but she wouldn't have fixated on you."

Lily handed three twenties to Dove. "Walk me out," she said. "Or we can share everything with the room."

After a quick word with the receptionist, Dove waved at Lily to follow her out the back door. As soon as it shut behind them, she said, "I can't take another damn thing, understand? Not one more problem. I'm at my wit's end." She began to cry, and Lily's anger instantly dissolved.

"When was the last time Reenie told you she saw someone in the woods?"

"Last week, before I left to take Brooklyn to Dom. She told me the devil was out there behind the house. She used to make fun of her father for all his tales of the devil, but she wasn't joking this time. That's why I decided to take her to Aunt Mimi's. I was scared to leave her alone for very long."

"Have you or Brooklyn ever seen anyone outside?"

Dove shrugged. "Well, sure. From time to time. Just the random hikers. That's what I told the sheriff, too. People park in the church lot and enter the woods on the path behind the old cemetery. I haven't seen anyone do that lately who wasn't a customer at the produce stand, though. I think something bad happened out there a long time ago, and Reenie's just mixing up her memories. She does that a lot when she's on medication. In fact, when you went over there in the middle of the night—"

"She called and asked me to come," Lily broke in. Everyone kept leaving out that important detail. "And if I hadn't gone, the church would have burned down, and it would have taken longer for the police to identify . . ." Her throat closed up at the thought of Josh's death.

"Do you know who it was?" Dove demanded. "Please, please tell me it wasn't anyone we know."

Lily couldn't find the words to tell her who they'd lost.

"Who?" Dove demanded, her voice suddenly shrill with anger. "Is Reenie in trouble? *More* trouble?" She turned and grabbed the door handle without waiting for an answer. "I need to get home. What if the police question her again? She'll freak."

"Wait," Lily reached out to hug her best friend. "Oh, Dove, the dead man is Josh."

CHAPTER SEVENTEEN

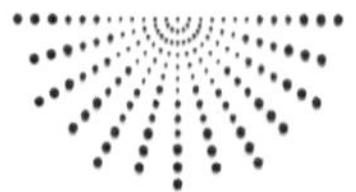

DOVE

As soon as Mallard Bay disappeared from her rearview mirror, Dove burst into tears. The harder she cried, the louder Lily's words resounded in her head.

Josh really was dead. She'd worried about it, told herself it wasn't true, and now she knew. His last words to her had been, "If you need me, call and I'll come."

She'd needed him, but she hadn't called. How could she? Dom was jealous of every man she spoke to, but he hated Josh—and he'd never even met him. Dove had left her marriage with only her baby, two suitcases, and Dom's words ringing in her ears. *If you see him, I'll kill him.*

Not long after their wedding, a wine-fueled dinner with her husband and best friend had forced Dove to see the real person she'd married. A random song on the restaurant's playlist had Lily laughingly describing their sophomore year in high school when she and Dove had been obsessed with dancing and boys. Dom had been a charming audience for Lily's story and her praise of Dove's talent.

"'Dirty Dancing' was our favorite movie, Right Dove? We had it on tape at my house, and the two of us tried to teach ourselves to dance. I don't exactly have two left feet, but I could never keep up with Dove. You should have seen her, Dom. Even my big brother thought she was amazing. He spent hours teaching us the latest steps. Those are some of my best memories."

They'd been Dove's too, until she and Dom got home that night.

Her thoughts drifted to the last time she'd talked to Josh. He'd promised to protect her, but she couldn't take the chance. Even after the divorce and visitation agreement were finalized, Dom still controlled her through Brooklyn. Josh was a risk she couldn't take, and Dove had cut all ties to him. Or thought she had.

A grinding noise from the right front wheel jerked her out of the miserable memory. She wrenched the little Civic back from the rumble strip at the road's edge. Why couldn't just one man she loved be worth the trouble he caused?

Snap out of it. Josh is in the past. He can't come back. Dove repeated the words until the churning wave of sorrow, guilt, and anger settled. Only then did her nerves steady. This was the reality she understood—the place where she'd lived most of her life.

A week ago, she'd allowed herself to hope. She'd waffled between two plans, neither much good, but she'd had options. The first one—her go-to daydream since she was sixteen—find Josh and disappear with him and their daughter—had evaporated in the parking lot behind Nail Elegance Salon. But Kyle had still been a possibility. With Brooklyn away for three weeks with Dom, she would have had the freedom to cement the new relationship she'd been nurturing for four months. With Kyle, she could take Dom on and win. She and Brooklyn would have a good life. A normal life.

She thought about the unseasonably hot day last May when Kyle Thatcher had shown up and changed everything for her.

Wearing her shortest cutoffs and a halter top, she had just taken over Irene's seat at the produce stand, and shooed her grandmother inside to the air conditioning, when a bright red Tesla rounded the bend and slid to a stop.

The man who climbed out of the car wiped out her bad mood in an instant. She took in the cocky grin, wide white smile and the too long lock of hair that fell across his forehead. He looked out of place in the countryside, and she decided he had to be famous. An actor vacationing in seclusion on the Eastern Shore. It happened all the time, but not here and not to her. Until now.

The long once-over he gave her stirred up feelings she'd thought three years of arguing and abuse from Dom had stamped out of existence. Best of all, he hadn't stopped to shop—he'd come to see Dove.

Introducing himself as Josh Travers's best friend and former partner in the Baltimore Police Department, he took his time explaining the sad state of Josh's current situation. According to Kyle, Josh had lost his job for using drugs and was in a residential treatment center. He was doing well but wanted to let Dove know he would be moving on as soon as his treatment was complete. He wished her well but couldn't handle a relationship with her or his family.

She wanted to take Kyle at his word, but none of what he'd said made sense. "I haven't seen Josh in five years," she explained. "His family thinks he cut them off, too. So, why would he want me to know any of this?"

He nodded as if he'd expected that reaction. "He said you're married and your husband—"

"I got a divorce," she'd interjected hastily. "I'm living here with my grandmother until I get back on my feet."

"Okay." He dropped the word slow and easy, full of nuance. "Josh has been really worried about you and your daughter but was afraid to contact you in case it caused problems."

"Which it definitely would have a while back," Dove said. "But not now. Can I see him?"

Kyle rubbed the back of his neck and wouldn't meet her eyes. "This is hard, so don't freak out on me, okay? Josh told me all about your, uhm, affair. And what your husband did to you. You're a part of his past that he can't go back to. It's part of his recovery program. But he needs to know that you and your kid are okay. He was good to me when I needed help. Now, I can repay him by hooking him up with a job and a new life when he finishes his treatment, but he won't move on until he knows you're taken care of."

Several dinners and long conversations slowly moved into nightly calls. When Kyle said he couldn't hide his feelings for her anymore, Dove cried with happiness. Josh was gone, but he'd sent this beautiful man to look after her, and a new path to happiness was opening up.

Between her schedule and Kyle's, they'd quickly settled into a routine that had her driving over the bridge to meet him on his nights off. She couldn't raise Reenie's suspicions by staying out too late, even with Lily babysitting. Telling her grandmother about a new boyfriend was out of the question. The woman saw devils as it was—who knew how she'd take the news of Dove's new lover? So, dates with Kyle were short but intense, and they made the most of each minute. Dove preferred to think of it in those terms, but she'd always been good at zeroing in on what pleased her and ignoring any inconvenient truths.

Eventually though, the signs of trouble were hard to ignore. Kyle had been hard to pin down. When she did catch him on the phone, he sounded distracted, and the calls were brief. Dove needed him today more than ever, but all her calls were going to voicemail.

She couldn't handle Reenie and Dom alone. Josh was dead, Kyle was ghosting her, and Dove wanted to hide from all of it. But there was nowhere to run and no one who would understand. Not even Lily.

CHAPTER EIGHTEEN

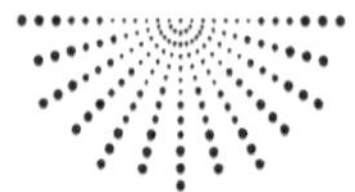

Grace returned home with a car full of groceries and a hungry toddler. Preoccupied with the lunch melee, she didn't notice that Mac was in a mood until she wound down her description of her conversation with Irene and he didn't respond. She realized he hadn't said anything at all after "hello," and that had been directed to Sonny.

She remembered his request that she get back as soon as possible just as he said, "You didn't mention you would be sleuthing this morning."

She glanced at the clock and blinked. How could it be one o'clock already? Should she admit she'd also forgotten to check the water levels in the drainage ditches or just apologize and make herself scarce. Mac was the calmest and kindest of souls—until he wasn't.

She tried changing the subject. "I was only there a minute. It was the grocery store that took the longest. I should have just gone to Baldy's Market, but I thought there'd be more of the basic items left at the Safeway in Chester."

He gave her a skeptical look but let it pass. "Any idea what your sister's plans are for today?"

Grace bit back the irritable response she wanted to make. She never should've left them alone. "No, I don't. How does she seem this morning?"

"No idea. She hasn't gotten up yet. But if you could move her car, I'd appreciate it. She's blocking the garage door and apparently took her keys to bed with her."

Stephanie didn't answer the first knock on the guest room door, or the second. Grace opened the door to find the room was dark. She could just make out her sister buried under a comforter with a pillow over her head. She called Stephanie's name and got a delicate snore in return. Fortunately, the keys to the Mercedes were on the dresser in plain view, and she scooped them up.

"Got them," she said to Mac when she got back downstairs. "My car's right behind hers. Where do you want me to park them?"

"She came in at four o'clock this morning," he said without turning around from the dishwasher he was loading.

"I didn't know she went out," Grace said in surprise, then remembered thinking that Stephanie was usually quiet when they came in from their tryst in the tool shed the night before. Stephanie and quiet always equaled trouble. "I'm sorry she woke you." She knew there was more, and she wanted him to spit it out. Her patience with juggling his feelings and her sister's behavior was wearing thin.

"She didn't wake me. The security system pinged my watch when she turned into the driveway. Just like the other times."

The security system he'd installed around their property was set to notify them when anyone passed one of the sensors. She still hadn't installed the app on her own devices, mainly because the alerts Mac received had all been for deer. Until Stephanie started visiting.

"It's happened before?" Grace was appalled.

"This is the second time this visit. She did it last time she was here, too, but I let it pass. You know, just because she keys in the right alarm code and doesn't wake you and the kids, I still have to check, especially since she's apparently incapable of locking up behind herself."

"I'm really sorry, Mac," Stephanie said as she entered the kitchen. "I'll pack up and have my things out of here in an hour, but I wonder if I can ask one more favor? I'd like to talk to my sister alone. Can I take her for a late lunch?"

Grace could see Mac wasn't even fazed, let alone embarrassed. He was mad far beyond irritation with a thoughtless houseguest.

"Yes, Stephanie, I will again rearrange my schedule and take care of the children and also get the house ready for a hurricane."

"We can talk here," Grace said, tired of trying to placate everyone. "All of us."

"I said I'd do it," Mac snapped. "Go to lunch. Do whatever you want, but this situation needs a resolution, not an argument, and I'm not changing my mind."

Neither of them had an appetite, so Grace parked at the head of a walking trail winding along Mallard Bay's riverfront. It wasn't raining, but she grabbed an umbrella, two water bottles, and crackers from her kid snacks, then led the way onto the trail. She'd already apologized for Mac's behavior, and small talk seemed awkward, so she walked silently, dodging puddles, and waited.

"You haven't asked where I went the last couple of nights, and I appreciate that. I'd prefer Mac think I'm just driving around. Anything other than the truth."

"We don't keep secrets," Grace said quickly. "I want to help however I can, and despite how irritated he gets, Mac will too. It's just—he's not flexible about the kids and our security. We both have unpredictable schedules, and he sees bad stuff as a cop. Stability at home is really important to both of us."

Stephanie said, "Tell him what you need to. But I don't want your pity, understand?"

"Not a problem." It slipped out before Grace could stop herself, and she softened it with a grin. "We can be as judgmental as you want."

"I've been going back and forth to my house."

"You're driving to New Jersey?" Grace was astounded. Three hours each way—whatever Stephanie was doing when she got home wasn't taking long.

"Last time I was here, Jerry went to our house to get some of his things. Now, my neighbor, Megan, lets me know if he shows up when I'm not home, so I can get back before he leaves. I've only caught him twice, but we've had good conversations—well, as good as that kind of talk can be. I thought I was making progress until last night. I left as soon as you went down to the beach and got home about ten. I blocked his car, so he had to talk to me."

"What about?"

"Listen and hold off on that judgmental attitude. I know how this sounds. I want him back, Grace. I know I can't have our old life, but I want my girls' father with me. I want my girls with me. They come as a package, so I've been talking to Jerry about a reconciliation. Last night he said it wasn't going to happen."

Grace struggled for something comforting to say, but came up blank. "Have the girls told you they want to stay with Jerry and this new woman?"

"They've always been daddy's girls—they'll stay with him."

Grace remembered that Rowen, the oldest, was living on campus at a small private college in New Hampshire. Carla lived with Jerry and his mother. She'd told Stephanie it was only to avoid having to switch high schools in her senior year.

"I have to keep trying. If I lose Jerry, I lose Rowen for sure. She rarely comes home, but when she does, she'll stay with her father, wherever that is. She's been difficult to raise, but I can't bear losing her. Carla will spend more time with me, but only weekends and vacations. After she goes to college next year, even that will slow down."

"That's sort of natural evolution, isn't it?" It was all Grace could think to say, though she couldn't imagine her own children leaving home.

"You don't understand. If the four of us stay together, I have a chance to mend my relationships with the girls—they blame me for the breakup. Me! Rowen said if I'd paid more attention to Jerry instead of taking care of Papa, he wouldn't have turned to someone else. They don't know about the other affairs, and if I told them, they wouldn't believe me. The more hysterical I've gotten, the calmer Jerry's been—in front of the girls, anyway. Plus, there's his mother, lavishing gifts and trips on them."

"Surely she doesn't want the two of you to divorce?"

"I thought she did, but now she says if we can make it work, we can all move into her guest house. If Jerry agrees to try, I can move in immediately and won't be homeless when we sell the house. And no, that's not a dig at you. I never wanted you and Mac as my safety net. Jerry owes me time to get on my feet."

"Sounds like you don't expect a reconciliation to last."

"No, I don't. I don't expect Jerry to be faithful or for us to have a physical relationship. I just want a few years as a family while I help my girls out into the world. I want a dignified ending to twenty-five years of marriage. Is that too much to ask?"

It wasn't, but Grace didn't see it happening. "Did you tell Jerry that?"

"Yeah. He actually teared up a bit, too. Then he said I'd be fine when I got over the shock. I'm a fool, Grace, and I have been all my adult life, apparently. I trusted Papa to do what was best, and I trusted Jerry. Know what that got me? Men who didn't respect me enough to tell me anything that would make their lives uncomfortable. I let them do it, and now I'm paying the price for being a coward. I have to fix it all if I can, and I'll do whatever it takes."

They'd walked nearly the trail's length, and the humidity was taking its toll. Occasional warm gusts rustled through the trees, bringing faint brackish harbor scents, but even that relief vanished when Grace took the shortest route back through residential areas.

They stopped in front of Delaney House, the elegant mansion Grace had renovated during her first year on the Eastern Shore. Stephanie looked horrified when Grace suggested they go inside for cold drinks and rest.

"Look at us! If my hair's as frizzy as yours, I don't want anyone seeing me. Let's just get back to your place. I have to pack, remember?"

"You know Delaney House is an inn now," Grace said, ignoring her last sentence. "The innkeeper runs the daily operations, but I own the property. Would you like to stay here while you work things out?" She tried not to think about lost revenues. With luck, Stephanie would get her life straight soon.

"I can't afford it," Stephanie said flatly.

"You don't have to," Grace insisted. "I checked while you were packing up, and there's a room available on the second floor. You'll be my guest."

Eventually Stephanie agreed but looked ready to cry again.

Grace knew none of them would be happy with this solution, but at least they would have a bit of breathing room. Stephanie needed time to think, and Grace needed to clear the air with Mac, but mostly they all just needed a break.

CHAPTER NINETEEN

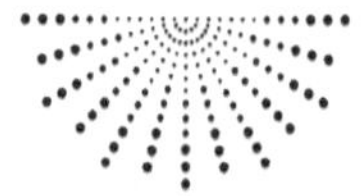

SUNDAY, SEPTEMBER 16

MAC

"We're gonna need a bigger boat," Grace said as she rescued the picnic basket from her children's swinging feet.

"This one's big enough for me," Mac answered absently. His mind was on the call he'd just gotten from Grant Carlisle. It hadn't lasted long, but the sheriff made clear there were no new developments in the Twin Corners arson or Josh Travers's death.

Carlisle hadn't said, *"Don't call me, I'll call you,"* but Mac recognized the brush-off for what it was. He'd worked well with the sheriff until now, so why was this happening?

A wail from Sonny brought him back to his family in the small motorboat. They were still tethered to the dock. In perfect parody of her mother, Fiona informed him sternly that her brother wanted to *go*.

It had been Grace's idea to take the children out on the river this deceptively calm Sunday morning. He'd agreed, hoping it wasn't her way of softening him up before delivering more bad news about her sister. Now he watched her distracting Fiona and Sonny with snacks and thought about how harsh he must have sounded yesterday as he'd effectively ordered Stephanie to leave. He needed to apologize for his behavior, but giving in to the boat ride and picnic was the best he could do.

"No putt putt, Poppy," Fiona said as he pulled away from the dock. "Go fast!"

"This little boat won't go fast, honey," he told his pouting stepdaughter. "Just putt putt."

"Wanna new boat," Fiona said disdainfully.

When he quit laughing, he realized she was right. His little outboard was big enough for him, but not all of them, and it had never occurred to him to do anything about that. What had been an extravagance when he was single was self-indulgent now.

Grace called it his lifeboat.

As he steered them into the creek's center, he wondered if her teasing covered resentment. Did she think he needed an escape from their family? His personal life had been slow and steady until, at the age most men welcomed grandchildren, he'd decided to trade quiet bachelorhood for two babies' bedlam and a high-energy wife. Sometimes he longed for a nap before breakfast, but today was the first time Grace had called him an old poop.

Unfortunately, Fiona heard her, and now everyone and everything in the house was a poop. To top it off, Grace had blamed him for making her mad enough to say it.

She'd been right about that too. When he'd lost his temper with Stephanie, he'd sounded like his grandfather—the one all the cousins avoided.

He cut the motor and let the little boat drift as he started a song the children loved, and Grace hated.

There was an old woman who swallowed a fly...

Fiona squealed, Sonny clapped his chubby hands, and Grace rolled her eyes before breaking into a grin. His beautiful family.

"There's a boat show on Kent Island next weekend," he said when he finished the last verse.

"For real?" Grace said, surprised.

"For real."

"Hear that, kids? Poppy's getting us a big boat!"

The next few hours were full of decisions, large and small. A larger outboard or one with a small cabin? Peanut butter or pimento cheese sandwiches? Carrot sticks or apples? For a few hours, it was a Norman Rockwell day, the kind of memory to keep close—a genuine lifeboat.

It wasn't until they were home, and he was making dinner while Grace bathed the children that he let himself think about Carlisle's call. The sheriff said he was checking in to share information, and after fishing for anything new Mac might have learned, he'd quickly backed off, ending the call saying autopsy results and a final fire marshal's report wouldn't be available until Wednesday—which was bull.

Mac briefly considered making an unofficial call to Desi Marbury. Detective Sergeant Marbury, his former subordinate in the state police, often assisted with his local investigations and could be trusted to keep his concerns about Carlisle confidential. But it felt too early for even that logical next step.

The sheriff was withholding information. And no matter how Mac looked at it, he couldn't figure out why.

CHAPTER TWENTY

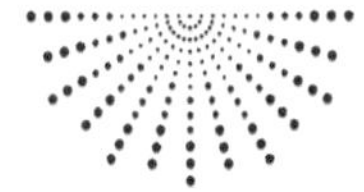

MONDAY, SEPTEMBER 17

The office atmosphere Monday morning was as off-kilter as Grace's home life had been over the weekend. Even though she arrived a few minutes early, everyone else was already at work, and no one was talkative.

Marjorie was in Mosley's office, and Jeff had his head down over a spreadsheet. He only spoke to return Grace's greeting, but she got a bright smile and decided things couldn't be too bad. She made coffee and headed for her office, pausing by Lily's desk. "Join me?" she said in a too cheerful greeting and was rewarded with a 'why not' shrug.

When they were settled in their usual conference spot—two upholstered chairs by the window overlooking the rear garden—Grace studied her assistant's tired face. "Tell me."

"Where do you want me to start?" Lily's words were blunt, but without heat. She sounded as exhausted as she looked. "I know more than I did Friday, but most of its family stuff, and I'd like to keep it that way as long as I can."

Grace would have argued with anyone but Lily. Instead, she said, "Tell me what you can."

"Mom needs a lawyer, too. And I've got four sisters, remember? And there's Uncle Gordy and—"

It was unlike Lily to whine, and Grace cut her off before she got used to it. "Are they all suspects in your stepbrother's death?"

"Sorry, boss. All I can tell you is that no one named Travers has been arrested. Yet."

"Start with your mom. I've been worried about her."

"She's a basket case. My sister Emily gave me an earful about that, and I learned how sheltered I've been regarding Josh. I've always known how he came to be with us, but I suppose I blocked the unsavory part. He was my brother who just didn't live with us. I thought everyone in the family felt the same way."

"And did they?"

"No. I was a self-centered kid, I guess. Counting Josh, I had four older siblings, and I'm the youngest by four years. I mostly hunkered down out of the chaos at home, ignoring arguments when I could. Josh always seemed older than my sisters, even though he wasn't. His childhood away from us was very different from our life, and this weekend I heard how the rest of the family felt in those years. Emily is the oldest—two years older than Josh—and she was jealous of him. The twins, Twila and Alexa, were born four months after Josh, and felt much the same way Emily did. They still do."

"But you didn't?"

"No. I was even worse. I used him, although my kid brain didn't see it that way. I was glad to have Josh around because when he was there, he was the focus. Nobody was picking on me or noticing when I read all day or spent the afternoon in the woods. Later, when I was sneaking out with boys, he even covered for me. In fact, he liked me better than my sisters did, and he was more fun. I was pretty self-indulgent and hell-bent to grow up and get off the farm. I was going to travel everywhere that wasn't the Eastern Shore."

That fit in with what Grace knew of Lily's early life. "So, you joined the Marines."

"Yes. We were all raised to be patriotic and do our duty, so no one fought my decision to defer college and enlist right out of high school. I was in basic training when Dad died. Josh came to the funeral, and we actually had a good adult conversation. We got together when we could over the next year, then I deployed to Afghanistan. Josh lost touch with Mom and my sisters, but he and I still talked by text and occasional calls."

"What was he doing during that time?"

"Bouncing from job to job. Then he joined the Baltimore PD and seemed to find his footing. We both had all-consuming jobs on opposite sides of the world, and when I finally landed stateside, I couldn't find him. I tried all the easy ways, but none of the addresses or numbers I had for him were good. I left messages at his precinct, but when he didn't return my calls, I decided to take the hint and leave him alone. I never saw him again. Not until Saturday when I identified his body."

"Wait! What?" Grace was appalled. "Who asked you to do that?"

"Carlisle. He said I had to see the body in person. I thought Mac would have told you?"

"I'm sure he didn't know," Grace said firmly. "He was home all day and wouldn't have kept that from me. But what was the point? Mac identified Josh from the photograph, too."

Lily had thought about that, too. "Maybe Carlisle thought he could get me to talk without my attorney. I didn't, of course, except to confirm my identification. I was emotional but careful with what I said."

"I'm so sorry." Grace wanted to wring Carlisle's neck. He'd played all of them, but he'd hurt Lily, and she'd see him answer for it.

"It was bad, but nothing on what he pulled next. He showed up at the farm a few hours later. Mom was there alone and let him in. She called me right away, but it took me half an hour to get there."

"Do you know what they talked about?"

"Mom swears she didn't say anything of consequence until I got there, but then she talked non-stop. Nothing incriminating, but not flattering. She made us sound awful. Carlisle didn't get out of line, and I recorded everything. I'll send it to your email."

"What did Carlisle want to know?"

"Anything about Josh. He was definitely fishing for something, but whatever it was, I don't think he got it. It sounds stupid now, but I didn't make a scene because I was grateful he hadn't shown Mom the photos of Josh. Even cleaned up, he looked awful."

"Well, it has been a long time since you saw your brother. Maybe—"

"Carlisle said I should expect the autopsy to report Josh was an addict and probably overdosed." Lily was rigid with anger. "I talked to Cy and Marjorie after you left Friday. They gave me some background on Josh."

"I'll bet The Bat enjoyed herself."

"It wasn't like that," Grace said. "Marjorie was sympathetic and spoke well of your family."

"Really? Huh. Well, we can use all the goodwill we can get. Believe it or not, Carlisle's game, whatever it is, wasn't the weekend's highlight. Emily and I spent the night with Mom, and Sunday morning, she got a phone call from a police captain from the Central District in Baltimore. He said that until two years ago, my brother was a police detective. This captain had worked with him and wanted to express condolences. According to him, the next of kin in Josh's records is Mom. Of everything that's happened, that's what broke her. She'd concocted this daydream where he'd married and had a good relationship with his mother and had left us in his wake. I think we all had a version of that dream for him." Her voice broke.

Grace put her hand over Lily's clenched fists and waited.

"Josh and Mom had an argument after Dad's funeral. She'd just found out Dad had a life insurance policy naming Josh as the only beneficiary. It was only enough to pay for a year of community college, but Mom was livid. She had a farm to run and needed every penny. There was a policy for her, too, but it wasn't nearly as much as she needed. She had to sell about a third of the pastureland."

"And that's what they argued about? Money?"

"Indirectly. You know Mom. She'd never do that, especially on the day of Dad's funeral. But when we were back home, Josh got her alone and asked if he could have our granddad's Bronze Star from World War II. It was a trigger, I guess. Mom told him he'd already gotten more than enough. She says she tried to apologize later, but I don't think she tried very hard."

Grace wondered how the sheriff would connect those dots. "If that's what Denise told Carlisle, maybe he'll move on to another angle. We still don't know why Josh died. Not for sure."

"I think I do. His captain offered condolences but skated around Mom's questions about why Josh left the force. I've seen this kind of thing before, and I knew where to go digging. My brother was fired from the Baltimore PD for misconduct. It's all a bunch of bull, and I don't believe any of it."

Grace decided not to push for details. "If you found that information so easily, then Carlisle probably did, too, before he interviewed your mother."

"I'm convinced it's why he interviewed her. He thought he could guilt her into saying something he could use against me. She may have given him reason to suspect her, too. But on a better note, this morning I had an email from Josh's former partner. He wants to meet, so I'm driving up to Kent Island in about an hour. I'm sorry, but I'm going to need time off, and I may not be able to give much notice."

Happy to finally be of some use, Grace quickly agreed. "Of course. Whatever you need."

"I'm not sure what this guy, Thatcher, is going to tell me, but he didn't want to do it by email or phone. He's legit, though. I checked him out with some buddies up in Baltimore. Solid background, okay rep on the force. One said he was a pencil pusher and a suck up, but that may be because Thatcher was promoted to a supervisory position. I'm hoping whatever he tells me will answer some of my questions."

"I hope so, too," Grace said. "I'm sure Carlisle is keeping information from Mac, so there's definitely a lot we don't know."

"Our reputation may have caught up with us," Lily said ruefully. "The sheriff probably views us as a posse. You, me, Mr. Mosley, especially Marjorie with her snooping. And Mac's one of us, too, whether he wants to be or not."

Definitely not, Grace thought, but she couldn't help smiling. A posse. She liked it.

"If one of us is under suspicion, it's not surprising that the sheriff is keeping information from all of us." Lily stretched. "I need another coffee for the road. Want one?"

"No thanks. If you're okay with it, I'd like to drop in on your mom and see how she is."

Lily tensed up again. "Think I'm holding out on you?"

"Yes, but not intentionally. I can't imagine how hard all of this is for you. If Denise will talk to me, I might pick up on something useful—"

"Or something she skipped when she talked to me," Lily finished for her. "I get it. It's a good idea. I feel like she's glossing over some of the details. Not related to Josh's death, but stuff with my dad. It's not that I'm asking you to interrogate my mother. It's just that she needs help, and we need information, and with any luck, you can get both."

As they were wrapping up, Grace asked if anything of interest on Irene or Dove had turned up in the state criminal or judicial public databases. Expecting to get a distracted 'no,' she was surprised when Lily stopped at the door and looked thoughtful.

"I totally forgot to tell you. Most of what I found we already knew about because we filed it—you know, trying to get sufficient records to substantiate a claim for use of the land the produce stand is on. But I also found where Dom had filed charges of child neglect against Dove, then withdrew the charge the next day. This was a couple of years ago, and I hadn't remembered it until I saw the record. He didn't like Dove leaving Brooklyn with Irene because of Irene's age and health. Dom told Dove he was showing her what would happen if she messed with him."

"Anything come of it?" Grace asked.

"A round of visits from social workers. Let's say Irene didn't interview well. After that, Dove dropped a petition she'd filed to raise her child support payments."

Lily left, and Grace tucked the information away for later consideration. She had a feeling it wasn't the last they'd hear about Dominic Pontello.

CHAPTER TWENTY-ONE

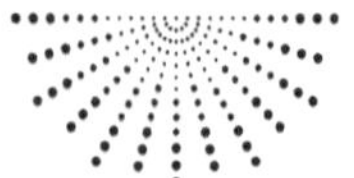

LILY

Lily hadn't recognized the name of the restaurant Josh's partner had given her, and when she finally located the battered food truck in the parking lot of a commercial waterman's offloading ramp, she knew why. The overcast sky cast a dull gray light over the scene as she pulled up, making the idea of eating even more unappealing.

All thoughts of lunch and food poisoning vanished when she met Kyle Thatcher. He wasn't particularly handsome. In fact, his nose skewed a bit to the right in a way that said he'd been on the losing end of a football scrimmage. Or a bar fight. The crinkles around his eyes made him look older than she'd assumed from talking to him, but his smile was charming, as was the warm clasp and gentle squeeze of his handshake. It took a full minute before she registered that he was only an inch or so over her five-six, which was totally counter to her usual taste.

Girl, get yourself together! She had work to do—work for Josh

—and she'd have to be especially careful with Detective Thatcher. She wasn't here to give information, but to get it, and the magnetism oozing off this guy was going to be a huge distraction.

Josh's former partner was guarded at first, but by the time they'd finished the rockfish nuggets and fries he'd insisted she try, they were talking easily. The conversation followed a casual trail, but she knew she had passed some kind of test when he said, "There are some things about Josh you should know, but they aren't good."

"I thought as much. I've put my life in your hands by eating fish from a food truck, so I'll trust you to give me the truth about my brother without sugarcoating it." She was proud that her words came out in her professional voice. Thatcher had disarmed her, and she felt foolish. Talking about Josh with a stranger who'd known her brother better than she had for the last decade was more than she'd bargained for.

"When was the last time you saw him in person?" Kyle asked.

"The day before I left for basic training. He told me he was joining the police force. We exchanged emails for a while, but that slowed down eventually. I tried to see him when I came home on leave a year later, but his phone number was disconnected, and emails and texts went nowhere. What can you tell me about the investigation into his death?"

If Thatcher took offense, it didn't show. "I've talked to Sheriff Carlisle, and I've seen the initial reports. The old lady who lives next door to the church," he hesitated. "She sounds a little unhinged. She told the responding officers she'd seen people behind her house, but couldn't identify them, except to say they were up to no good. Do you think she would have recognized Josh if she'd seen him?"

Lily thought that was an unusual question to lead off with. "I don't know. Were you in the observation room when the sheriff questioned me?" She knew in her gut that he was, and if he lied—

"Yes." A red flush crept up his neck. "The sheriff and I

worked together a few times back in Baltimore. He was good enough to bring me into the investigation on the BPD's behalf, but only in the background. He doesn't want to spread that around. If it makes you think any better of me, I'll share that I don't think you're even in the running as a suspect for the arson or Josh's death."

"If you wanted to question me—"

"I wanted to meet Josh's sister and talk about him. I . . . I miss my friend."

Lily couldn't get a read on him. The man was a puzzle, but she only saw sympathy in his gaze. "Josh and I drifted apart, but he was always my brother."

"He was really proud of you, you know," Thatcher said. "He kept up with your career, and he bragged about you. I know you had the resources to find him if you wanted to. Why didn't you?"

"Because my mommy told me not to," wasn't a reasonable answer, but she dressed it up and delivered it. "Josh didn't part well with my family, and he rebuffed all my attempts to connect. I assumed he had his own life, and he didn't want to be part of mine. Now, is this where you're going to tell me I'm wrong?"

There was a flicker of reaction, and when he spoke there was a bite to his words. "No, this is where I'm going to tell you that you're missing a big chunk of Josh's story."

Over the next hour he talked, and Lily listened, her emotions swinging as he described Josh's police career and gradual decline. At some point during his recitation, she fell back on her training, and without even realizing it, cataloged expressions and wording and formed an opinion she couldn't shake. She felt sure he'd been truthful in his description of Josh's early police career, but then Thatcher lied.

Before he could refine his fiction, she said, "Somewhere in there, you changed what you'd planned to tell me."

"You're wrong. Everything I said was true."

She ignored his protest. "Maybe. Maybe not. But you changed what you were going to tell me."

This time he didn't hide his irritation, but his voice was mild. "Josh said you were sharp. What was your assignment while you were in the military? I'm guessing you ended up in security intelligence of some kind. Interrogation?"

He was looking less attractive and more petulant by the moment, and she was losing patience. "Josh was pretty deep undercover, wasn't he?" It was a total stab in the dark, but it was the first thing she'd thought when she'd left the morgue after identifying her brother. It was the only explanation for Josh's appearance and his death that made sense to her. The only one she could live with. Kyle's description of a washed-up drug dealing cop was too painful to leave unchallenged.

He shoved the remains of their lunch into the greasy paper bag it had come in. "Look, you have it all wrong. Josh was fired from the force two years ago. He called me a couple of weeks ago and said he was leaving town. He sounded rough. I thought he was using again, and that was the last straw for me."

"I don't believe it." Lily leaned across the small table, forcing him to look at her. "You. Are. Lying." But the thought of Josh as a junkie was now firmly planted in the back of her mind, and she hated Kyle Thatcher for putting it there.

"I'm not. I'm telling you this so that your family won't feel guilty."

She had no comeback for that. He'd gone right to the core of her grief and shoved it in her face. And he wasn't finished.

"Josh felt bad about avoiding you, but he was ashamed. He'd wanted to prove to you he could be a success, but it all fell apart."

"How?" she demanded. "I know him. He wouldn't—"

"You knew your stepbrother, Lily. You didn't know my partner."

The wind had picked up, and the weak sunshine that had briefly broken through disappeared behind a bank of heavy gray clouds. Rain began to fall just as a weather alert chirped on Lily's phone. The hurricane had shifted course and was now predicted to make landfall near Newport News.

She got the hood of her rain jacket in place and jiggled the zipper that always stuck. Then she stood and took a business card from her jacket pocket. "Here. Email me if you have any real information, but stay away from my family." She walked away but heard his footsteps crunching on the gravel as he followed, both of them getting wet as the rain picked up.

"I'd like to come to the funeral," he called out. "Is that okay?"

"What?" She stopped long enough for him to catch up and step in front of her, rainwater dripping from the brim of his Baltimore PD cap.

"Josh's funeral. I'll stay away if you insist, but he was my partner for years, and I would like a chance to say goodbye."

"I don't know what will happen with a funeral." The lump in her throat stopped the rant she wanted to unleash on him.

"He was dishonorably discharged from the force," Kyle said slowly. "But the department will still be represented, and I want to be there."

"No. Not if you're still trying to sell this garbage about Josh."

"God, I suck at this. Look, I've already made you so mad you won't listen to me, but I didn't mean to. I only wanted you to have context, so you'd understand what Josh did. Somebody in your family should know the truth."

Whatever he was going to lie about next, she didn't want to hear, but his meaning was clear. If she didn't listen to him, he'd find someone who would. Maybe her mother. She crossed her arms against whatever was coming next and said, "I'm listening."

"Josh has a daughter." A gust of wind buffeted his words, but she heard them plainly enough. He stepped closer. "I know the woman he was involved with. She was married, and she let everyone think the kid was her husband's. I've known her for a while. God, this is hard. I don't want to hurt either of you. She's a great person—really great. She's a close friend of mine."

Lily studied him as the words sank in. "You're really here on her behalf, aren't you?"

He looked embarrassed. "We've been dating, but only for a few months. Her name is Dove Pontello, and their daughter's name is—"

"Brooklyn," Lily said. She felt numb, while at the same time wanting to hit something.

"Yes. They live with the woman who accused you of arson. Dove won't tell you, and she's going to need you. I couldn't lie to Sheriff Carlisle about this, so you'll hear it sooner or later. Josh wouldn't want you to find out like that."

She turned away without speaking, got in her Jeep, and locked the doors.

Kyle Thatcher left without looking back, but Lily sat watching the rain for a long time.

CHAPTER TWENTY-TWO

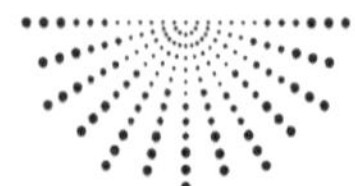

Grace walked into Delaney House and paused in the grand entry hall. Her gaze automatically swept up the cantilevered staircase to the domed ceiling above. She wouldn't change anything about her life with Mac and the children in their cottage by the river, but this place was hers. No matter who occupied it, it would always be hers.

"Admiring your handiwork?" a cheerful voice said, breaking into her reverie.

Grace turned to smile at the inn's housekeeper, Margo Lapin. "Always. I'm still trying to make up for the first time I saw this place and wanted to turn and run back across the bridge."

"That's not what I've heard," Margo said. "You took a pile of rubble and made it into a showpiece that I'm so happy to spend my days in."

"Well, that's an exaggeration—about the condition of the house, I mean. But it was definitely a labor of love for a lot of people. Now that we've been down memory lane, can you spare a few minutes?"

Grace peeked into the elegant and immaculate rooms they passed on their way to the large kitchen at the back of the house. The last time she'd been here was a few weeks ago when her cousin and business partner, Niki Malvern, had come down from New York for their monthly meeting. They had created Delaney Inns, Inc. two years earlier, combining Niki's established Victory Manor Inn with Grace's property, now called The Inn at Delaney House. While Niki was still the general manager, she had moved to New York with her fiancé, leaving daily operations of both inns to Margo and a small staff. So far it was working, but both women were careful not to micromanage Margo, who was more than capable of running their business, but didn't take well to suggestions from the owners.

As they entered the kitchen, Grace said, "You know, one day you're going to come in here and the table and my rocking chair are going to be gone."

"I'm not worried about that. I don't sit down much, and there isn't a spot in your house big enough for the table." Margo patted the top of the sturdy 19th century farm table that took up most of the inside wall of the large Victorian kitchen.

"Apparently, a grandfather a couple of centuries back brought it over from England. Looks like it's been through the wars, doesn't it?"

"And still standing to serve through a few more." Margo glanced at her watch.

Taking the hint, Grace said, "I can't stay but a minute, and I know you're busy too, but I wanted to talk to you face-to-face and thank you for putting my sister up. Make a note for the accountant to charge the lost revenue to me if you have to turn down any rental opportunities while she has it tied up."

Margo looked relieved. "Happy to help."

"The cottage is too small for long-term company, and I'm sure she's much happier staying here than in our guest room."

The innkeeper lost her smile. "You mean *when* she stays here, right? Mrs. Rogers left yesterday morning. She said she'd be back, but she didn't say when."

Grace thought she should have known Stephanie wasn't here as soon as she entered the house—it was too quiet. "All right. Let me find out what happened to her, and I'll be back in touch with you."

"No worries. We're getting cancellations right and left. The hurricane has everyone spooked.I should have plenty of room for her if she comes back."

Again, with the hurricane. In Grace's mind, the long-awaited storm and her flighty, thoughtless sister were twins. Both seemed determined to wreak havoc in her life.

CHAPTER TWENTY-THREE

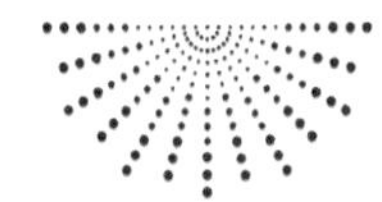

It was difficult for Grace to push thoughts of her missing sister aside and focus on the conversation she needed to have with Denise Travers. Lily's mother had her keen intellect and wicked sense of humor, but Grace had never seen the woman upset.

She drove slowly down the lane to the Travers farm and pulled up in front of the long bungalow-style home. Carefully tended hanging baskets hung from the porch railings in stark contrast to the sandbags piled around the foundation. She was surprised to see that hurricane hysteria was alive and well this far inland from the riverfront.

The screen door opened before she could knock. Denise welcomed her with a hug and led her through to the formal living room.

Grace settled onto a floral print sofa and made small talk while Denise produced iced tea and brownies. When she finally sat on the wingback chair opposite Grace, it was only to perch on the edge. "Josh was a sweet boy," she said without preamble. "I wish I had done more for him."

"Just like your daughter," Grace said, smiling. "Straight to the point."

"I wanted to start with something true, but kind. Josh was an adorable baby and a sweet little boy."

Grace wondered if that was what Denise thought she should say, rather than her true memory of the child her husband had fathered.

"That's what you wanted to know, isn't it?" Denise set her untouched tea aside. "I thought I was beyond being embarrassed about the whole thing, but apparently not. When you're barely twenty and have one baby, leave your husband, make up long enough to get pregnant again, and then learn he was screwing a girl in Baltimore..." She smoothed an invisible wrinkle from her slacks. "Super Daddy had two women pregnant at the same time and got three babies in one year."

Grace paused mid-sip. "Did you tell the sheriff that?"

"Isn't that why you're here?" Denise squeezed her eyes shut. When she opened them again, she looked calmer. "My apologies. I know you're here to help. Do you ever get pedicures?"

"What?" Grace laughed in surprise.

"Pedicures. Talking to Sheriff Carlisle was like that. You know, a so-called beauty treatment that hurts like hell if you have ingrown nails. A quasi-medical procedure all dressed up with glossy polish. For some silly reason, I thought telling him everything, even though it hurt, would remove the guilt I've felt for thirty-six years."

"Did it?" Grace asked.

"No. My husband has been gone for a long time, and I still haven't forgiven him for Josh."

Denise pointed to a family portrait above the fireplace. A dark-haired boy stood between three blonde girls of similar age. Next to them was Wayne Travers, holding a baby girl.

"Our first three girls take after me," Denise said. "Joshua and Lily were Wayne's little clones."

"I'll bet that was the last time you got her into anything with ruffles," Grace said, but the joke fell flat.

"They look happy, don't they?" Denise asked wistfully. "I took that photo, and I keep it up there to remind me of my place in our family. I stayed behind the camera in those days, keeping everything steady. At least I tried to. Sometimes I ran out of patience, or goodness, or whatever it was that let me pretend I was happy, too."

If this was how the meeting with Carlisle had gone on Saturday, Grace thought he had left with all sorts of interesting ideas. "It would help me to know what the sheriff asked you. That way, I'd know what direction he was leaning."

Thunder rumbled in the distance. Denise went to close the windows against the approaching rain. "The sheriff was nice. Led me along like a puppy. First, he skirted around everything, then asked about Irene's claim that Lily had been a juvenile delinquent and threatened to burn down the church. I told him it was all ridiculous. He agreed with me, and I relaxed a little. Big mistake. That's when he switched to Josh and Wayne." She turned back and came to sit next to Grace. "I said more than I should."

Grace leaned forward. "Such as?"

"That I never wanted Josh and always resented him." The words came out in a rush. "Learning to live with that kind of wound was hard. Poor Josh is dead, but like everything else he did, he even managed to hurt us in the way he died."

Even though Lily had her father's coloring, she had Denise's stubborn expression and the same defiant tilt of the chin. But Grace didn't see Lily's strength and adaptability in her mother. If it had ever been there, it had worn away.

"Lily thinks I need an attorney," Denise said abruptly.

"I think everyone does. But what do you think? Do you want an attorney?"

"No. Not unless it's you. I'm already so embarrassed to be in this position. And just thinking about Sasha Blayne—Josh's mother—tears me up. Always has. Back when it all started, everyone looked at me like I was some kind of fool. Which I wasn't." Denise took a shaky breath. "Wayne was a good man, a good father, and a much better person than I am. I told the sheriff that, too."

Grace could imagine Carlisle licking his chops over that admission. "What else did you tell him before Lily joined you?"

"I said Sasha was a tramp, and if he wanted an unbiased opinion of her, he'd have to go somewhere else. He really perked up when he heard that."

Over the next half hour, Denise shared her story—one Grace knew she'd never have gotten if Lily had been with her.

"Wayne and I were separated when we realized how much we loved each other. We got back together, and the twins were born. Sasha showed up with Josh when they were four weeks old. Wayne and I were kids who grew up fast. We made mistakes. I've told you and the sheriff all this because I want you to understand how I feel about Josh."

Grace leaned forward. "I can appreciate that. But I have to ask, do you know anyone from Josh's past, or his mother's, who might've wanted to hurt him?"

Denise looked miserable. "Sheriff Carlisle asked that, too. The answer is no! And I didn't want to hurt him, either. It just happened, my feelings I mean, but I worked very hard not to let them spill over onto Josh. Not until Wayne's funeral. I feel worse about that than anything."

"How about recently?" Grace asked. "We're not getting much from the sheriff's office. Did Josh's captain in the Baltimore PD tell you anything that might indicate someone held a grudge against him?"

Denise paused, then said, "No. It was a family visit, a formality. Very nice, but light on details."

Grace said, "Somehow, Josh went from being a police officer to ending up in an abandoned church that was deliberately set on fire. If you have any idea why he was here on the shore so close to your home, it could help us figure out what happened."

Denise stood abruptly and left the room. When she returned, she was holding a small wooden box that she opened to reveal a Bronze Star medal. Its red, white, and blue ribbon was as pristine as the day it was awarded.

"If he wanted anything from me, it had to be this. It was Wayne's father's. He was wounded in World War II."

Grace studied the medal. "Lily told me Josh had asked you for this the day of the funeral and you said no. So why would he come for it now?"

Denise looked defeated. When she answered, the words came in a rush, as if she wanted to rid herself of the painful memory. "He called me on Sunday before the fire. I hadn't heard from him in ten years, and I nearly fainted when I heard his voice. For a second, I thought it was Wayne. They always sounded alike. Josh didn't say much at first, just asked how the girls and I were doing. Then he said, 'I know I made you mad when I asked for the medal at Dad's funeral, but—' and I just lost it." She stopped abruptly.

"Did you tell the sheriff about this?"

"I was too ashamed," Denise said. "I cut Josh off before he could finish. Said I didn't want to hear about that damn medal again and hung up. It was a knee-jerk reaction." She was bright red with embarrassment. "I hung up on him, and now he's dead. I keep telling myself that none of this is my fault, but maybe it is. What if he wasn't calling about the medal at all? What if he was trying to apologize, or if he needed help?"

"You hadn't heard from Josh at all before that call? Not in ten years?"

"No," Denise said eagerly. "I swear."

"What about his mother?"

"Sasha? She probably would still be harassing us, but she died a few years ago. Cancer. I used to look her up from time to time. I'm not proud of it, but I always felt better when I knew what she was up to."

Grace tried to piece it all together, but too much information was missing about Josh's last days. "Do you know if Josh ever went to Irene Jensen's part of the woods? Or had any connection to the Twin Corners church?"

The abrupt change of subject seemed to confuse Denise. "Have you ever seen a map of our property?"

"No," Grace said slowly.

"If you look at a map of all the parcels Wayne and I bought over the years, you'll see they're contiguous and run down to Deer Creek. The creek is the border between Irene's land, the church's parcel, and our farm, but Josh and Wayne camped all over those woods. Nowadays, hikers do, too, and I can't be bothered with trying to stop them." She hesitated, then said, "Was Josh really homeless? I regretted having him in our lives, but I would have never left him alone and sick out on the street—or out in those woods! I didn't know any of that when he called." Like her daughter, Denise pulled her grief inward, her posture not inviting any physical sympathy.

Grace watched the wind blow leaves past the windows and let her cry in peace.

Eventually the sobs eased, and Denise wiped her face. "Throughout all of this, I've been given chance after chance to rise above the fallout from Wayne's one bad decision. I tried to be a good stepmother, but I never once thought of Josh as my child. He was an obligation. And when I might have saved him at the end, I pushed him away again."

Grace said, "You couldn't have known what kind of shape he was in, Denise. You aren't responsible for what happened to him."

"Lily always says you're kind. You drive her crazy with it sometimes. I didn't tell her about Josh's last call. I'll do that when she comes by this afternoon."

"Good. I think you should tell the sheriff, too. I won't say anything to him but keeping it to yourself might cause problems down the road."

Denise nodded slowly, but whether she was agreeing or just trying to end the conversation, Grace couldn't tell.

CHAPTER TWENTY-FOUR

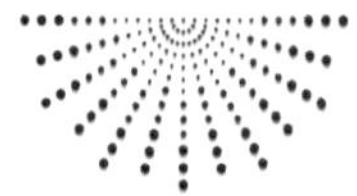

MAC

Mac looked across the conference table at two of his oldest friends and knew his wife was going to be irritated when she found out about this meeting.

Correctly interpreting Mac's hesitation, Mosley said, "Are you sure you don't want to wait for Grace?"

"No." Mac gave Marjorie a pointed look. "And I don't want either of you filtering your thoughts out of consideration for my marriage." As he intended, this brought a chuckle from Mosley and a wry smile from his former sister-in-law.

"Seriously," he continued, "I've got time right now, you're both here, and Grace will hear it all eventually. But the three of us knew Josh—at least to some degree." He paused, then jumped in. The story wouldn't get any better if they ignored it. "Cyrus, I know you helped Wayne handle the legal side of the custody question. And

Marjorie, as I recall, you were in the women's guild at Saint Mary's with Denise Travers."

"Yes," Marjorie said flatly. "She has a bloated opinion of herself —and her family. Her birth family, I mean, not Wayne and the kids. Her parents are Boston come-heres, and when Denise lowered herself to marry a farmer from the Eastern Shore, you'd think she gave up royalty to join the country folks like us."

Mac let the comment go. "Here's my dilemma today—" He paused, considering how much to share. "Carlisle told me the medical examiner's office is slow walking the autopsy reports on Josh Travers." He let that hang in the air. Neither of them looked surprised.

"They aren't giving it priority, or Carlisle isn't sharing the results with you?" Mosley asked.

"Lee wouldn't be here if he and the sheriff were on the same page," Marjorie said. "I stopped by the courthouse this morning to file a deed transfer and saw the State's Attorney."

"Did she run before you could catch her?" Mac teased.

"Like a scalded cat." Marjorie threw up her hands in mock bewilderment. "I was only going to ask about her new grandbaby, but she ducked into the ladies' room before I could even say hello. I followed her in, of course, but she brushed me off."

Mac absorbed that tidbit. It wasn't only the sheriff and the medical examiner's office, but the SA was also avoiding people connected— even tangentially—to the investigation. Maybe he wasn't as off his game as he'd thought. "I'm considering my next steps, and I wanted to coordinate with you two. Make sure there's nothing I'm missing."

"Such as?" Mosley asked.

Mac leaned forward. "Let's start with this. Carlisle has only been around Kingston County about ten years. The three of us were here in the years of Wayne and Denise's marriage and the scandal around Josh's birth. Can either of you think of something that would cause Carlisle to close us locals out of his investigation? Anything that could make him believe we'd cut one of the Travers some slack, or even help them with a coverup? Something that would get traction all the way up to the State level?"

"You don't want my help. You want gossip." Marjorie's face tightened. "I *do* have other skills, you know."

Mosley reached over, patted her shoulder and said to Mac, "She's been with me nearly forty years because she's smart, perceptive, and very good at her job."

Mac thought Mosley was deftly avoiding defining exactly *which* job Marjorie excelled at: the one where she was a secretary and de facto paralegal, or the one where she was a clearinghouse for every shred of gossip—true or not—circulating in Mallard Bay. "I need help, Margie. Can you climb down off your high horse and give me a hand?"

Marjorie continued to sulk, but said, "Well, you and Wayne were good friends, right? How about the times you helped out when young Josh's mother complained about Wayne or Denise?"

"That's right," Mosley said. "I was in on those sessions, too, since I represented the Traverses in the custody fight over Josh. None of it amounted to much. The boy's mother was... let's call her contentious. She used any excuse to paint Wayne, and especially Denise, as villains so she could squeeze more child support out of them."

Mac leaned back, relieved. He had already talked to Avril, who'd said much the same thing. Then he thought of something he hadn't asked her. "What do you know about Josh's life growing up in Baltimore?"

"It wasn't like the life he had here," Marjorie said, then gave Mac a look that dared him to ask how she knew, but Mosley spoke up, changing the subject.

"The logistics were complicated. Wayne wanted to keep both women happy, and every time Sasha crossed the Bay Bridge, she found some way to upset Denise, so having her come here didn't always work out."

"Did you act as a go-between?" Mac guessed. He hadn't known, but wasn't surprised. Mosley would have kept any hint of conflict away from the authorities, even him.

Mosley said, "My staff and I did."

Mac got a wide smile from Marjorie. "I would be the staff in question. I got the afternoons off to go and get the boy, and young Josh was no trouble. He usually read a book on the drive to the Traverses' farm. And that only went on for about a year. Then things settled down a bit, and they started meeting at the Annapolis Mall."

They'd gone off track, but something about this nagged at Mac. He asked if either of them knew of any trouble Sasha or Josh had gotten into in Baltimore. The question earned him surprised looks and another sharp rebuke from Marjorie.

"So that's what this is all about? Why didn't you say so? Do you mean the time Josh was arrested, and you went up there, got him out of jail, and made it all go away?"

Mac sighed. He'd been right all along.

"You saved him, Mac. You and Wayne, and the time he spent here on the shore. That boy would have turned out just like his trashy mother if it hadn't been for you."

"That's harsh, Marjorie," Mosley said gently. "Ms. Blayne lived hand to mouth in a bad neighborhood, but she did what she could for Josh. And Social Services kept an eye on them. I talked to the boy on many occasions, and he seemed to love his mother. I also tried to keep up with him after Wayne's death, but eventually I lost track of both of them."

Marjorie looked thoughtful, then sad. "Everyone liked Wayne. He was a good person. What he did, cheating on Denise, that was wrong. But he admitted the truth and did his best by his boy. And Josh worked hard, too. It hurts to think of him dying that way."

After a moment, she added, "Guilt doesn't die with the one who earned it, you know. What Wayne and Sasha did, no matter how they tried to make up for it, still affects some people. Denise most of all, I would imagine."

Mosley sighed. "Mac, I don't know what Carlisle and the State's Attorney are keeping from you, but you'll probably find out before long. I hope whatever it is won't impact the memory of Josh's career and the good work he did."

There wasn't much to say after that, and Mac left feeling as if he'd somehow made things worse for a dead man. When he reached his own office at the police station, he called Grant Carlisle and said, "We need to talk."

CHAPTER TWENTY-FIVE

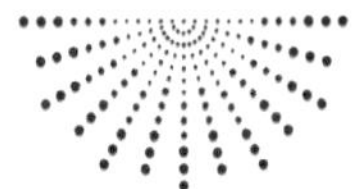

MAC

"I'm sorry, Chief Mac," the clerk in the reception office of Kingston County's public safety building said. "Sheriff Carlisle is still on a conference call. He knows you're here, and I'm sure he'll be free soon. Want a refill on the coffee?"

The last thing Mac wanted was more lukewarm, burned coffee. But he smiled and held out his cup. He was determined to remain upbeat, but it was getting harder with each passing minute.

His appointment with Carlisle had been at one—a half hour ago —and his presence was becoming awkward. He knew almost everyone who'd passed through the large space and wondered if Carlisle was making a point by keeping him waiting.

After the former Kingston County Sheriff, Weiland Jones, suffered a fatal heart attack, Carlisle, a retiree from the Baltimore Police Department, had run unopposed in the interim election. Mac had enjoyed an easy working relationship with the new sheriff. Until now.

His concern that he was being shut out of the investigation into Josh Travers's death grew, and when Carlisle's door remained closed, his suspicions seemed justified.

As he was leaving a message with the receptionist, her intercom crackled to life. Mac was close enough to hear Carlisle say, "Send McNamara in and buzz me in ten. I don't have time for this crap today."

"Sorry for the wait, buddy." A tall man with stork-like legs, Carlisle crossed his office in long strides, his hand out, palm up and fingers spread for a see-how-strong-I-am shake. "We're covered up and short-handed. If you weren't a good friend, I'd recruit Tremaine Harper for my staff. We sure could use him. That guy has it all."

He waved Mac to a low armchair across from his own seat, an executive desk chair that emphasized Carlisle's six-foot-five frame.

Mac added the chair—and the comment about poaching Harper —to his growing list of reasons to dislike the sheriff. "Harper's a good man. Sharp and hardworking. Reminds me of Joshua Travers when he started out."

"You seriously comparing Harper to Travers?" Carlisle's surprise might have looked genuine to Mac at one time, but not now.

Instead of answering, Mac said, "Did you ever work with Josh in Baltimore?"

"I'm sure I saw him around, but I never heard of him until he got fired." Carlisle smirked. "What does that tell you?"

"Gotcha," Mac said conversationally. "You were... remind me again? In logistics and supply?" It was a stupid thing to do, but he couldn't resist. And he enjoyed watching Grant Carlisle's smug expression evaporate. The sheriff might have been a captain in Baltimore, but not in the criminal division, which was the impression he had liked to give when he campaigned during the election.

"I held a lot of positions over the years," Carlisle said. "And I can tell you that those boys over in Criminal Investigations run dark sometimes. Travers decided the pay was better on the wrong side of the law. It was only a matter of time before he took a tumble."

The little speech was straight out of an old, bad movie. Mac could almost hear Grace huffing in exasperation. "You might not be aware of Josh's background. I've known him all his life—"

"But not in the last five or six years, right? Thanks, Chief, but if that's all you're here for, let me save you some time. I have intel from Travers's old partner. The guy spent the last few years trying to save Travers's ass, not that he got anywhere for his efforts. I don't need your help with this investigation. I know how you operate, and I don't like it. My department runs strictly by the book."

Mac leaned forward, stunned. Keeping his tone mild, he said, "You obviously have concerns about me. Do me the courtesy of allowing me to address them."

"Courtesy? That's rich, coming from you. This murder occurred on my patch, not yours. The deputy on the scene should never have involved you, but he did, so now I'll make my position clear. You and your wife and whoever else you want to play with can handle Mallard Bay's Police Department, but all of you need to stay out of my operations."

"Why?" Mac asked. "What's happened, Grant? I can't think of any reason you wouldn't cooperate with anyone who can help solve this murder."

Carlisle studied him, then said, "Why don't you have my job? From what I've been told, all you'd have had to do was file for candidacy and sit tight until election day."

It didn't sound like a challenge, just curiosity, but Mac was careful with his answer. "I am where I want to be, doing what I want to do. I only want to take care of my home patch." He hesitated, then added, "Except in circumstances where I can be of value to another agency—"

"Or where your friends and family are involved," Carlisle cut him off.

"I don't deny that both Irene Jensen and Lily Travers are friends of mine. And Josh was once a very good friend. Are you saying you'd sit on your hands in a similar situation?"

"Of course not, but the difference is I follow the letter and spirit of the law, you don't. And while we're on the subject of our differences, I don't interfere in other jurisdictions, or spread confidential information," he paused to give Mac a sly grin. "And I don't assault people I don't like."

Mac didn't give him the satisfaction of reacting to the provocative statement. Instead, he decided to cut through Carlisle's insinuations. "And you think I do?"

"I know it," Carlisle said. "You got a disciplinary warning for assaulting a citizen and restraining her against her will. I'll admit I was amazed when I heard that, but I guess I wouldn't run for a position of any consequence, either, if I had something that big hanging in my background."

This time, Mac didn't hide his surprise or his disgust when Grant Carlisle smiled, showing every one of his capped teeth. "If you ever want the details of how I helped Josh Travers pull his drug-addled mother out of a prostitution ring, just ask me. I'm not ashamed of it, and I don't hide it. I'm sorry you're letting my actions color your view of Josh and his life."

Carlisle clapped slowly. "Bravo. That's a great speech. What I can't understand is how it all got swept under the rug. You kept on racking up commendations and promotions when any other officer would have been stalled right where he was until he quit."

"You read my state police personnel file."

Carlisle looked uncomfortable, but his next words were pure

bluster. "I have connections in a lot of areas. I know things you don't. So, yeah, I know what you did and how you still caught break after break in your career with the state police. I've got to ask myself why? Who else have you crossed the line for, and what do they owe you?"

Torn between wanting to walk out and poking Carlisle a bit more to see what he would spit out, Mac said, "If you expended as much effort looking into Joshua Travers's file as you have mine, you'd know that it's highly unlikely he ever chose to take drugs. Whatever brought him to his death in that church isn't a case of a junkie meeting a bad end."

Carlisle stood and came around the desk to tower over Mac, forcing him to look up. "Travers is a waste of resources. A crooked cop. I won't spend a single taxpayer dollar more than I have to closing out the investigation into his death, and you are not going to make it any harder for me with your sob stories. If you want to cry over someone, how about that old lady Travers terrorized before he died? Irene Jensen was half crazy to start with. Maybe she got scared enough to do something drastic to defend herself. No jury will convict her if she did."

Mac wondered if the man knew that his nose hairs needed a trim. The petty observation eased his need to sucker punch the ass.

"I'm busy." Carlisle stepped back and pointed at the door.

Mac took his time walking across the room. He opened the door and raised his voice to carry into the reception area. "Thanks for filling me in, *buddy*. Josh Travers was a good man and a decorated officer. I'll do everything I can to help your investigation."

He could feel Carlisle's glare as he left, stopping to exchange pleasantries with several people before the front door of the Sheriff's Office closed behind him. He kept a smile on his face until he reached his patrol car, but his mind was racing.

At the administrative end of command in the Baltimore PD, Carlisle wouldn't ordinarily have had access to information about an undercover officer or their active cases, but he would have been told the cover story that protected Josh and his work. If that was what he still believed, then the investigation Josh had been working might not be closed, and Josh's name wouldn't be cleared until it was. Carlisle could bluster all he wanted, but Mac was sure there were other eyes closely watching the sheriff's work. If Carlisle was being kept in the dark about Josh's status, there was a very good reason.

As painful as it was, Mac needed to step back and wait for either Carlisle or the agencies above the Kingston County Sheriff's Office to take the next steps. But that still left him with a dilemma about Carlisle's knowledge of Mac's State Police personnel file. If someone had leaked information from his record, it was a problem. And if Carlisle had gotten access to the entire file, he may have seen much more than a favor done for a fledgling police officer.

He made a call as he pulled out of the parking lot. It was time to bring in reinforcements.

CHAPTER TWENTY-SIX

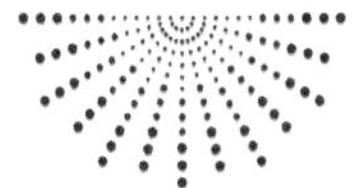

MAC

"Grant Carlisle has a, uhm..." Desi Marbury paused, looking embarrassed. It had been a long time since Mac had been one of her supervisors, but she was still careful with her language around him. "...burr under his saddle," she finished. "And he definitely has a problem with you, Chief."

They were in McDonald's in Centreville, Mac dressed for the pre-hurricane chores he hoped to get in after they were finished, and Desi in her off-duty uniform of ripped jeans and a well-worn Van Halen tee. Her long red hair, which was usually in a low, braided knot at the nape of her neck, fell loosely over her shoulders in waves. Except for its color, she was unremarkable, as was he. Neither looked like what they were—skilled, decorated police officers carrying concealed weapons and discussing arson and a suspicious death.

"Does Carlisle talk about the problem he has with me?" Mac asked.

"He gave Captain Binks an earful. Son of a... gun told my boss that he didn't want me on the Travers case in any capacity because of my connection to you. Said anything you learned would go straight to Grace and compromise his investigation. Carlisle says none of us can keep our mouths shut."

A surge of anger almost put Mac off his Quarter Pounder. "When was this?"

"Cap called me in as soon as I reported for duty this morning and ripped me a new one before he heard my side. When I told him I hadn't had any connection with the sheriff's investigation, he cooled down. I went back over all the recent cases I've worked with you, pointing out our brilliance, naturally, and when I finished, he was still pissed, but not at us. When I told him you'd called and wanted to meet, he said to read you in on Carlisle's request and the active case on Travers's death so you wouldn't be caught out when the MSP ramps up their inquiries."

Mac knew Captain Binks was a straight arrow and was relieved to know he hadn't bought Carlisle's narrative. "So, read me in. Is the analysis of Josh's autopsy and the crime scene evidence still being slow walked through the system?"

"No. It never has been. Cap made a few calls, and whatever he'd learned wasn't favorable to the sheriff. He said to tell you Grant Carlisle is just a legend in his own mind, and the Baltimore brass couldn't get him retired fast enough. Carlisle's the one holding things up. After his first five years, most of his career in Baltimore was spent in administrative positions. This is his first major crime investigation, and he doesn't know what he's doing. Keeps changing his mind about what he wants and what to do next, so naturally information is slow to come together."

Mac felt better. Five years ago, something like this wouldn't have been more than a headache, but now there was more on the line than the mud Carlisle was slinging. Lily, Desi, and who knew how many other good people might be hurt by the sheriff's insinuations. "So, what can you tell me? Have you seen the test results? How did Josh die?"

Desi wiggled a hand and leaned over the table. Her eyes shining, she said, "That'll be an argument for a prosecutor and a jury. Seriously, Chief, this is a strange one." 'Strange' in Desi's world meant exciting. "Sorry. I know he was your friend, and I don't mean—"

Mac waved off her apology. "He was murdered. How did it happen?"

"Travers was stabbed. Small knife wound, left side, lower back. Easy for the paramedics at the scene to miss as they tried to revive him. Medical examiner said there'd been some superficial first aid, but the cut to Travers's liver caused slow internal bleeding. It might not have incapacitated him right away, and the stabbing could have happened as much as forty-eight hours before Josh entered the church. Smoke inhalation didn't help and undoubtedly sped up his death, but the stab would have done the job eventually."

"He was out in those woods slowly dying for as long as two days?" Mac thought of Josh as he'd last seen him. They'd gone to an Orioles game. What had been so important that neither one of them had followed up their promises to get together again? He'd have to come to terms with his feeling of loss and regret at some point, but it was an indulgence he couldn't afford right now. "How much of this is being released to the press?"

"Only that Travers's death was definitely a homicide. No details, at least not right now. Carlisle didn't want that much released, but he's trying to look like he's cooperating with us."

Mac pushed a bit more. "Not that I'm ungrateful, but in light of all the crap Carlisle is spewing, I have to ask why Binks wants me to have the information if he's keeping it out of the press."

"It's precisely because of Carlisle that Binks wants you on

board. State Police and Baltimore PD have been watching everything and are ready to step in. They've waited about as long as they can, but Carlisle is getting close to screwing up more than this death investigation. He's monkeying around in Travers's personnel files, and since your friend spent the last two years undercover, you can see how that might be a problem." She sat back and beamed at him. "Feel better about things now Chief?"

'Better' wasn't the right word.

"Cap said he'll fill you in on the details as soon as he can, but we only have one goal—solving Josh Travers's murder fast and clean without jeopardizing the case he was working on. So, Cap is letting Carlisle push the story that the autopsy is the delay, and it's an easy sell if you don't know much about stab wounds and asphyxiation. One dead guy, two causes of death and two killers?" She gave him the hand wiggle again. "It plays for now."

Mac thought about how it would play out in the press. Two killers. One who stabbed Josh and left him to die, and one who set the fire that sped up his death.

"Chief?" Desi leaned back in.

Mac glanced around, relieved that no one was interested in their intense conversation.

"One more thing. You won't like it, but Cap says to tell you it's crucial. Nobody is going to set Carlisle straight until MSP and Baltimore PD take over. No matter what the sheriff says, does, or implies, he's the face and voice of the investigation into Detective Travers's death. Cap says he'll explain everything to you in person when you get together. Cap still thinks Carlisle's clean, but ignorant and arrogant. He's furious that we're encroaching on his authority. Plus, like I said, he's got a bug about you and it's driving him crazy."

"That's ridiculous!"

Desi stuffed a fry in her mouth and chewed, shaking her head at him. "Not really. Every big name who backed him in his election tried to get you to run first, didn't they?"

"A few people mentioned it."

"Bull...crap, pardon my French, sir. Hell, Cap was on the committee pushing the grassroots effort to find a candidate. You were the number one choice. Carlisle was a distant second. He wasn't even close, and he had to work for that. I think along the way he learned not only how impressive your career was, but how many of us you raised up through the ranks before you retired from the State Police."

"That explains what Carlisle said, I guess."

Desi grew serious, then angry as Mac described the meeting in Carlisle's office.

"He hacked into the state personnel database!" Desi whispered, wide eyed. "Holy—" she stopped when Mac shook his head.

"I doubt he did it personally. Our sheriff can barely open his own emails. But he got the information somehow."

Desi looked uncomfortable. "Josh isn't the only messed up kid you took some heat for, and none of us will ever forget it."

"I'm not doing anything about it at this point, but I want Binks to know that Carlisle has an in with someone who's feeding him information from the state's archived files."

"*Someone* as in?"

"Don't know. Who's aware that you're meeting with me today?"

"No one but the Cap. I eat half my meals here, so nothing new."

Mac said, "Good. I'm at Lowe's shopping for supplies, or I will be."

Desi slurped the last of her shake. "Leave it with me. I have a feeling this is another nasty development Captain Binks will want to handle himself."

CHAPTER TWENTY-SEVEN

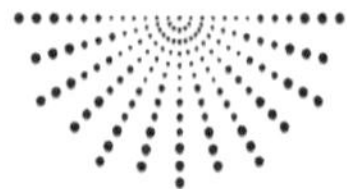

"Where does this leave us?" Grace asked. She noticed her open office door and asked Mac to wait on hold. Lily was still out, and a quick check told her Jeff was manning their phones. She had no reason not to trust their administrative assistant, but now wasn't the time to test his ability to keep his mouth shut in the face of juicy gossip.

Carrying her phone, she walked to the bay window where she could see the late summer flowers swaying in the pre-storm breeze. Maybe looking at something beautiful would make this ugly situation easier to handle. Returning to Mac, she said, "Okay, I guess I'm being unfair to ask, but naturally I want to know everything Carlisle had to say."

He didn't answer immediately, and when he spoke, he sounded tired. "We're in the same situation we were in this morning before I found out what the sheriff really thinks of me." He relayed Carlisle's accusations, and when she calmed down from that, he added the leak of his personnel file and sat back while she exploded.

"That's reprehensible! If he read your *classified* records from the state police, what else is he capable of?"

"We don't know that's what happened," Mac said. "But he does have the most salacious details from my one disciplinary action. Lots of people knew I was a mentor to Josh, and, according to Marjorie, everyone in Mallard Bay knows I helped Josh when he was arrested."

"You were a mentor to a lot of people, and you saved his career," Grace argued, not ready to give up being mad. "But how many people know that you both were arrested after you saved his mother's life?"

"Technically, I wasn't—"

"Handcuffs, Miranda warning, and a ride in the back of a squad car."

Mac sighed. "I talk too much to you at night."

"It may have all been explained eventually, but how many people actually knew what happened?"

"Actually, the misunderstanding was cleared up on the ride to the precinct. I wasn't booked, and I got Josh released the next day after Sasha Blayne regained consciousness at the hospital. She testified that Josh called me to come help both of them after her pimp had beaten her senseless. It was a squalid mess, but it all worked out."

Grace didn't let it go. "How many of the people who knew what happened might be inclined to tell Grant Carlisle?"

"About the incident itself? Any number of people could have, but it doesn't seem like the kind of thing that would pop up in conversation this many years later. He's only been hostile to me lately."

"And you think this is why? Because you had a stellar career even after receiving a disciplinary warning?" When Mac didn't answer, she said, "You have to find out who told him."

"State officials need to handle it. I'm serious, Grace. I can't do anything right now, and you can't interfere. No one else can know about this. I need you to trust me and let it go. I gave someone my word it wouldn't go anywhere, and I'm only telling you this so you'll understand how Carlisle feels about me. About us. Don't provoke him."

She had asked him to trust her often enough, and he'd never let her down. "I'll let it go, but I won't forget it."

"You can avenge my honor when it's all over, okay?"

"Looking forward to it. Meanwhile, I'll still give you everything I can. Lily's got a lot of support in the community, and Marjorie says all kinds of rumors are flying about her being railroaded by the sheriff. Marjorie heard from her nephew—the deputy, not the HVAC tech—that Irene Jensen is being looked at for the arson and Josh's death. Can we talk about that?"

"Maybe later. Right now, I've got another hurricane video conference to get through. We have to get ready to evacuate tonight, too. The storm could still change course, but it looks as if it's coming up the bay."

After he disconnected, Grace leaned her forehead against the cool glass of the windowpane and studied the peace rose she'd planted in the little garden last year. Would it still be here when the storm was over?

A soft tap on the door announced Lily's arrival. She joined Grace by the window. "You look like your day has been as fun as mine. Learn anything new?"

"Trying to sort it all out right now," Grace shared Marjorie's latest gossip and then said, "How about you?"

"Josh's partner had some news—big news. I've got to go talk to Mom, but I wanted to stop here first and find out how your conversation with her turned out."

Grace knew Lily would be out the door as soon as she heard about Josh's call to Denise. "Your news first," she said, gesturing for her to sit down.

Lily looked both defeated and agitated as she dropped onto the chair. "Guy's name is Kyle Thatcher. He was Josh's partner in Baltimore until Josh was supposedly fired for misconduct."

"He confirmed Josh was fired?"

"Not to my satisfaction," Lily said firmly. "But yes, that's what he says. And there's another complication, a big one."

Grace waited while Lily seemed to search for the right words.

"I was buying his concerned partner routine, but then Thatcher lied to me. He said Josh was an addict who fell apart when a woman he was seeing broke it off. She was married, had a baby, and later got divorced. Josh told Thatcher that the child was his."

"And you think it's all a lie?" Grace asked, even though she knew from the tears glistening in Lily's eyes that the story wasn't finished.

"I know my brother wasn't an addict. And 'falling apart' isn't in Josh's playbook. So, all that's a lie. But I also know he would have moved heaven and earth to do what was right for his child. And if he couldn't do that out in the open, he'd do it secretly." She looked at Grace. "Maybe from the woods behind Irene and Dove's house."

"Brooklyn," Grace guessed.

"That's what Thatcher says, and I believe it. Which means I've been babysitting my own niece for five years. Dove has to know Josh is Brooklyn's father, but I'm damned sure that her ex-husband doesn't. No way Dominic Pontello would support some other man's kid."

"Well, wait. How can you be sure of anything? Did Josh get a DNA test done?"

"I don't know. But I was there all through Dove's marriage and pregnancy, and it fits. Dove gave Dom the divorce on his terms, and she never reports him when he's late with support checks. She's a basket case about him filing for full custody, though, and she's said more than once that Dom would kill her if she had an affair."

"None of that means anything, Lily. Why are you so quick to believe what some stranger tells you?"

"When did you last see Brooklyn?"

"Ages, I guess."

Lily held out her right arm, pushing up the sleeve of her shirt.

"Nice. But what does your Celtic cross tattoo have to do with anything?"

Lily pointed to a brown birthmark near the bend of her elbow. "Brooklyn has one that's similar. So did Josh. They aren't identical, of course, and I never thought much about it until today. But more than one person has mistaken me for her mother when I've taken her on outings." She pulled her wallet out of her back pocket, teased a small photo out, and handed it to Grace. "This was taken last month."

"Wow." Grace had to smile at the mini version of Lily. "Even with a snaggle-tooth grin, she looks like you."

Lily sighed. "And Dad and Josh. And I never saw it because there wasn't any indication that Dove and Josh had ever reconnected. I got another surprise from Thatcher, too. He and Dove have been dating. Unless he's lying about that. But I tend to believe him."

"What are you going to do with all this?" Grace asked.

Lily leaned back in her chair. She looked spent. "Don't know yet. I have to talk to Mom about most of what Thatcher said, but it isn't fair to spring Brooklyn on her until Dove admits she's Josh's child. Or until I can get proof some other way. Unfortunately, Thatcher also told Carlisle everything. You were right about someone watching my interview. Thatcher. He's helping Carlisle with the investigation, but not publicly."

"You've got a lot going on," Grace said. "And I'm afraid there's more. We have another problem with your mother."

"Let me have it," Lily said abruptly. "What else could happen today?"

"Did Denise tell you that Josh called her right before he died?"

"Mom says she hasn't talked to him in ten years. That's not true?"

"I'm sorry," Grace said quietly. "But Denise told me Josh called her a week before he died and asked if he could have your grandfather's Bronze Star medal. She hung up on him and then was too ashamed to tell the sheriff."

"Or me," Lily said. "And it explains why she's such a wreck. Does it change anything?"

"It looks bad that she knew where Josh was in the days leading up to his death and lied to the sheriff. If she tells him now, she can say she was upset and ashamed of her reaction to Josh but wants to set the record straight."

Lily reluctantly agreed.

Grace pushed her point again. "Don't waste time. Go home and get your mother to make that phone call. It may already be too late. Carlisle is on a witch hunt, and we don't want to give him a new victim."

CHAPTER TWENTY-EIGHT

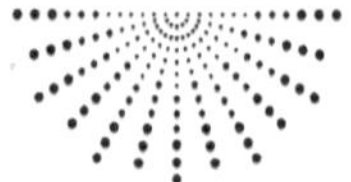

LILY

When her mother finished describing her last conversation with Josh, Lily understood why she hadn't told the sheriff. They sat together, holding hands, as Denise called Carlisle's office and left a message detailing everything—Josh's request for his grandfather's medal, her response, and why she'd kept quiet earlier.

Her mother's distress only reinforced Lily's decision to keep quiet about Dove and Brooklyn. She only had a stranger's word that Josh was Brooklyn's father, and it wasn't enough to act on. Not yet. It was possible Carlisle might bring it up to Denise, but he hadn't said anything so far, and Lily decided to take the risk.

Emily arrived to spend the night, and after bringing her sister up to speed on their mother's upsetting day, Lily found herself at loose ends. She needed space to process everything that had happened, but sitting still wasn't an option. The office would provide a distraction, and there was plenty of work waiting for her.

It was only five o'clock, but the porch lights were on at the office and the windows were dark. It looked like she could work in peace and quiet. That was the plan until she got out of her Jeep and heard a man call out, "Hey! Wait up."

Kyle Thatcher trotted down Main Street toward her, his energy a stark contrast to her exhaustion. "Sorry," he said as he reached her. "I didn't mean to startle you, but I'm glad to see you again."

Lily returned his smile despite her earlier reservations. He had changed her world with the news he'd given her that morning and now looked like he had more to tell her.

"I know I dumped some heavy stuff on you today. Have you told anyone yet?"

She didn't ask which explosive topic he was referring to—Josh's supposed addiction or Brooklyn—so she kept her answer vague. "Yes. My attorney and a couple of other people. It's a lot to absorb."

"I'm sure." Thatcher broke off, stepping aside when two women with shopping bags squeezed past them. "I feel so bad about how I've handled this. Can we go to your office? This is it, right? I'd like to smooth things over. You'll have questions when things calm down, and I want us to keep the lines of communication open."

Lily agreed, partly because she was curious, but mostly because she didn't want to lose contact with him, either. Kyle Thatcher had the sheriff's ear and might prove to be useful down the road.

He made small talk about Grace's choice of artwork and antiques in the reception area. His interest wasn't excessive, but Lily was grateful Jeff had cleared the desks and closed Grace's office door. For once, he'd followed protocol.

When they reached Lily's desk, he continued, "I realized after you left this morning that I forgot to tell you I have some pictures of Josh from before... you know, before everything fell apart. I'd like to give copies to your family, but I'll need your email address."

"It's on the business card I gave you earlier. It's a kind offer.

Thank you." When he didn't respond, she added, "Can I do anything for you? I really do have to work. But I can see that something's weighing on you. Is there more about Josh that you haven't told me?"

"I need to make you understand what happened to him, but I don't want you to get mad again."

He wasn't going to let this go. She crossed her arms and told him to get on with it.

"I don't want to speak ill of your brother, but I knew Josh, the cop, and you didn't. What he experienced working undercover broke him. He never wanted you to know that he was an addict, but he couldn't keep it from me."

Just as it had that morning, Lily's bullshit alarm went crazy. She had felt the truth in what he'd told her about Dove and Brooklyn, but she was equally as sure that he was lying about Josh. "Look, I understand your need to clear your conscience, but—"

"I'm trying to tell you how Josh died! Dove and Brooklyn are in danger, and so are you."

She hadn't been expecting *that*. Thatcher rubbed the back of his neck, then smoothed his tousled hair down. She thought it was a soothing ritual. If he'd been a teenaged girl, he'd be twirling a lock of hair.

Speaking rapidly now, he pressed on. "Josh was worried about the dangerous people he crossed when he worked undercover. Later, when I met Dove, she told me more about that. Everything she's done has been for Brooklyn, and I'll stand by her, no matter how things turn out. She's done the best she could."

"I'm going to need you to explain all that. You've left too much out."

"Dove was afraid of Josh, of course! He had a dangerous job, and he kept disappearing for long periods of time. She didn't want him near Brooklyn, so she cut ties with him. But he kept coming back here."

"And how do you fit in?"

"Your brother was always a loner—it made him good at his job, but he was isolated from those of us who could help him. And that led to paranoia. The last time I saw him in Baltimore, he'd given up his apartment, and cut his ties to our friends. He said he was going to live off the grid—camp out for a while. I managed to follow him once. He came to the Eastern Shore, but I lost him. Do you have any idea where he may have been before he was killed?"

Lily had a very good idea of where Josh's campsite might be. The same place their father had taken them when they were kids. If there was anything of value there, she had to get rid of Kyle Thatcher and find it.

"No. Sorry." She forced what she hoped was a sincere look of understanding. "I think I finally get what you've been trying to tell me, and I'm sorry I've given you such a hard time. Is there anything else? Can I do anything to help you?"

"Oh, no. I've already told you enough to get my ass thrown in jail. Plus, I don't have any jurisdiction here. I've told Sheriff Carlisle everything, and he assured me his people will look for the camp. You have my number, so we'll keep each other up to date, okay? Call me if you learn anything, or if you need help. I'll do the same. Maybe one day, you and Dove and I can all be friends. She's got a lot on her, and a hard road ahead, I'm afraid."

So, he wanted to know what was happening here, but he couldn't stay around, *and* he wanted her to look out for Dove, who apparently had even more problems than she 'd told Lily. She pushed all that aside for now.

"Thank you for confiding in me. I'm sure the sheriff will follow up on your tip about the Josh's camp. He's got a good team." Lily wasn't at all sure that Grant Carlisle would follow up on anything that might cast doubt on his own theories.

Thatcher seemed relieved. "I'm glad you can see that, even with the way the sheriff has treated you. He wants me to back off, so that's what I'm going to do. I don't really have much choice."

"You're going back to Baltimore?"

"Not directly. Don't know if I mentioned it, but I'm supposed to be on vacation, and I'm taking a couple of days off."

"With Dove?" she asked. He did his head rubbing thing again and looked embarrassed. "Sorry. None of my business." But it *was* very interesting.

As they walked to the front of the building, she made herself thank him for coming to see her. She thought her words sounded insincere and robotic, but she couldn't be sure she wouldn't need his cooperation again. She regretted it, though, when he gave her one of his dazzling smiles. The guy really was a jerk.

A gust of wind hit as he stepped onto the porch. He reached out and brushed an errant strand of hair from her face, his hand lingering a bit too long. "Don't guess you'd let me hug you?"

"Wrong time." She stopped herself from adding that there would never be a right one. As soon as he turned to go, she shut the door and reflexively turned the brass deadbolt lock.

What had just happened? It was too much information, too many sensations to process while everything was still raw. She hated that she couldn't put Kyle Thatcher squarely on the side of good or bad. She had to admit much of what he'd shared made sense, but he had to be dead wrong about Josh being an addict. Surely, her brother couldn't have changed that much. Not with the scars he carried from his childhood.

And Brooklyn? The way she tilted her head when concentrating —just like Josh had done. The slight furrow between her brows when she was thinking hard about something was identical to the one Lily's father had passed down to all his children. If the child turned out to be her niece, it would mean that a little bit of Josh was still here, and the family would have a chance to make up for the time they had lost with her.

But first, Lily needed to find a killer.

Across the street, Dove Jensen watched the exchange between her friend and her lover and felt foolish. She'd hoped to catch Lily at the office alone and talk things out, but instead she was hunched down in the front seat of her car, crying as her heart broke.

She knew as soon as she saw them that Lily and Kyle were perfect for each other—similar backgrounds, their connection to Josh. They even looked like lovers standing on the porch, his hand caressing her face.

Dove had been wrong about everything. No one was going to help her. She was on her own.

CHAPTER TWENTY-NINE

TUESDAY, SEPTEMBER 18

By Tuesday morning, Hurricane Florian had made up her mind and was heading up the Chesapeake Bay. The weather alerts shifted from yellow to orange overnight, and Mac was once again insisting they move inland.

"I'll call you as soon as I get to the office if there's any additional news there," he said, giving Grace a quick kiss. "Now aren't you glad I insisted on making that supply run to Costco? If the forecast holds, I'll still have time to put plywood up over the patio doors and we'll get more sandbags set up on the river side. Benny pulled the boat out for us yesterday—did you notice? At least we don't have to worry about that anymore."

Grace wanted to say she hadn't worried about his boat but kept it to herself. She'd have to remember to thank their friend Benny Pannel, though. She was sure the busy contractor was all over Mallard Bay helping clients and friends prepare for the storm.

She followed Mac to the front door. "With the boat secured and the sandbags in place, if you board up the glass doors, we don't have to evacuate today, do we?"

Mac gave her a look that said he was tired of not being taken seriously. "The first time someone goes through a hurricane threat on the Eastern Shore, they laugh at the way the locals prepare. Afterwards, they usually apologize—if they're still here."

"Can I apologize in advance and stay here?" She was tired of the entire conversation. She wanted her sweet husband to come back and the argumentative person who was glaring at her to go to work.

"As I have said..." He stopped and took a breath before repeating what he'd already told her a half dozen times. "The threat to us is not only the flooding. If the river and the other tributaries around us overflow and take out the roads, we could be stranded here on the second floor—or the roof—and have to be rescued by people who were smart enough to listen to the warnings and move to higher ground."

"I hear you, but—"

"No buts. You have to trust me on this. I have to go, but we're moving to either Avril's or Delaney House tomorrow if the current forecast holds. You can decide which and make the arrangements."

She gave him a salute as he went out the door, proud of herself for using four fingers to do it. A check of her phone showed the forecast still matched her mood—gloomy with a chance of chaos.

Rocky chose that moment to start barking hysterically and running around in circles, drawing attention to her empty food bowl, waking the children, and giving Grace a taste of what mornings at Avril's would be like when the little spaniel joined forces with Avril's German shepherd, Louise, and a five-pound Chihuahua mix named Leo.

The thought of three barking dogs, two cranky babies, and four unhappy adults trapped in one house during a hurricane made Grace decide to check with Margo Lapin and see if the attic apartment at Delaney House was available. The innkeeper had already alerted her to the number of cancellations rolling in. The inn might be full soon, but not with paying guests.

As Fiona and Sonny ate their breakfast—Fiona methodically separating her scrambled eggs into neat little piles before eating them and Sonny rubbing his in his hair—Grace compiled a list of things for Hallie to pack during the children's nap times. It would take both of them to get this circus relocated five miles inland to the relatively high ground of Mallard Bay's historic district. When she was finally ready to leave for work, there was only one task she needed to handle before the morning got away from her.

The break from Stephanie had been great, but Grace was getting worried about her sister. Knowing she was deliberately stepping into quicksand, she tapped out a text. *Where are you? Are you coming back?* She quickly erased the last sentence, not wanting to give Stephanie any encouragement to return. *Hope things are going well. We're prepping for a hurricane.* Maybe that would be enough to scare Stephanie into staying put.

Feeling guilty and conflicted, she hit send and almost immediately saw the dancing dots of a pending message on the screen. Stephanie was already typing, and as usual, her message was more of a letter than a quick text.

Everything OK now. But Carla has been suspended for two weeks. She went skinny-dipping with a bunch of boys in the school pool. She's being so vile to me I'm taking her to Jerry and his mother. Have a few things to do here but should be back there soon. Will explain new plans when I see you.

Through the kitchen window, Grace watched waves forming on their normally placid creek. Like the storm, Stephanie's drama was building, and it was heading right for her home. Hurriedly, she typed, *Hurricane is coming. Wait another week at least. Call if you want to talk.*

The very last thing they needed was Stephanie arriving with a new problems they couldn't do anything about.

She hit send and then realized she hadn't made any comment about her niece. Unable to think of anything else, she sent back, *Good luck with Carla. Hope everything will be all right.*

But nothing felt right, and Stephanie didn't respond.

CHAPTER THIRTY

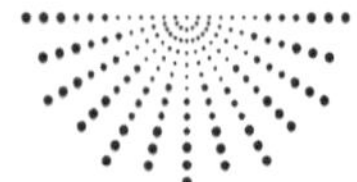

Grace arrived at the office determined to get ahead of the mounting complications in Josh Travers's case while she could still work. The old building seemed sturdy despite the strengthening wind, but she worried about the crape myrtle tree beside the front porch.

The coffee was brewing when Lily joined her in their kitchenette. She looked as if she hadn't slept. "Have you seen this morning's paper?"

"I was waiting for coffee." Grace picked up two clean mugs from the dishwasher and waved one toward Lily, who answered with something that sounded like *Duh.*

"Someone leaked details about Josh to the press." Lily handed over a copy of *The Chesapeake Times* as she accepted her coffee. "And they know a lot more than we do."

The headline made Grace wince. "Local Man Found Dead in Twin Corners Fire." The article included a press release from the Baltimore Police Department.

"Joshua Wayne Travers, Jr., a former employee of the Baltimore Police Department, was found deceased under suspicious circumstances near his family home in Kingston County, Maryland. Mr.

Travers's employment ended under circumstances involving serious misconduct. Despite the complicated nature of his departure from our agency, we mourn his loss and extend condolences to his family and friends."

Grace said, "I'm so sorry. This is really heartless."

"It's also not true," Lily insisted. "Well, not all of it."

Grace read the rest of the article. "This says funeral arrangements will be private. Has anyone contacted you or Denise?"

"No." Lily checked her phone screen. "Here's something new. This just popped up on Birdie Jones's page."

"Oh, don't read her crap."

But to Grace's surprise, Lily defended the popular local blog. "The Bird's cleaned up her act—sort of, and she has some actual sources. Unfortunately for us."

"Who?"

"The *Baltimore Bugle*'s online edition."

"That source isn't any better than *Birdie's View*," Grace protested.

Lily continued reading. "An unnamed source claims Josh was seen frequently in the Twin Corners area over the past five years." She gave Grace an exasperated glance. "There is no community in Twin Corners, only the Jensens and the church." She flicked the screen and kept reading. When she put the phone down, her face looked pinched with worry. "The article says a man fitting Josh's description had been stalking a woman in the Twin Corners area. She filed two complaints with the Kingston County Sheriff's Office in the past year."

"Irene," Grace guessed. "Or Dove?"

"One or the other of them," Lily agreed. "If it's true. But why wouldn't Carlisle tell us about this?"

"Why wouldn't Dove or Irene tell us?"

Lily threw her hands up. "I'm so lost in this mess, I can't begin to guess. But I do know that I've made it worse." She quickly filled Grace in on Thatcher's visit to the office.

"He sounds like a lame detective—"

"Or he's a damn good liar," Lily finished, then her expression changed to uncertainty. "He says Carlisle will end up arresting Irene for Josh's murder."

"Lily, just stay away from him—"

"Oh, hell, Grace. You don't know the magnitude of my screwups. The way he talked about Irene and Carlisle's investigation, he must be working with the sheriff. And instead of pressing him for information on that, I got all wound up in what he said about Brooklyn." Lily took out her phone, punched an icon, and a second later said, "Can you talk?"

Grace listened as Lily asked Trey Harper if he knew a Baltimore Police detective named Kyle Thatcher. They spoke for a few minutes, then Lily asked if Trey had thought anymore about what she'd asked him that morning. After a moment, she ended the call with a soft, "Yeah. Tonight." She turned to Grace, her expression a mixture of relief and confusion.

"Does he know Thatcher?"

"No," Lily said. "But he's making some calls—discretely. If the sheriff wants to shut us out, there's no need to alert him that we're aware of it. This morning, I asked Trey to think back to the days that Dom was still around and try to remember if they talked about Josh."

"I take it they know each other, Trey and Dom?"

"Since kindergarten," Lily confirmed. "I was there, too, but Trey knows Dom as a guy, if you get the distinction. Around the time Dom and Dove were breaking up, he and Trey worked out several times a week at the same gym, up in Stevensville. Trey would sometimes complain to me that Dom never shut up. He ran off at the mouth about everything. Dom asked Trey about Josh once, but Trey didn't know him well, and didn't have much to say."

"And that means?"

"That Dom was interested in Josh for some reason. He might have suspected Dove was cheating. Or maybe he didn't and was just curious about any guy Dove had known in high school."

Grace considered another possibility. "Maybe Thatcher lied to you and Dove and Josh never had an affair. I mean, you didn't suspect there was anything between them, and if Dom watched her that carefully, it wouldn't have been easy for Josh and Dove to get together, would it?"

"No," Lily said slowly. "But six years ago, Dove was twenty-six and miserable. If she and Josh met up again and he gave her any encouragement, she may have forgotten she was wearing a wedding band. It would only have taken one chance encounter."

"But even if you're right, and Josh is Brooklyn's father, I can't see how it ties to his murder."

"That's because you don't know the whole story. Do you remember that old Dixie Chicks song about two best friends from high school?"

"Oh, for heaven's sake—" Grace stopped. "You mean *Goodbye Earl*? Are you telling me you and Dove wanted to kill Dominic?"

"No. I'm telling you she asked me to, and I said no, but now I'm wondering if she killed Josh."

CHAPTER THIRTY-ONE

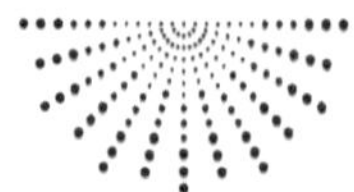

LILY

"There were all kinds of reasons why that marriage was a bad idea. Dove didn't love him, but she loved the idea of marriage and a life outside of Twin Corners." Lily paused to stare at the full cup of coffee she wasn't drinking.

"Did Josh know about the wedding?" Grace prompted.

"A week ago, I would have said no, and I'm sure Dove wasn't seeing him. She was all wedding and all Dom, all the time. About a year later, Dove told me that Dom hurt her. She had bruises and wanted help to get away from him, but she wouldn't let me call the police. Then he was sorry, yada, yada."

Grace nodded sympathetically.

"The next time it happened," Lily continued, "she asked me to help her get a divorce. She wanted alimony and their new house. I told her she'd been watching too much daytime TV and explained how divorce in Maryland works. She wouldn't file charges against him, but she wanted the divorce, so I agreed to talk to him. You know how this story goes, don't you?"

"He promised to be good, she went back to him, and it happened again."

Lily knew how many battered spouse cases Grace had handled over the years, most of them in pro bono divorce proceedings. "I should have told you sooner," she admitted. "Anyway, that time, I paid Dom a visit. We talked—again. There was a lot of shouting and threatening, but in the end, he packed up and moved out. A month later, he was back, and Dove was happy, but too busy to talk. I told her I was done, and if she came to her senses, to go to the police. I had this job and a life of my own, and that was that."

"Until it wasn't?"

"Yeah. This firm was still in the Easton office back then, and I lived downtown near the Avalon Theater. One day Dove was waiting when I got home. She had walked to my place from the hospital emergency room. She had two black eyes, a cracked rib, and was missing her two front teeth. She told the police she'd been mugged and didn't know who'd done it." Lily stopped and waited for the jolt of anger from that memory to ease. "Dom hadn't damaged her face before. He was escalating, and she wanted me to stop him. Permanently."

"She flat out asked you to kill her husband?"

"Best friends don't always use filters, you know. They say all kinds of crazy things to each other. That day, she was in pain and medicated, but she said she wanted to be free of him forever, and that was a good thing."

"So, you did—what?"

"Made a phone call." Lily gave Grace a sheepish smile. "Mr. Mosley. He did what he does, and Dom ended up in the Talbot County Detention Center overnight. When he got out, Dove was at Irene's and after a talk with Mr. Mosley, Dom left her alone for a while. Then Dove realized she was pregnant."

"She took him back."

"She panicked. But Dom is smart, in case I haven't mentioned it. He never touched her again. The last time I saw him, he told me they were toxic, and he wasn't going to jail for her. She made him crazy, and he had anger management issues. After a shouting match when she was six months along, he left her. But his parting shot was a demand for full custody of the baby as soon as Dove gave birth. He didn't get it, of course." Lily sat back and waited for Grace to process what hadn't been said. It didn't take long.

"So, again. Did Dove actually ask you to hurt Dom? Not just make him go away, but physically hurt him in doing so?"

"Yes. But—"

"Don't." Grace's voice was sharp. "Don't you dare equivocate. She asked you to hurt someone for her."

Lily said, "It makes me sick, but I'm forced to consider the idea she may have had someone kill Josh. Look at it from her point of view. She needs Dom to support Brooklyn because she barely makes enough to cover their living expenses, even sharing with Irene. She was already in an untenable situation when, if we can believe Sheriff Carlisle, Josh showed up and started watching them."

"You think he scared her?"

"Worse. Imagine if he walked out of those woods looking the same as he did on the day he died. And what if he knew Brooklyn was his? He wouldn't leave, even if Dove told him to. He'd blow up what little stability she's managed to put together."

"You mean if Dominic found out."

"Exactly," Lily said. "Dom talked about going back to court even before he made his big announcement at the airport last week. Dove had hoped to talk him out of it because a new court proceeding would mean social workers' home visits and a lot of questions."

Grace knew it was a valid concern. "And Dominic might learn

Dove and Irene had reported a stalker in the woods but had stayed there with Brooklyn."

Relieved that Grace had made the same assumptions she had, Lily added, "I'm thinking he already knows, and that's why he's refusing to give Brooklyn back at the end of his visitation. Dom could have checked the same databases I did when I researched records on Irene. He might have even thrown it at Dove at the airport, and she didn't tell me. I'll look into it as soon as I finish what I'm working on right now."

"Do I even want to know what that is?"

Lily thought about her response for a long minute. This was not going to go over well. "After Kyle left yesterday, I drove to the turnaround at the bridge on Deer Creek Road between Twin Corners and the lane to our farm. You know, the place where you pulled off when your car broke down last month?"

"I do," Grace said slowly. "It took an hour for AAA to get a tow truck out. I was nervous sitting in a locked car in the midafternoon sunlight. Are you telling me you went into those woods at dusk? What were you thinking?"

"It wasn't dark. Early twilight." Lily had been in much worse places in the dead of night but didn't think this was the time to bring it up. "I thought I knew where Josh would have camped, and I wanted to check it out. I was right, too. Someone had been staying there, and it wasn't a vagrant's camp. There was expensive camping gear. And I found this." Lily pulled out her phone and pulled up a photo of a small spiral notebook. She could tell that Grace wanted to chastise her for tramping through isolated woods to a possible crime scene.

"You looked at it?"

"Yes. I wore gloves. I just flipped through it. It appears to be mostly a surveillance record. Dates and times of people coming to Irene's house and other places I can't identify. I'm betting Josh's phone has photographs to go with the notes."

"You're sure it's his?"

"It's my brother's handwriting. I photographed every page, then left it in the tent, but I think that may have been a mistake. I want to talk to Mac and get a forensics team out there before Kyle or the Sheriff's people find it. Those two may both be upstanding in all of this, but something tells me they aren't. The camp is well hidden, off the footpaths the hikers use, but eventually, someone will find it like I did." She swiped through photos of the notebook's content, stopping at one and handing it to Grace. "The name on the inside flap is Josh Travers."

"And you think you're the first one to find it since he left it the last time?"

"I think so," Lily said. "It was neat and organized, just as Josh would have kept it, except for the sleeping bag. There were blood-stains on the inside. He'd hung a trash bag in a tree. It had bloody bandages and bandage wrappers, along with a used-up tube of antibiotic ointment and an empty bottle of rubbing alcohol."

"Someone doctored him? We should be calling Mac but finish your thought first."

"I only saw signs of one person. Single sets of footprints, unless two people were wearing the same style shoe in the same size with the same amount of wear in the tread. I think Josh patched himself up from a first aid kit." Lily stopped, remembering the scene. "There was a bloodstain, like a bandage had leaked while he slept."

"Where—" Grace started but stopped. "I'm so sorry."

Lily was grateful Grace didn't try to fill the silence as she mopped up her tears. When she could talk again, she said, "The middle of the bag. Josh must have been wounded in his lower back. I'm thinking he was stabbed and had internal bleeding. If he'd been injured in his abdomen, he wouldn't have been sleeping on his stomach, but with a back wound, the pressure might have helped."

"So, he was stabbed before he went into the church."

"Yes. I'm guessing that was as far as he made it looking for help. Maybe he'd called someone to come get him."

"Do you mean Kyle?"

"Yes, possibly, if Dove is the one who stabbed him. Or maybe he called Dove because Kyle stabbed him. Or maybe he didn't trust either of them." Lily's voice broke again, and she left the rest of her thought unspoken—why hadn't he called her?

Grace took over. "Let's call Desi Marbury. She's on lead for the state police. It'll only cause infighting if I call Mac because it isn't his jurisdiction, but I'll tell him everything. Before I make the call, though, I have to ask—there is any reason that I shouldn't involve the police?"

Lily said, "Make the call. I'll admit to tampering with evidence. I think, in light of everything that's happened, it's an understandable move. But even if they don't agree, I'm going to get justice for my brother."

CHAPTER THIRTY-TWO

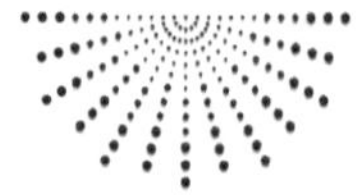

LILY

The interview with Desi Marbury was brief, but she told Lily to standby for a follow-up session once the state's forensic team had finished cataloging evidence from Josh's campsite. Lily had been investigated by Marbury once before and wasn't looking forward to their next meeting. They'd developed a friendship in the intervening years, but she wasn't counting on getting any breaks.

In the meantime, she decided to go home, pack a bag, and move out to her mother's house until the hurricane threat was over. Her apartment was in a squat cinderblock building three blocks from the harbor and should be safe enough, but Denise was nervous. Why should they both be alone and anxious?

As she drove through the north end of town past the large waterfront homes on Americus Street, she wondered if the landscape of the pretty neighborhood would be the same when Florian was through with Mallard Bay.

She saw Dove's car as soon as she turned into the parking lot of her small complex.

They really needed to get straight about Kyle's claims that Josh had fathered Brooklyn, but now that the opportunity was here, Lily had no appetite for another confrontation. There was comfort in waiting for the information to emerge in its own time. She turned the Jeep off but didn't get out.

Was it possible that Dove had killed Josh? Had she literally stabbed him in the back and left him to die? Memories to support these fears had been popping into Lily's mind since Thatcher turned her world upside down.

Could Dove kill a man?

She had talked about killing her husband just a few years ago, and she'd been much more serious than Lily had let on to Grace.

We need to make Dom go away permanently. You know people. You know how to do that, right? Lily could still hear Dove's plea—and the whistle of her words through her missing front teeth.

Dove apologized later, but their relationship had never been the same. Lily gave advice when asked, money when needed, and always had time for Dove and Brooklyn. She was a rock of support, but not a fixer. She guided Dove through her divorce and custody fight, but they never talked about murder again.

Dove held her life together by never planning too far ahead. No problem was ever solved, only denied, then deferred, and when necessary, adapted into a new reality that she accepted with a fresh layer of resentment. Each time it happened, Lily felt guilty.

Now, she was scared. Anyone could kill, given the right motivation, and Dove's was powerful. What comfort and peace she'd managed to maintain depended on Dom's money and his acceptance of the custody agreement. Josh threatened both.

She was so lost in this thought that she was startled when Dove got up from the front porch steps and yelled, "Get over here!"

Please, Lily thought as she got out of the Jeep and race-walked to her front door. *Please don't say anything that makes you sound guilty. Let me find the real killer before you ever know I suspected you.*

But Dove no longer read Lily's mind in the way she'd done when they were kids. "I saw you with Kyle Thatcher," she announced when Lily was still ten feet away. "I saw how he acted. How long have you been with him?"

Caught off guard again, Lily gave up trying to guess the answers to any of the questions that were piling up around her. She unlocked the door, pushed it open and told Dove to get herself inside.

It was time to air the truth.

She didn't waste time on preliminaries. Dropping her backpack onto a chair, Lily turned to face her oldest friend, trying to keep her anger from exploding. If Dove wasn't guilty of something, she was at least keeping secrets, and now, more than ever, that was a problem. "Spill it. All of it. How do you know Thatcher?"

Dove wasn't fazed. "Oh, don't pretend with me. How long have you been sleeping with him?"

"I just met the man. Now answer me! How do you know him?"

Dove stalked into the kitchen, grabbed a glass from the dish rack on the counter and filled it with water.

Lily watched the performance with growing unease. Dove hated drinking tap water. "Quit stalling. How do you know a detective from the Baltimore Police Department, and when did you meet him?"

"About four months ago. Josh sent him to find me."

The dam broke with Dove unveiling a part of her life she'd kept hidden, and Lily growing even more confused and concerned. She had thought she was prepared to hear Dove admit to being in contact with Josh over the years and keeping their relationship a secret, but she wasn't. And Dove's total lack of remorse for betraying their friendship was infuriating.

"You talk like he's in the past!" Lily finally cried, interrupting Dove's description of her brief dalliance with Josh. "Like he meant nothing to you."

Dove looked startled, her single-minded anger stalled. "What? I *loved* him, Lily. You know I did. But I grew out of it. I'll always be grateful that he stepped in to save me when I was in trouble with Dom, but he also messed up a big part of my life, you know? Kyle was Josh's last gift to me. Don't you see that? He sent Kyle to take care of me, because he couldn't do it himself anymore."

"Really? How well do you know this guy?"

They glared at each other until Dove said, "I thought he was like Josh used to be, okay? Strong and brave. Someone who could keep Dom in check and get Brooklyn and me out of our miserable life in that shack in the woods. But Kyle's a liar. All men are, and I should have known he was too good to be true. There. Are you happy?"

Lily shook her head. "No. But we need to get this straight. For all our sakes, so help me here. Did you know Thatcher worked with Josh in Baltimore?"

Maybe it was because she'd used his last name, but Dove seemed to back down a bit. She looked like she was weighing her responses, then shrugged. "Yeah. That's how Kyle knew about me. Josh sent him to see if I was all right."

Lily recognized Dove's sly sideways glance—her tell when she was holding back. But before Lily could call her on it, Dove went on the attack.

"You wouldn't know anything about being locked into a relationship and not able to get out. When you came back from the Marines and fell into that great job with Mr. Mosley and had the cute apartment in Easton and started dating handsome guys and partying on the weekends, I got married. Something you still haven't managed, although I wouldn't wish Dom on anyone."

Lily didn't know which she wanted more, to slap Dove or pour herself a large glass of wine. Neither would be helpful. "Did you and Josh get together after you married Dom? Did you even tell him you had a husband?"

"Once, when things were bad with Dom, I ran into Josh and told him what was happening."

"When was that exactly?"

Dove looked angrier than ever. "When I went to a dentist in downtown Baltimore to have my teeth replaced. You said you couldn't get off work, and I had to drive myself."

Lily remembered very well. Dove had been livid and refused to postpone the dental appointment by two days to a Saturday. "You met Josh at the dentist?"

"As I was leaving. It was a big office building, and we ran into each other in the lobby. We talked for hours. Then he followed me here to make sure I made it okay. I was still weak from the dental work, and he made me go to Reenie's. The next morning when I went home, Dom was gone. Later, I found out he was at his parents', recuperating from a mugging. He had a broken nose and a dislocated shoulder. He never hurt me again." She laughed bitterly. "That was the first time Josh took care of me."

Lily kicked herself for believing that a couple of nights in jail had checked Dom's need to beat up his wife, but she never could have guessed that Josh had been the real deterrent. She pushed Dove a bit more. "Why didn't you leave Dom if you had Josh?"

"You know why! I found out I was pregnant, and I had my choice of a software designer and a five-bedroom home, or a cop I could see whenever he surfaced from chasing the scum of the earth. Guess which one I chose. I thought having the baby would keep Dom in line."

"Why didn't you and Josh get together when Dom was gone for good?"

Dove gave a short, ugly laugh. "Like sister, like brother. Josh's work was more important than I was. He was working undercover, and I couldn't even see him. He sent money, though, and even that was risky. If Dom ever found out . . . Forget about it. Four months ago, Josh went into rehab and sent Kyle to look out for me. And that's all you're getting until you explain what you and my boyfriend are doing together."

"I was going to tell you all of it, but I've been tied up with Mom and the police, remember?" Lily only got cold silence for an answer. "Thatcher called me yesterday morning and introduced himself. We met and he told me about his work relationship and friendship with Josh. He told me a lot about my brother I didn't know. Some of it broke my heart."

Dove now looked more worried than angry, but she didn't let it drop. "And yesterday afternoon at your office? What was that all about, and don't you dare lie to me."

"I'm the one who's been lied to," Lily said. "Thatcher just showed up. Said he wanted to give Mom some photos of us that Josh kept on his desk when they worked together."

"That's ridiculous. Kyle knows Denise wouldn't want pictures of Josh. I told him about what happened when your dad died." Dove stopped, then barged on. "Oh, don't look so surprised. Kyle asked me why Josh was estranged from your family."

"How much did you tell him?"

"Everything. Why not? Josh trusted him. I needed someone to talk to, and Kyle was Josh's best friend."

"Did Josh tell you that himself?" Lily knew the answer before Dove opened her mouth.

"Of course not. He was in rehab, and he sent Kyle to check on me. How else would Kyle have tracked me down?"

Lily could think of several ways but was too exhausted to try to make Dove see reason, or even the obvious. "You were seeing Josh before Dom knocked your teeth out, weren't you? Why didn't you tell me Brooklyn is Josh's child?"

"You don't know that," Dove said coldly. "*I* don't know that. Not for sure. And I don't want to. Denise will never accept Josh's daughter, and Dom will kill me."

Lily couldn't leave it unsaid. "But you told Kyle she was Josh's, didn't you? And he told me."

The shock on Dove's face told Lily everything. They had both been played by Kyle Thatcher.

CHAPTER THIRTY-THREE

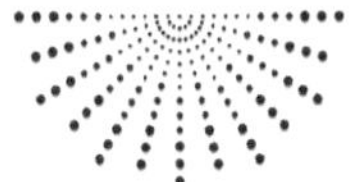

DOVE

Heartbroken and angry, Dove drove home on autopilot. She knew from bitter experience when a guy was into her and when he had moved on. Kyle hadn't been exactly subtle. He wanted Lily badly enough to tell her Dove's biggest secret. That betrayal would keep her awake all night.

She called the traitorous jerk, composing a scathing message for his voicemail as the rings went unanswered. There was no way he was going to dump her without getting a piece of her mind.

"Dove, baby!"

She was so startled when he answered, she almost steered her Honda Civic into a drainage ditch.

"I was just about to call you!" Kyle said. "I've finally gotten a few days off, and I've reserved a room for us at the Holiday Inn Express."

Dove's heart raced. Why had she let Lily get into her head?

"You there, Sweet Cheeks? I've got big plans for us. Get your granny over to her sister and then we'll have our own hurricane party."

"Don't know if I can. I have stuff to do."

If only Josh would stay out of her mind. She didn't love him. Hadn't in a long time. But whenever she saw that little birthmark on the inside of Brooklyn's elbow—the one that looked like Lily's—her pain felt very much like a broken heart.

Kyle groaned. "Don't talk like that! I need you, baby."

"Reenie's been alone all day, and she's not well. She's been having those spells again." Dove knew she'd give in if she stayed on the line any longer, and she couldn't stand the thought of running to him so soon after he'd been with Lily.

"Huh," Kyle said. "The spells where she sees people out in the woods? Did she recognize anyone?"

Dove heard the now familiar shift in his voice. He wasn't playful anymore. "I stopped listening to the details ages ago, but I've got to get her some help. And . . . I've been talking to Lily." He didn't respond, and she thought she'd lost him. Then the connection crackled to life again.

"I guess I know what that means. She told you that we've met."

She was crying too hard to answer him, and she knew he could hear her sobs.

"Do you still trust me, Dove?"

She didn't, but she wanted to. She couldn't think of anything she wanted more, and in a burst of need she told him so. The last thing she expected was that he'd yell at her.

"Then listen to me, damn it! You and Lily are both in danger. The sheriff knows it and is keeping an eye on Lily and her family, but I said I'd make sure you're safe. Josh had enemies, don't you get it? They need to make an example of him, and killing him wasn't enough. They're going for anyone he may have talked to."

"Oh, my God! But I hadn't talked to him in years—"

"Which is why the sheriff isn't buying my argument that you need extra protection. I'm not leaving you here alone."

Those were the words she'd been longing to hear, but Dove was too scared to be happy. "Should I call Dom? He can keep Brooklyn safe. I'll just tell him I'm in trouble."

"No. Don't do that. You'll never get her back. Things will settle down. It will just take some time. I can't give you any details about the investigation, but I think you know I love you, right?"

Her panic eased as he told her everything she wanted to hear. When they ended the call, the plan was in place. Dove would leave work early tomorrow, take Reenie to Mimi's, then meet Kyle at the hotel.

"Are we good?" he asked her. "Be firm with your granny, Dove. Tell her you're getting home at one to pick her up. If she knows you have a schedule, it will go easier, don't you think?"

"I'll write it down for her," Dove said eagerly.

"Is there any chance you can't pull it off? You're not expecting anyone to come by the house, are you?"

She laughed for the first time in days and loved him even more for thinking her family was normal enough to have anyone to their home. "No. The stand is closed, and we're not expecting visitors. I'll pick her up at one and be with you by two-thirty."

She hung up smiling. They would wait out the hurricane and talk everything through. Kyle could fix anything.

Just like Josh used to do.

CHAPTER THIRTY-FOUR

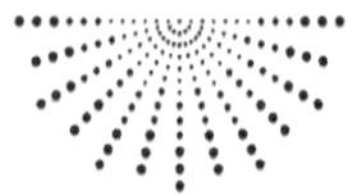

"You haven't packed yet," Mac said, looking around their bedroom. "I thought we agreed that you would get bags ready for you and the kids in case we need to leave in a hurry."

Grace sat next to a mountain of clean laundry that covered their bed and finished folding a dress of Fiona's before answering. "I've just now found time to finish up the washing I started over the weekend. You know what happens if I leave it too long." Actually, she was pretty sure he didn't, but he was wise enough not to say so. "Do you still think we'll have to evacuate? I heard Florian could stall before it gets here." Moving into town would be a headache and she already had too many of those.

"How many hurricanes have you lived through?"

She rarely heard that tone in his voice and looked up at him in surprise. "You get a pass on that one, mister. Give me a hand here and tell me what's really happening. I can do the packing before bed."

It was already nine o'clock, and she was exhausted. Packing was the last thing she wanted to do, but the Baltimore Orioles were playing the Yankees and Mac was in here, instead of camped out in front of the television. They had discussed their day over dinner. She had filled him in on the arrival of Kyle Thatcher and his claims about Josh and Brooklyn, but nothing Mac had shared so far warranted this level of agitation on his part.

He shifted the pile of clothes to the center of the bed, sat down, and started folding one of Sonny's T-shirts. "I just got a weather update. Hurricane's losing strength and slowing down, but we'll still catch the outer bands of the storm."

"But isn't that good news? If it's slowing, maybe the river won't overflow this far upstream."

"Maybe. It's more likely we'll get high winds, flooding, and random tornados. High tide will peak tomorrow about the same time we're supposed to get the worst of Florian. Even if the creek water doesn't reach the house, we could still be cut off here."

Grace sped up the folding. This no longer felt like a battle of wills. "Has that happened to you before?"

"My folks were once on their own here for days. My dad took a rowboat down the lane to check on our neighbors, the Silvas. Mom wouldn't let me go with him, and I was a jerk. Later, I learned he pulled Mr. Silva out of the water near what had been their garden. He'd probably gone for help for his wife. She'd had a heart attack. Dad never got over finding their bodies. The roads out here aren't in much better shape today than they were back then."

That explained a lot, she thought, feeling guilty for not paying closer attention to his concerns. "We'll pack the bags tonight, and I'll take them and the kids into town with me tomorrow morning. Hallie can keep them at Avril's. If we need to come home before the storm's over, we'll use your truck."

He gave her a grateful look, then said, "When this is all over, we should get you something with four-wheel drive and a high ride."

She was glad he didn't suggest trading in the BMW. Her mother's car was 14 years old and had a second home in their mechanic's shop, but she couldn't bring herself to let it go. "Maybe," she said.

"Right now, though, why don't you tell me what else is bothering you?"

"Witch," he said, giving her a brief smile as he handed her a stack of sleepers. "Bet you can guess."

"Let's see. Stephanie isn't here, so . . . Carlisle giving you as much grief as he is Lily's family?"

He gave her a sideways look she couldn't interpret, then described his visit to the sheriff's office and Grant Carlisle's rant.

Grace struggled to make sense of it. "That's unbelievable."

"He thinks I funnel confidential information to you. He also thinks I should've been thrown out of the state police years ago, and he considers Josh to be no loss to society." Mac shook his head. "I read Grant wrong from the get-go. The man has been carrying a huge grudge since the election, and I had no clue."

"He knows a drafting committee approached you about running?"

"Some of the same people backed Carlisle when I declined, but it was at the last minute. Now he seems to be bent on showing me up."

He looked so worried, it surprised her, and she reached out to give him a hug and whispered, "I'm sorry."

He chuckled. "That's nice, honey, but I didn't mean the jackass hurt my feelings. Only that I haven't been on guard with him while he's been looking at me as a competitor. And now he's withholding information from me and smearing other good cops in the process."

"He's badmouthing Josh?" Grace asked but wasn't surprised when he didn't answer. "Go around him then," she said. "Get the information you need from other sources. You don't have to be tight with the sheriff to do your job."

"No," he admitted grudgingly. "But it makes my job that much harder."

"Did he give you any idea of who they're investigating? Or Josh's cause of death? Anything?"

"Carlisle? Hell no. The only idea I got from him was that I should get out of his office." He fell silent and seemed to give his full attention to folding a fitted sheet, finally saying, "To hell with it," and handing it to Grace, who tucked the corners together and folded it into a square.

"Was that to hell with the sheet or Carlisle?" she asked.

"Both. If he continues to give Lily and Denise grief, or if he turns on Avril, who right now, no one is showing any interest in, you'll want to contact the Medical Examiner's office. Go right to the top and take a subpoena with you. If the verdict is inhalation as the cause of death, I believe Carlisle will arrest Irene. Those were her trash barrels that were on fire next to the church. Even if it isn't carbon monoxide poisoning or asphyxia due to smoke inhalation, they could still charge her with felony arson, or something along those lines."

"What about Lily?"

"I don't see how they can charge her with anything. The time-line doesn't fit. Her phone records will prove she was home when Irene called her, and she wouldn't have had time to get to Twin corners, move those cans to the back of the church and get all three of them burning to the point the church burned, too."

"We've already put in requests for the cell phone records," Grace said. "It's Denise who's looking bad in Josh's death now. But I agree, Irene would be the most likely suspect, except for the fact that she's ancient and will come across as feeble and incompetent to a jury."

"Especially if she has the right attorney," Mac said drily.

They had finished folding clothes, and as she sorted outfits for packing, Mac went to the attic for suitcases. When he returned, she said, "Is this what Carlisle objects to? Us discussing cases like this?"

"He should be so lucky to have a sounding board like you. Let me ask you something. If Carlisle had accused a client of yours yesterday, before we had this conversation, what's the first thing you would have done?"

"After causing him enough grief to reconsider being so stupid?" She shrugged. He'd made his point. "I would call the medical examiner's office and schmooze someone. If I didn't get what I needed, I'd get a subpoena, then drive over to Baltimore and camp out until I had information on the cause of death."

Mac looked at her speculatively. "You've already established that with her trip to Richmond, her evening with Trey, and the cell phone records, Lily is in the clear. Avril has Hallie as an alibi. If you find that Denise, or Irene, or Dove killed Josh, are you going to cover it up?"

"No, but—" She stopped and sighed. "It will be especially hard for me if it's Irene."

"A cranky old woman left on her own in an isolated house who routinely imagines there are strange men sneaking around?" Mac looked thoughtful, then sad. "According to the statement Dove gave Carlisle, she and Irene routinely burn trash and yard waste in those barrels."

"See, I don't get that at all," Grace said. Her earlier exhaustion was gone, chased away by the pleasure of being in sync with Mac again. "Irene's a tall woman, and she looks strong, but she's in her eighties. She couldn't have moved all three barrels from her property over to the church."

"If they were empty, and she tipped them on their sides and rolled them, sure she could."

Grace frowned. "Okay. But then she'd have to carry trash and leaves over there to fill the barrels. Wouldn't Dove have noticed whacky behavior like that? And it's been raining off and on for more than a week. Everything in those barrels would have been wet. She'd have to use an accelerant. I'll need to check with Marjorie's nephew to see if there was any evidence."

"Gasoline," Mac said. "One of the firefighters told me there were no empty cans left behind, but the smell and the burn pattern told the tale. You'll have to ask our sheriff for the crime scene tech's report, though."

"So even though Irene's ancient and afraid of devils and bad men, she goes out in the dark—" Grace stopped and pictured the scene. "Carrying at least one heavy can of gasoline and some dry, flammable materials. She lights up those cans she's dragged, what —forty feet?—over to the church, and fills them. She waits until the fires get going good, then calls Lily to come over, hides in her house—"

"Stop! I get it. Jeez, woman. I hope I'm not on the witness stand in front of you. You'll have her out of court in five minutes."

"Maybe not," Grace said quietly. "I can see her pulling it off."

"And Denise?" Mac asked. "Or Dove? What about them?"

"Let's finish the hurricane prep," she said as he set the packed bags by the door. "One crisis at a time, or we'll never get any sleep."

CHAPTER THIRTY-FIVE

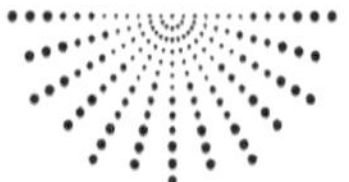

WEDNESDAY, SEPTEMBER 19

The bedside clock said 5:45 when Mac woke Grace on Wednesday morning. When she sat up, she saw he was fully dressed and holding the suitcases. "We should've gone last night," were his first words.

"How bad is it?" She scrambled out of bed, went to the window, and looked out at the heavy gray sky. There was enough light to see that their creek was now fast-flowing water. Grabbing up the jeans she'd worn yesterday, she said, "I'll get the kids ready. I only need to get a few things."

"I was just on a conference call with the emergency operations center," Mac's face was tight with worry. "Florian shifted trajectory and will make landfall somewhere around Pocomoke City. The outer bands will hit here tonight around 10 p.m."

"Tonight? That's sooner than they said yesterday."

Mac sighed but let it go. "I don't know how fast the water's rising, but at least it's stopped raining, for now. Tremaine's at the office, and last reports are that Route 791 and Killian Road are still clear enough for us to get out. I finished prepping the house the best

I could last night after you went to sleep, so just get dressed and grab the kids. Everything's already in the truck."

"Oh, Mac." She yanked a sweatshirt on and tried to wrap her mind around what was happening. "But the sandbags. We didn't—"

"I did. Now hurry!"

Minutes later, she had Fiona and Sonny dressed, Rocky's harness and leash on the barking dog, and the bulging diaper bag Mac had packed over her shoulder.

"What happens next?" She'd heard the drill often enough over the past week, but her mind was numb with shock.

"Evacuation alerts are going out about now.The next few hours will tell us if the governor needs to expand the evacuation orders and make them mandatory."

"And if she does?"

"Later, Grace." Mac swept Fiona up in his arms and took Rocky's leash.

Desperate to contribute, she said, "I'll take Sonny with me in the BMW."

He stopped at the door and looked at her, his voice firm as he told her no. "We can't take the chance. The water is rising near the end of our lane and Bilby Creek is nearly up to Route 791."

"But it's not flooded yet. If we hurry—"

"You could make it. But if you should stall out in water, you'll block the road. I've already put the car in the carriage house. It should be okay. But we need to leave—"

"Now," she finished for him. The carriage house was a rustic holdover from the days when it actually housed the McNamara family's horse buggy. She hated to think of her mother's pride and joy crammed in next to the riding mower and generations of old equipment.

The children happily ate their makeshift breakfast in their car seats, excited at the new adventure Mac spun into a story as they drove past fields with standing water and overflowing drainage ditches that lapped the edges of the asphalt.

"Do you think we'll make it to Avril's before the roads are covered?" Grace asked, trying to keep her voice steady for the children.

"We'll make it," Mac said with more confidence than she suspected he felt. "But I can't stay once we get there. I've activated Mallard Bay's emergency plan, and I'll be tied up all day with the fire department and other emergency responders. The high school is being designated as a shelter."

"Should we get Hallie and Avril and go there now?"

"You'll be safe at Avril's—that area is all high ground." He glanced at her, then back at the road. "The safest thing is to take the children and go north. You would be out of the storm's path entirely."

"No," Grace said firmly. "We stay together with our family and friends. Or as together as we can be with you running the emergency response."

Once they reached the main road into Mallard Bay, Grace called Avril, then Cyrus, and finally Marjorie. After conferring briefly with Mac, she called Margo and told the housekeeper to get ready to host an inn full of refugees. Not only was Delaney House the largest and tallest house in town, but it also sat on the highest point and had a full English basement. She tried not to think of it as a holding pond for rising water.

When she finished making arrangements, Mac gave her a dubious look. "Avril agreed to leave her house? It should be safe enough there."

"Agreed? She had already set up the exodus and was about to call and tell me what we were doing. No wonder Margo sounded irritated when I told her to get the inn ready for all of us. She already had her orders and thought I was calling as an afterthought.

I'll have some serious relationship mending to do with her when this is all over."

Mac said, "Avril's probably spooked remembering the hurricane in 2002."

"Whatever. She's definitely on a mission. She said Cy refused to come to her place because it would be unseemly, and he was moving into the office. He agreed to Delaney House because Avril told him there would be lots of people and she was going, too."

"And Margie?"

"Was already driving to our house. Why in the world she thought we were in a better location than she is, I can't guess, but Avril said she reversed course for Delaney House without a complaint."

"She wanted to be with family," he said.

Grace snorted. "She wanted to be with you and the kids. Rocky and I could float away for all she cared."

"That's not true," he protested. "She loves Rocky."

Their amusement evaporated when Grace's phone lit up and she read the incoming text from Stephanie. *Leaving Newark around 7. Traffic looks good, so should be there about ten.*

"Didn't you tell her to stay home?" Mac's voice was cold again.

"I told you I did!" Grace snapped, angry with her sister and the tone in Mac's voice. "You heard me leaving her that voicemail last night. And that was the second time I told her."

"You know she never pays attention to messages she doesn't like. She'll claim it didn't come through. You should have kept calling until you got her."

From the backseat, Sonny began to cry.

Switching to her 'happy mommy' tone, Grace dug through the diaper bag at her feet for animal crackers and said, "Oh, don't worry, Poppy, it will all be fine." The look she gave Mac said if he wanted anything to ever be fine again, he needed to get off the subject of Stephanie. "Auntie Stephanie will turn around when she realizes she's stuck in traffic, but she'll come see us soon and bring lots of goodies."

"I don't think that's what he's crying about," Mac said dryly. "Better try to call her."

But her call went straight through to voicemail, as did her next three attempts.

"You've done what you can," he said when she pocketed her phone and stared out the window.

Through the rain-streaked glass, she could see water puddling on the road in front of them. "Maybe she'll check her messages and call me."

"So she can join us at Delaney House?"

Grace made herself pause before answering him. "I'm not having this argument again. Yes. If my sister makes it here, she'll be at Delaney House with us."

"Or we can stay at Avril's in peace," he said, smiling as the idea took hold. "Avril and Hallie can hold down the fort at Delaney House with Stephanie, Margie, and Cyrus, and we'll keep the kids and dogs at Avril's."

"That's why they made you Big Chief," Grace said, relieved but not ready to forget she was mad. "You get to tell Avril and Marjorie."

CHAPTER THIRTY-SIX

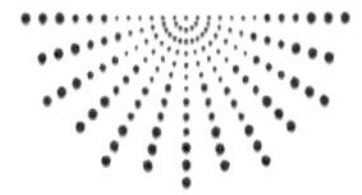

IRENE and DOVE

Irene was tired. Tired of watching the woods, tired of listening to her granddaughter argue, tired of waiting for something to happen. She dragged her ladder-back rocker to the den window so she wouldn't have to look at Dove. Behind her, the local weather channel continued to warn of impending disaster. The hyper commentator's bouncing and arm waving had given her a headache —at least that was her excuse to face the outdoors and ignore everything else around her.

"Reenie, the rain's getting worse, and they've called for everyone to evacuate to high ground before sundown. We have to leave as soon as I get home from work. One o'clock, remember?" Dove asked for the third time.

Irene wondered if the girl would ever understand that repeating herself didn't make anyone listen better.

"You're scaring me, Reenie. Answer me!"

"We're okay for now," Irene answered on autopilot, never taking her eyes off the woods. "I haven't seen anyone else since that one devil died. Besides, I have a headache. I don't feel like going for a car ride."

Dove clenched her hands so hard her gel-hardened nails cut into her palms. "That's good, but we have to leave because of the hurricane." She was too harsh and earned a side-eye glare from her grandmother. "You're going to stay at Aunt Mimi's. She's inland, and her brick house will be safe. I have friends expecting me in Chestertown, so I'll be safe, too. It's only for one night." The lie made Dove's stomach twist, but really, what choice did she have? If she ever got Reenie to Aunt Mimi, she wasn't bringing her back here.

Irene didn't argue. Let Dove think what she wanted. If the Little Wye River and Deer Creek had flooded every time those ninnies in town got all worked up over a forecast, her house would've washed away long before now. If she went to Mimi's, her dear baby sister and her granddaughter, who thought she knew everything, would decide she was better off staying there permanently. Irene had heard them talking on the phone last night. Dove seemed to think Irene went deaf when she watched the woods.

Even the people she loved most in this world underestimated her.

Maybe she should listen to Dove and go. Whatever was coming couldn't hurt Aaron. Her work was done, and she needed to let it all go.

"Tomorrow," she said, still watching the woods. She'd leave tomorrow. Maybe.

Dove watched her grandmother with mounting frustration. She knew Irene wasn't being obstinate to cause trouble; she was tired and sick and shutting down.

Dove's memories of her grandmother as the strong woman who'd raised her were fading. Grandpa Harvey had been gone since

Dove was ten. At an age when most people leaned into retirement, Irene had picked herself up and pieced together odd jobs to supplement the produce stand and keep the bills paid. She cobbled together a quiet but productive life with one goal—to take care of Dove, the child her own daughter had abandoned.

Dove had heard the story so many times, she could recite it word for word. Thirty-one years ago, Debbie Jensen had appeared on her parents' doorstep, wild-eyed, dirty, and skeletally thin. In her arms was three-month-old Dove. Debbie stayed forty-eight hours— long enough to shower, eat, and catalog all her parents' faults before leaving with everything of value she could carry. Everything except her baby.

Every time Dove thought about taking Brooklyn and leaving the Eastern Shore, she looked at her grandmother and wondered what her own life would have been like if Irene and Harvey had placed Debbie's malnourished crack baby in the state system. She owed Irene everything, but there was still the problem of the hurricane.

I'll be back here no later than one, and we're going to Aunt Mimi's." When Irene didn't react, Dove exploded. "All right, you stubborn old woman. Now, you listen to me. You always told me to do the right thing no matter what it cost, and that's what I'm going to do. I'm taking you to Mimi's, and you are staying there until this storm is over. Get your stuff together while I'm gone. If I have to carry you to the car when I get back, I will."

Irene was three inches taller and twenty pounds heavier than her granddaughter, and she smiled at Dove's threat. Her own stubbornness was replicated in that girl.

But maybe it *was* time to pack.

CHAPTER THIRTY-SEVEN

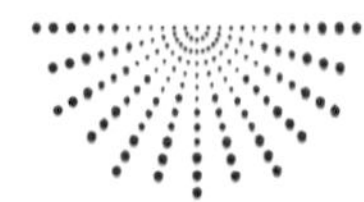

Delaney House was more like a fraternity house on an Ivy League campus than a three-hundred-year-old mansion with a distinguished, and occasionally scandalous, history. Laughter pealed out from the kitchen at the rear of the house as three harried cooks tried to prepare breakfast for a growing clientele of rain-soaked, worried people.

"It's a buffet. No special orders, I'm afraid," Hallie said when Cyrus Mosley asked if he could have an egg white omelet with soy sausages.

Mosley surveyed the spread of toast, egg casserole, and scrapple. "I think I'll have some juice and walk over to the office."

"You have to eat," Hallie insisted. It had taken a lot of convincing to get the stubborn old lawyer to join them, and she wasn't about to give him a reason to leave.

"I will," he said, "but first, I need to check the tree by the porch at the office. It's older than I am, but I'm not sure it's as strong." He paused and gave her a wink that made her giggle.

Hallie played her trump card. "Well, okay, but the best rooms are going fast."

Mosley leaned in close to whisper, "Is there one with a private bath still available?"

Hallie nodded. "Number five. You'd better grab it. Unpack your clothes and spread them around. Nothing like underwear on the floor to mark your territory. I'll have your omelet ready when you're done."

His face on fire, Mosley hurried to the door just as Mac pushed it open, carrying Sonny on one hip. Grace followed with Fiona clutching her hand, and Rocky on a leash.

"Hi!" Grace sang out, then stopped, looking around the large room crowded with people eating and talking over each other in nervous excitement.

As Mosley edged past her, she was sure she heard him say, "Run for your life."

Mac placed Sonny in Avril's waiting arms and gave Grace a quick kiss. "I got a call from Jason Binks. He needs to see me in Easton Barracks right away. I've got to run down there before I go to the fire department."

"The state police captain?" Grace asked. "Another hurricane conference now?"

"It never ends. But the roads are okay out to Route 50 so far. I'll be fine." Fiona thought otherwise and wrapped herself around Mac's leg. He knelt down to her level. "You be good for Mama, okay? I'll be back as soon as I can."

"Go," Grace said, giving him a gentle push. "We've got this."

In short order, Avril and Marjorie had relieved Grace of the kids and told her if she wanted to help, she could leave their things in the rear parlor, which had been designated the downstairs nursery.

Grace had just finished doing as instructed when Lily and Denise arrived.

"It's coming down in buckets out there!" Lily said, setting her mother's bags down. "Mom insisted on being part of the excitement. I figured I'd drop her off and go check the office."

"Cy was just fretting about that tree by the porch," Grace said.

"Oh, no you don't," Avril joined them, hands on her hips and a 'don't mess with me' look in her eyes. "The tree will come down or it won't, but there's work to be done here first. You two can round up the animals for me and get them over to my house. Grace, you and Mac are staying there and supervising the zoo. Lily, you can join them if you want. Hallie and I are keeping the children with us on the third floor. Everyone will sleep better that way." She pointed at Rocky, who was sniffing around Lily's boots. "Leash that sassy girl first. The other animals are scattered around here, so make sure you get them all."

"Now wait a minute." Grace didn't want to argue, but felt she had to try to hang onto her own children.

"Oh, don't worry," Avril said, rolling over her. "Hallie and I will stay with the children, but someone has to be responsible for the animals, too. Lily, I saw you brought Denise's station wagon. It'll be a tight squeeze, but you aren't going far. After you finish at my house, you may as well go to the office and check on things there so Cy will stop worrying. Have a look around town while you're at it, and if Baldy's has milk or eggs left, grab it all."

It had been a while since Grace had seen Avril so animated, and it was hard not to smile at the transformation. She'd keep her children with her tonight, but she and Avril could have that discussion later. For now, she'd follow directions.

The last voice she heard as she left the kitchen to round up all the four-legged refugees was Fiona's.

"Bring cookies, Mama!"

It wasn't a request.

CHAPTER THIRTY-EIGHT

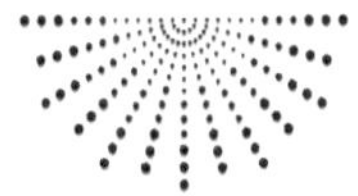

STEPHANIE

The moderate rain that had been falling steadily since she left Newark drummed on the roof of her small Mercedes as Stephanie navigated I-95's southbound lanes. Wind gusts occasionally buffeted her car, but nothing she couldn't handle. She smirked as she turned up her Metallica playlist, drowning out the weather reports until a special bulletin interrupted with the latest hurricane alert.

Hurricane Florian has shifted trajectory overnight, with landfall now expected near Pocomoke City, Maryland. Officials are reporting severe backups north and south on all major routes with heaviest congestion at the Chesapeake Bay Bridge and the Chesapeake Bay Bridge Tunnel.

She tapped the screen, cutting off the newscaster. "Bunch of drama queens," she muttered. But by the time she crossed into Maryland, the northbound side of Route 301 had slowed to a near standstill. She watched the vehicles fleeing the upper trajectory of the storm and felt the first nudge of worry. "So much panic over a little rain," she reassured herself.

Grace's warning voicemails sounded like typical overreactions from her perpetually anxious sister, but now Stephanie couldn't get a call to go through.

Even as the weather worsened and the traffic slowed, she kept going. This storm couldn't possibly be worse than the situation she'd left behind. On impulse, she pulled off at an exit in Elkton and found a grocery store. If everyone was going to be gathered at Grace's house, she could make up for her unscheduled arrival by making dinner. She'd show Grace she knew how to take care of a family.

By late morning, Stephanie was navigating the back roads to Mallard Bay. She'd stop at Grace and Mac's, prepare a feast, then slip away to her quiet, comfy room at Delaney House. She could use some pampering after the week she'd had.

A few cars passed her heading in the opposite direction, but she dismissed their worried expressions. The roadside drainage ditches were full to overflowing, but the pavement still had clear patches.

"This is why I never listen to weather forecasters," she said aloud. "Total overreaction."

She almost changed her mind when she turned onto the winding lane leading to Grace and Mac's cottage and had to drive through water that splashed her windows, but she made it through. The next surprise was more ominous. The barricade of sandbags across the front door and the taped windows sent a clear message: everyone was gone.

Her phone still showed the same old warnings—disaster everywhere—but it had stopped raining, the sky was looking lighter, and she had ice cream in the car that was already getting soft. "Oh, screw it!" she yelled, and tackled a sandbag.

In the kitchen, everything looked perfectly normal—a total mess

—but she'd take care of that, too. She walked to the windows facing the creek but saw nothing too concerning. The little beach had disappeared, and water was almost up to Mac's workshop, but she barely registered this change to the landscape. The rain had stopped, hadn't it? This was as bad as it would get.

She tried to call Grace, but her phone showed no service. "That's weird," she muttered, trying again. Nothing. The landline in the kitchen was dead, too.

Deciding it was a normal inconvenience that came with living in the country, Stephanie unpacked her groceries. She'd surprise everyone with a wonderful dinner when they returned. Grace might have her nose out of joint, but Mac would surely appreciate a real meal after all the wasted effort preparing for a storm that would be gone by evening.

CHAPTER THIRTY-NINE

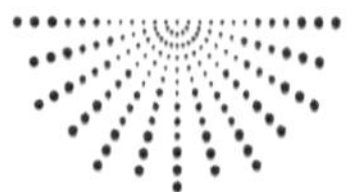

DOVE

Dove Jensen checked her phone again and had to force herself to set it down on her workstation instead of flinging it across the salon.

Why wasn't Reenie answering?

Angry thoughts of her grandmother's stubborn behavior shifted briefly to the mother who'd abandoned her, the father she'd never had, and then to Dom's brutality. The litany of injustices she'd endured and survived eventually wore thin, leaving her emotionally exhausted and still facing the same issues she'd had when she'd started her mental whining.

She tried to focus on Kyle waiting for her at the Holiday Inn Express, his dark hair slightly damp from the rain, curling over his forehead. This led to other thoughts, and another half hour crept by.

"Mr. Nguyễn?" she called out to the small man who sat in one of the pedicure chairs flipping channels on the television. "I'm leaving early today, remember?"

"May as well," the shop owner said. His wrinkles doubled as he smiled at her. He clicked off the weather alert that had been cycling through the local stations all morning. "Go get your grandmother and be safe. I'm waiting on a delivery of sandbags for the doors, and then I'm out of here too. For once, I'm glad I lease this place and don't own a waterfront home."

Dove waited until she was in the car to turn on her phone. No messages, no missed calls. She swore under her breath and called Irene again, disconnecting without leaving a message when her grandmother didn't answer. Reasoning that the shortest route home would also be the most heavily traveled, she took a back road out of Mallard Bay.

She didn't pass anyone, but she still kept her speed down and avoided any standing water as best she could. But going slower meant a longer trip, and eventually, her thoughts turned to Irene.

She could have gone back to bed, although Dove couldn't imagine her grandmother doing such a thing. Unless...Dove gripped the steering wheel as she counted back through the long hours of last night to the time she'd insisted Irene take a dose of antihistamine to help her sleep.

Reenie had taken that pill at midnight. Seven hours later, Dove gave her another to calm her nerves after a restless night. Had Reenie taken one, or even two, more doses during the night? It wouldn't be the first time. What was the maximum someone that old could take? What would an overdose do to her? Dove's mouth went dry at the thought.

A panicky little voice in her head said Irene might be dead.

Was that possible? The windshield began to fog, and Dove jabbed at the defrost button before remembering that it didn't work.

She's fine, she's fine, she's fine.

Dove hung onto that chant, whispering it under her breath. One way or another, she was taking her grandmother to Aunt Mimi, and once this storm was over, they would decide where she was going after that. It would be somewhere that she'd get real medical attention from professionals who didn't use generic antihistamines to keep her calm.

There was a flash of lightning and an ear-splitting boom. Instinctively, she slammed on the brakes, but it was too late. The impact caused her to briefly lose consciousness. She opened her eyes to see her windshield filled with tree branches and water dripping through cracks in the glass. A gigantic pine had fallen directly in front of her car. Judging from the crumpled condition of the front end and steam rising from the damaged hood, the old Civic had seen its last ride.

Her head and shoulder hurt from the airbag deployment, and a dull throbbing intensified when she tried to move. There was dust everywhere inside the car, and the acrid smell of chemicals made her eyes and throat burn.

Eventually, she managed to get out of the battered Honda, the door creaking in protest as she pushed against it. She breathed deeply and tested her limbs, making sure everything worked properly. Her left wrist ached when she rotated it, but nothing seemed broken.

Fumbling for her phone, she tried 911, but the call wouldn't connect. Small wonder, she thought. Reception in this area was iffy in good weather, let alone with gusting wind and surges of rain. Maybe she'd have better luck up the road. She grabbed her backpack and stumbled into the woods around the fallen tree, grabbing branches to steady herself and grateful she was on a short stretch of road without drainage ditches.

She was about a mile from home. She could make it, and when she got there, she prayed her grandfather's old truck would start up. It had been fine the last time she'd taken Reenie for a ride. It would get them out to the main road to Centreville and Aunt Mimi's place.

She walked faster, chastising herself. No more mental wanderings and silent temper tantrums. Reenie might be losing her mind, but Dove certainly wasn't. She needed to take charge.

She would get Reenie, call 911 on the landline and report the location of her wrecked car and the downed tree. She'd call Kyle to pick her up at Mimi's. It was about time he met her family.

She plodded on, head down, her resolve hardening with each step. Another tree fell nearby with a splintering crash, the ground trembling beneath her feet. She sped up, her heart racing. None of her plans would work out if she didn't make it home.

CHAPTER FORTY

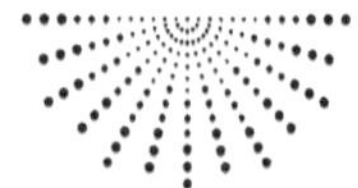

"Do you think it's going to hold?" Lily asked, peering through the station wagon's rain-spattered windshield.

The old crape myrtle looked the same as it had in last week's sunshine, only wetter. Since Grace knew even less about trees than she did about hurricanes, she just shrugged. "Don't know, but maybe we should park around back."

The Victorian home that housed Reagan and Mosley, Attorneys at Law, had a new roof, and its original shutters were closed tight. Grace hoped it would be enough protection. They had gone through a major renovation last year, and she couldn't imagine repeating the process.

Once inside, they paused in the back hallway to dry off. Lily began flipping on the overhead lights. "Power's still on. That's something."

They walked a slow circuit of the first floor, checking windows and doors. "I'm not sure there's anything for us to do," Grace said, "But I'll check messages."

"Coffee?" Lily asked, already heading toward the kitchenette.

"Please. I didn't get any this morning." Grace played back the few messages they had. Three clients canceled their afternoon appointments, and Jeff had gone to his mother's house in Salisbury to move her to the nearest shelter.

"That poor guy," Lily said. "And his poor mother. Can you imagine being cooped up with a social media fanatic when the Wi-Fi goes out?"

They settled into the small conference room with their coffee. Grace said, "Jeff's resourceful. He'll save enough selfies and reels to post for a week when he gets home." She scrolled through the weather forecasts on her phone. "According to this, we're just in the outer reaches of the storm. I'm glad we got the groceries to Avril before coming here. I feel guilty leaving her, but I barely cleared the kitchen door before she shut it behind me. She enjoys being in charge at Delaney House."

Lily was staring out the window and didn't answer.

"Oh, come on! You aren't in hurricane panic, too, are you?"

"Not yet. But since we have a minute to ourselves, I need to tell you about my conversation last night with Dove. She was waiting for me when I got home." Lily quickly filled Grace in, wrapping up with, "We have everything out in the open now, but I am still processing my feelings about the whole situation."

"I'll bet," Grace said sympathetically. "That's a lot to digest. Do you believe everything she said?"

Lily hesitated again. "She insists she hadn't talked to Josh in a long time and never told him that Brooklyn could be his. She did tell Kyle, however, and was incensed to learn that Kyle had told me. What's surprising is that she hasn't put two and two together and asked Kyle if he told Josh."

"Is that pertinent?"

"I guess not. Just the former cop in me getting odd vibes. Thatcher is either the type of career officer who stays in desk-bound positions, or he's orchestrating something. Either way, I think he's definitely manipulating Dove and me. I'm not saying he's bent, exactly. But I wasn't surprised when Dove assumed Kyle was hitting on me. He was definitely leading up to it."

"Dove's an attractive woman, and so are you. You're even the same type—physically, I mean. Brunettes, slender—"

"Shorter than him."

Grace burst out laughing. "That's an issue?"

"Who knows?" Lily shrugged. "He may have a tall Swedish wife and a bunch of monster-sized kids for all I really know about him. And I'm guessing Dove doesn't know much more. They apparently talk a lot but haven't spent much time together. Except for meetups."

"Hookups?"

"I was trying to be polite."

Lily's phone burst to life with a "Gimme Three Steps" ringtone.

"Seriously?" Grace said, laughing. "Lynyrd Skynyrd?"

"Classic. And it seems right for life lately, you know?" Lily answered the call, then toggled the volume button. "I can hardly hear you," she shouted. "Are you all right?" She gave Grace a worried look. "Where are you now? Forget about your car. We can handle that later. If Bronson Road is impassable, maybe I can take Route 57 and come to you from the north. Either way, just stay there and try not to panic. Since you called 911, they might reach you before I do." There was a pause, then Lily sighed in exasperation. "Okay, okay. I'll be there as soon as I can."

"Dove?" Grace guessed. "What's happened? Is Irene all right?"

Lily drained her coffee and got up. "I have to make a rescue. Dove tried to take her old Civic down Bronson Road. She's lucky to be alive. A tree fell across the road in front of her. She tried to walk home but only got halfway before twisting her ankle. Fortunately, she's in a clearing and has a weak phone signal."

"Did she call 911?"

"Yes, she reported the crash and the blocked road, but told them she could get home on foot. That was before she actually tried to walk any distance. The bigger problem is she can't reach Irene and is worried she may have had one too many doses of antihistamine. She doesn't want to call emergency services again, or Mimi, because Irene will go nuts, especially if she's fine and has a good reason for not answering."

Grace sighed. "Okay. Well, Irene seems to like me again, sort of. I may be able to help with her. And it will give us an excuse to ask both of them some questions."

Lily looked uncomfortable. "I'd rather drop you back at Delaney House. Remember yesterday when we were discussing both Irene and Dove as possible suspects in Josh's murder? Nothing's changed, Grace. In fact, I'm thinking that's why Kyle Thatcher is all up in their business, you know? Mac will be upset if you come with me and Thatcher turns out to be right."

"We need to talk to Dove and Irene. Irene doesn't like you, and I have a phone full of photos of Mac and the kids to entertain her with. You talk to Dove, and I'll handle her grandmother."

"While we evacuate them in a hurricane. Mac will kill me."

Grace smiled. "Mac won't be surprised in the least. Besides, he had to go to Easton, he won't even know. Let's go."

As Lily locked up the office, Grace gave in to her inner nag and tried to call Stephanie again. The call went immediately to voice-mail, but she saw she had a new message of her own. Stephanie was on her way.

"Avril or your sister?" Lily said, correctly interpreting Grace's grimace.

"Steph should be at our house by now if she didn't get washed off the road."

"Looks like we're running a taxi service today. Let's get Dove and Irene, then backtrack to your place and get Stephanie before Mac finds out."

Grace said, "He's a busy guy, especially today. He probably

already knows about Steph, though. His security app will have given him all the details as soon as she hit the driveway."

The rain had eased up while they were inside, but they had to dodge large puddles of standing water as they made their way to the parking lot. Grace stopped at the sight of the huge, battered truck Lily was headed toward. "We aren't taking your mother's station wagon?"

"Don't you think we did enough to it hauling all those animals to Avril's? I'll have to have it detailed as it is. Besides, do you want to go swimming today, or get back here in one piece? This is Dad's old farm truck. I drove it in case I needed a hurricane-proof ride."

"There is no such thing, and I can't believe this thing runs," Grace said, watching as Lily wrenched the dented driver's side door open and climbed up behind the steering wheel.

"It's an F-350. Biggest, baddest truck ever. It's indestructible." Lily fired up the engine and laughed when it belched black smoke out the exhaust pipe. "We don't bring her out in polite society except in emergencies, but this old girl will carry us through anything, just ask our cows." She glanced over at Grace, who was trying to find her seat belt without touching anything on the dirty seat. "You'll want to hang on to that grab handle over your head. Dogs chewed off the belt on that side."

Grace grabbed the grimy bar above her window and glared at Lily. Then looked harder and forgot about the missing belt. "Are you wearing a holster under your jacket?"

"Of course. Where else would I keep my Glock? You don't want to know what gets flushed out of those woods in a flood. Now hang on."

CHAPTER FORTY-ONE

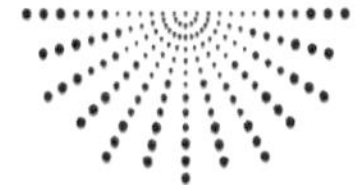

MAC

Mac's windshield wipers struggled against the downpour as he drove from Easton to Mallard Bay. He tightened his grip on the steering wheel as he relived his meeting with MSP Commander Binks.

Confiding in Desi Marbury had paid off and he was now part of a state and federal task force looking into a large Eastern European trafficking syndicate operating from the Port of Baltimore. He wasn't sure if he'd been excluded until now because his former colleagues thought he was getting too old for the fight, or that he was too close to Josh. Grace's involvement in Lily's defense didn't help either.

Binks had been blunt. He was only bringing Mac in because of a Baltimore Police Department detective named Kyle Thatcher.

"This isn't only about Detective Travers anymore, Mac," Binks had told him as he handed over a file folder. "His sister is right. He was still working undercover, and it looks like that's what got him killed. His assignment started out small. Just the Baltimore Police Department looking into rising crime in an area of the harbor that had been relatively quiet, as those places go. Travers worked alone until evidence began piling up. The state joined in, and the task force was formed about a year ago when it became clear that the scope of the operation was larger than initially thought. Then the Feds joined—FBI and Homeland Security."

"What's the focus?" Mac asked.

"A growing syndicate trafficking drugs, electronics and stolen data, but mostly, people. So far, we have two dead port workers and an undercover agent—Travers—to add to the homicide tally." He handed Mac a folder with photos of Josh, clean-cut and in uniform, alongside surveillance shots of him looking haggard and disheveled.

"Sham charges of Travers's addiction and dishonorable discharge were his cover," Binks continued. "Damn convincing one, too. It held for the whole run of his assignment until last week. We've known for months that information was leaking out to the syndicate somehow, but now we have evidence that Travers's former partner, Kyle Thatcher, has been playing both sides—supervising undercover agents while feeding information to the syndicate Travers infiltrated."

"And Josh found out," Mac guessed.

Binks nodded. "We believe Thatcher either killed Travers personally or ordered it. He died of internal hemorrhaging from a lacerated liver, and he was dead before the fire caught. A blessing, I suppose."

Mac pulled his mind back to the present and slowed his speed as the road ahead disappeared momentarily in a sheet of rain. He was sticking to the better side roads to avoid the slow rolling traffic on northbound Route 50 and cursing himself for not insisting that Binks hold their meeting virtually. Not that either one of them would have been comfortable risking that. Binks had been cautious in answering Mac's question about Grant Carlisle's status in the investigation.

"Unclear," Binks said in a tone that didn't invite more questions. "Your sheriff is cooperating with Thatcher, but he likely thinks everything is on the up and up. We've lost track of Thatcher, but in an abundance of caution, we're not sharing that with Carlisle." Binks handed Mac a surveillance photo of Kyle with Dove Jensen, and another of him with Lily. "Intelligence suggests he's in Mallard Bay now."

Binks's final warning echoed in Mac's mind: "If this organization feels threatened, they'll eliminate anyone Travers might have talked to, as well as anyone Thatcher identifies as a risk to them. If their usual pattern holds, Thatcher will be told to clean up his messes, permanently, and if he doesn't, the syndicate will, and Thatcher will suffer the same fate."

"So where does it all stand right now?" Mac was already on his feet, ready to leave.

Binks joined him and said, "Kyle Thatcher is many things, but stupid isn't one of them. He's stayed safe operating out of his office and by phone without ever setting foot near the docks and the trafficking operations. Tracking Travers down and killing him was probably a new experience for Thatcher—one he screwed up royally. There'll be pressure on him now from all sides, and that will make him especially dangerous. If you or your sergeant makes contact with him, alert us, but don't approach him. We can't afford to bring down the whole operation when we're this close to concluding it safely."

The road ahead cleared, and Mac called Tremaine Harper. When his sergeant was up to speed, he thought about calling Grace. And say what, he asked himself. "Stay away from Lily and any man you don't know?"

He was still wrestling with that when his phone pinged with a notice that someone had turned onto their property. A few minutes later, the house alarm was cleared with the correct password.

Stephanie. It had to be.

Now he had a good reason to call and check on his wife. And after that, his sister-in-law would get a piece of his mind.

CHAPTER FORTY-TWO

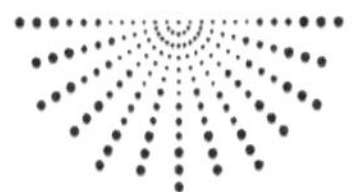

KYLE

Despite all his years on the force, he had never even come close to killing anyone until a week ago. Now he was about to take two more people out—while he was supposedly on vacation, no less.

The irony of that little twist kept popping into his mind at the most inopportune times. His co-workers back in Baltimore thought he'd shaved a few days off his Ocean City vacation to lend a hand to a former colleague who was in over his head trying to be a sheriff. Everyone knew Grant Carlisle had barely made it to retirement pushing papers for the BPD.

The Eastern European thugs who had been feeding Thatcher's offshore accounts thought he was completing the assignment they'd given him.

But all he had managed to do so far was screw up both scenarios. Now instead of killing one man, he also had to kill two women. Kyle wanted to throw up. Again. His expertise was in planning and organizing other people's work, and he was out of his depth with murder. But he wasn't in any position to argue with a cartel of criminals. He'd made promises he had to keep.

If only Irene Jensen hadn't come into the woods when he stabbed Josh.

He kept reliving the scene, and every time he did, his anger grew. Remembering the old woman's piercing scream infuriated him. She'd distracted him long enough for Josh to turn and the knife to miss its mark.

Kyle had planned a clean, fast kill, face to face. Josh deserved that much. But instead, he'd stabbed his former partner in the back, literally and figuratively, and he'd been paying the price ever since.

Later, when he was calmer, he realized Dove's grandmother couldn't have seen his face—she'd been behind him. But she'd heard his voice. Heard him tell Josh he had no choice. If she ever heard him speak again—well, Kyle knew he couldn't take that chance.

The past week had been horrible. Over and over, he relived the moment his knife sank into Josh and his friend's gasp as he pulled away. Josh had stumbled off, disappearing into the woods, while Kyle had waffled between chasing after him and shutting the screeching woman up.

Then, Irene Jensen stopped yelling and started moving toward him, and he ran. He barely remembered charging through the woods to his stolen car and the dubious safety of an Annapolis motel where he'd stayed hidden for two days. Then came the miraculous news that disgraced former detective Joshua Travers had died in a fire.

It wasn't the clean solution Kyle had hoped for. The local cops were investigating the odd death of a man who'd been stabbed, only to turn up forty-eight hours later in a burning church.

So far, nothing connected Kyle to Josh's death, and soon the only witness would be gone. It made him sick to think of killing

Dove, too, but at least he wouldn't see what happened inside the house when he hit the detonator.

It wasn't supposed to be this way. A propane gas explosion? It had sounded easy. Easy and clean, and best of all, he didn't have to see the aftermath. He just had to get away and hide for a while.

So it was cowardly. *He* was a coward. But he was a rich, *live* coward, and he intended to stay that way.

Besides, what choice did he have?

He walked through each step of his plan. It should work. Yes, he'd made mistakes initially, but today's solution was a testament to his ingenuity, and that would go a long way to restoring his standing in the syndicate's eyes.

Of course, he hadn't counted on a damn hurricane, but he reasoned it could work to his advantage. There was nothing to be done about it now. It wasn't like he had the luxury of waiting for good weather.

He checked his watch, then the Jensens' house. The old woman chose that moment to walk out into the backyard. He took a small taser from the duffle bag on the seat beside him, then waited for her to go back inside.

It would all be over soon.

CHAPTER FORTY-THREE

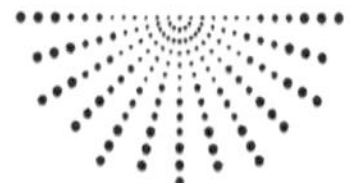

IRENE

Irene craned her neck to look up at the strange sky. The winds were still low, but she knew better than to get her hopes up. The surrounding silence was enough warning. Still, she didn't move. The air was thick and heavy with moisture, and she thought she could taste the storm that was coming. Everything felt wrong.

She had been wrong to fight Dove like she had. Yes, Aaron's resting place was still Irene's responsibility, but her boy was gone. Her granddaughter was alive, and Dove would never leave her alone. Resolving to go pack her clothes and all the valuables they could fit into the little Civic, Irene blew one more kiss to her boy and went back inside.

She had just zipped up her suitcase when she heard the squeak of the screen porch door. She might have missed it with rain pounding outside, but a person who spent as much time alone as she did, knew which sounds belonged and which didn't. Had Dove come back early? Her gut said no.

The man saw her as soon as she stepped into the kitchen. Her reflexes were still good, and she darted for the nearby block of knives, but he was faster than she, and he was ready. She only had time to register the small box he held, and the red dot on her denim apron.

"Get out!" she screamed, too frightened to make her feet move.

He stepped forward. There was a sharp *pop* and something struck her. Her abdomen was on fire. Then she was on the floor, her muscles spasming. She had no control, not even over her own screams. When the black dots that danced behind her eyelids grew larger, she welcomed them and didn't hear his footsteps fade away.

When Irene woke, she was surprised to find that she was alive. She had died, hadn't she? The stillness told her she was alone, but it was too quiet. Her chest felt funny, and her stomach hurt, but it was bearable. She wondered how bad her injuries were, but she wouldn't know for sure until she tried to sit up. A broken hip was her biggest fear—it would be the end of independent living. A mirthless laugh escaped her lips and echoed around her. She hadn't been independent for a long time, but something told her she'd better get that way fast.

"Act like you've got some sense," she scolded herself, then looked around. She was still on the kitchen floor. Immediately on the heels of that realization, she remembered how she'd gotten there and covered her mouth with both hands to keep from crying out.

She hadn't been delusional after all. She *had* seen two men in the woods. Josh Travers and the man who'd stood in her kitchen and shot her with his little weapon. There had been a devil after all.

The memory infuriated her. She wanted to give him a taste of the pain that had rocketed through her body. Give him the squeezing, burning spasms—

As her rage drove out the last of the haze and shock, a new thought came to her. God was giving her a chance to clear her debts before she died, and she couldn't waste a gift like that. There was so much to atone for.

Josh's death was an accident. Irene hadn't even known he was inside the church. She'd only wanted to get rid of the building and all the trouble that came with it. It had been hard, rolling the empty trash barrels over to the church, and then filling them, one armful at a time, with the recycling materials she'd stored in the shed. She still didn't remember setting the fire, though. It had been raining, hadn't it? Yes, that was why she'd pulled the barrels closer, under the eaves and up next to the wall with its peeling paint.

She tried as hard as her aching head would allow, but she still couldn't remember lighting the fires. She was, however, sure of one thing. She hadn't known anyone was in the church that night.

Her thoughts swam, and she closed her eyes against the memory of the news report. Josh Travers, that kind boy, had died while she watched the church burn.

Debbie's gaunt face took Josh's place in her mind. Surely Debbie's terrible choices weren't Irene's fault? She'd done everything she knew how to save her girl—but God forgive her, she'd been relieved when Debbie had left home for good.

She'd given up on her child. On both of her children. She hadn't fought hard enough for Debbie, and she hadn't fought at all for Aaron.

She had been so weak when she was young.

You're a sinner, girl. Whoring around and lying. That shovel's your punishment. Pick it up and help me dig. Can't put a stillborn bastard in my churchyard. It belongs out here in the wild.

Father would be so angry if he could see her now.

Her eyes closed, and she drifted again. She wanted to shake her head until her brains rattled and jumpstarted her sanity, but pain and fear immobilized her. That realization puzzled her for a minute. Fear of what? She was alone.

Then she smelled the gas.

Pain took her breath as she pushed herself up, but she made it, falling forward to catch herself on the tall stool next to the stove. The knobs had been pulled off the burner controls, and try as she might, she couldn't remember what to do, but she had to move—the fumes were gagging her. Lurching across the room, she grabbed a chair, then the table, then the porch door. She froze. What if he was still in the yard? Or on the other side of the door?

She dropped painfully to her hands and knees and crawled toward the bedroom, holding her breath as she went.

CHAPTER FORTY-FOUR

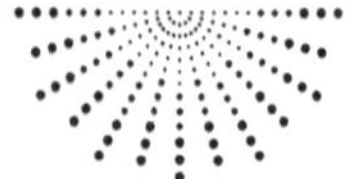

KYLE

Furious with himself, Kyle Thatcher darted across Irene Jensen's soggy backyard in a panic, making a beeline for the car he'd left behind the half-burned church. He told himself he wasn't running away again—he was just in a hurry to get to the next phase of his plan.

The battered Chevy Malibu was a world away from his Tesla, and he was grateful for its grimy anonymity. Inside the locked car with its cracked upholstery and mingled smells of fast-food wrappers and motor oil, he wasn't Detective Thatcher. He was deep undercover, but not like the officers he supervised. He would never be one of them again.

It took a while before his hands stopped shaking, but eventually he got himself together. He couldn't finish the job stressed out like this. Messy or not, he'd checked off everything on his list. Now there was nothing to do but wait for Dove.

He tried not to think about how she'd looked the last time he'd seen her. If he could have thought of any way to spare her, he would have. But there was only one way out for him.

For the hundredth time, he wondered if he should have trusted the local cops to do their job and maintained his distance from this God-forsaken place. He might have had that option if the local fire department hadn't shown up and put out the fire before it could burn the church and any trace evidence that Josh had been stabbed.

Whoever had filled those barrels with cardboard and paper had all but left a sign that said *Burn Me*. He could hardly be blamed for taking such an in-your-face opportunity, could he? He could still hear the *whump* as the sparks from his road flare ignited the trail of gasoline he'd poured into the barrels and on the church walls.

His brief streak of luck had run out at the worst possible moment. The church might have burned to the ground unnoticed—except Irene Jensen hadn't stayed in Centreville with her sister after all. The second her porch lights snapped on and lit up the yard like a crime scene, he'd taken off.

But things had gone bad much earlier—his good friend Josh had seen to that.

Just turn yourself in, Kyle. I'll go to the captain with you. I'll tell him how the syndicate blackmailed you and you couldn't get out. None of the information you gave them was really important. We can make this right.

Kyle hadn't wanted to make it right. He didn't want the steady stream of easy money to dry up. And he sure as hell didn't want to end up in pieces, dumped from a syndicate-owned cargo ship into the Atlantic Ocean.

Josh Travers had no idea what Kyle had actually told the local syndicate boss. He'd believed Kyle's sad tale of his mother's medical bills and bankruptcy, and there was no one more loyal or supportive than Josh.

Kyle had always exploited that weakness, but within minutes of talking with Josh's sister, he knew she'd never buy his crap.

That was why he was here now. No one was going to believe him once Dove started talking to her best friend. She and her grandmother had to die before that happened. Before her Irene convinced everyone that there really had been two men in the woods on the night Josh was stabbed. Kyle's cover wouldn't last long after that.

He ran through his mental checklist. The knife he'd used had been cleaned, soaked in bleach overnight, and placed in the back of the utility drawer in Irene Jensen's kitchen. All the burners and the oven of her gas range were on with the pilot lights blown out. Both doors leading into the kitchen were shut—he'd lucked out there. No open concept floor plan meant the propane would accumulate faster. Now all he needed was Dove. He just had to wait.

Nervous, he fingered the small plastic box in the jacket of his raincoat—then froze.

What the hell was he doing?

Kyle yanked his hand free and clutched the steering wheel. No more stupid mistakes. He'd worked too hard. The last step was to push the button as Dove entered the house, and the resulting flash from his remote grill igniter would do the rest. The explosion would remove the only two people who could tie him to Josh on the day of the stabbing.

He thought about the interview he'd give to explain everything away. He'd spin a story about a mentally unstable woman who took her own life out of guilt. It would be tragic but believable. Irene Jensen, overcome with grief and confusion about killing Josh, had turned on the gas in her kitchen and sealed herself inside.

Then her granddaughter had come home unexpectedly. Opened the kitchen door. Sparked the blast.

Collateral damage.

As for Josh, Kyle would say he stalked Dove and threatened to tell Dominic Pontello that Brooklyn was his daughter. To stop him, Dove stabbed Josh and left him to die while she rushed Brooklyn across the county.

It all fit. Josh going for help and only making it as far as the church. Irene Jensen discovering the scene and setting the fire to destroy the evidence of her granddaughter's crime. It was tragic. Desperate. It could almost be true.

And who would blame the old woman for setting up a painless suicide while her granddaughter was supposed to be away from home? Or for miscalculating and creating an explosion instead?

Kyle's racing heart slowed a bit as he thought about each event that only needed a bit of embellishment—a suggestion here, a bit of misdirection there—to deliver plausible explanations for all three deaths.

Explanations that didn't land anywhere near him.

He checked his watch. The propane fumes had been building for over an hour. He'd been worried there wouldn't be enough time before Dove arrived. Now he wondered how big the explosion would be. Where was she?

A large truck suddenly came around the bend in the road just past the house. He ducked down, waiting for it to pass and cursing when he heard tires hitting gravel and the engine fall silent.

If Dove hadn't gotten herself a new ride, he was in trouble.

CHAPTER FORTY-FIVE

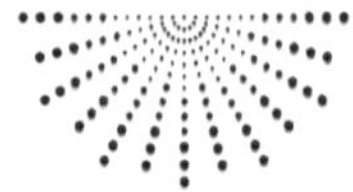

MAC

Mac knew Stephanie was inside the house as soon as he pulled up behind her Mercedes. The sandbags that he had dragged into place as they'd left that morning had been shoved around, and he heard the thumping of a bass guitar. His idiotic sister-in-law was waiting out a hurricane with her own private party. So far, the creek had only risen halfway up the back lawn, and he knew that would only make it harder to talk her into leaving.

He opened the door and yelled her name at the top of his lungs. It felt great but only got him a shriek from the kitchen where Stephanie, judging from the dirty dishes that covered every surface, was preparing a feast.

"You scared me," she yelled back at him before silencing the music. "Another surprise ruined. I wanted to have a big dinner ready for you all when you came home tonight."

"Came home? There's a hurricane—"

"Oh, for heaven's sake. We haven't lost power, and the storm's mostly over. Now don't you feel silly?" She opened the oven door, releasing a mouthwatering aroma of roasting chicken. "Chicken, four sides, and homemade rolls. All you'll have to do is heat it up. And a chocolate cake for dessert. I'll move right over to Delaney House when Grace gets home."

Mac wished there was something, anything, that he could arrest her for. "This is just a temporary lull. In another hour, rain and wind will start building up again. Tornado watches have already been announced."

Stephanie paused, then shrugged. "This morning wasn't so bad, was it? I mean, except for all those crazy drivers on the road. Go on back to work and let me finish this food."

He gave it one more try. "We'll pack it up and take it with us. Let's go."

"There's a chicken in the oven and I've got these rolls ready to go in next. Seriously, you're sweet, but no."

It was *sweet* that got him.

He went out to the utility room, rummaged around and returned with his arms full.

"What? No!" Stephanie grabbed the pan of rolls from the kitchen table just before Mac dropped a large pile of rope on the counter right where the resting dough had been.

"Pay attention because I'm only going to go through this once. Don't turn the music back on. If you hear a roaring sound like a train, drag the mattress from Fiona's bed into the tub in the kids' bathroom and cover yourself with it."

"I know what to do in a tornado, Mac! But look outside. There isn't—"

Ignoring her, he pointed to the rope. "This is a ladder. Take it up to your bedroom, open the window, put these hooks into the metal rings that are right under the windowsill, and throw the ladder out."

"But—"

"Don't wait until water is in the house. Get it in place while you have plenty of time. Make sure it's set up before dark at the latest. The biggest blast of the storm will be around ten." He ignored her squawking and went back out to get a collapsible metal ladder. Propping it up against the pantry door, he said, "In the closet in your bedroom there's a panel in the ceiling. Load up a bag with water and food, and a flashlight. Put all your supplies on the top shelf in the closet and keep the ladder nearby." He tossed an odd-looking can onto the rope. "This is a mini foghorn. If you think a rescue team is nearby, open a window or climb out on the roof and hit that top button."

Stephanie's voice shook with anger. "And I suppose if the water comes up to the roof, I should climb up the chimney?"

"No. If it gets up that high, you'll drown. I'm leaving in five minutes." He left her there, silent for once, as he went to check the rest of the house.

It was hard to ignore the hateful voice in his head that said he didn't care if she came with him or not. But leaving her here wasn't really an option. Each new bulletin he received was worse than the one before.

He checked the living room and found the stuffed elephant Sonny slept with every night.

He scooped up toys into a laundry basket along with all the baby items off the top of the dresser in the nursery. The matching silver baby brushes with their initials, the small pink jewelry box, all of Fiona's little girl finery. The wooden rattle his grandfather had carved.

In the room he shared with Grace, he grabbed everything that spoke to his heart and would fit in a pillowcase.

Later he would realize it never occurred to him to go upstairs to his office and take the mementos from thirty-five years of policing. Photographs of his parents and grandparents joined the few of Grace's family and he was done.

Stephanie met him at the door with a suitcase at her feet and two bulky garbage bags in her hands.

He picked up the suitcase and reached for one of the bags. "Is this the food?"

"No," she said in a small voice. "I put everything in the fridge. Traveling with a half-baked chicken didn't seem like a good idea. You must have left in a hurry this morning. I grabbed the kids' toys. I think I got their favorites."

As he turned to the door, he heard a soft, "I'm sorry."

She sounded so much like Grace it took the fight out of him. "Don't forget your backpack," he said as he opened the door.

The rain had started again.

Mac balanced the suitcase, garbage bags, and his own hastily packed belongings while Stephanie huddled against the intensifying wind gusts, clutching her backpack to her chest.

"Truck's this way," Mac shouted over his shoulder. "Watch your step. The ground's slick." He glanced back at Stephanie, who was stepping carefully in her impractical sandals.

He had just shoved the last of the bags and the laundry basket into the back of the truck when he felt it—a jabbing pain above his right ankle. A burning sensation immediately spread outward, and he knew exactly what had happened.

"What's wrong?" Stephanie demanded. She was moving toward him, bare legs under her tennis shorts and sandaled feet.

"Freeze!" he yelled. "Don't come any closer!" His leg was on fire, the heat searing through his calf muscles.

Stephanie's shrill voice cut through his shock. "What did I do wrong this time? Honestly, Mac—"

"Snake," he yelled. "I'm bit. It's under the truck."

"Oh my God, I see it!" Stephanie danced backward while

digging frantically for her phone. "I see it! It might be a copperhead."

Mac caught a glimpse of the thick-bodied snake as it slithered away from the truck in the direction of the woodpile. He tried to slow his breathing. "Water snake," he said, but the searing pain radiating up his leg argued for Stephanie's call. His heart was racing too, whether from fear or the venom, he couldn't tell.

"We need to get to the hospital." Stephanie was at his side now. "I got a photo of it so we can look it up." She slid an arm around him. "Try not to panic."

He straightened up and jerked away from her. He was only dizzy, not panicked. Copperhead bites weren't supposed to be this bad, this fast. Stephanie and her damned chicken dinner...

"Mac? Mac!"

She was holding him again, and her voice seemed to come from very far away. His vision tunneled, darkening at the edges. Then he was on the ground, though he didn't remember falling. Rain splashed on his face as Stephanie bent over him, her features fading.

"Don't leave me!" she cried, but it was Grace's voice that he heard. Then there was nothing.

When he came to, he was in the front hall. He was wet and muddy, and Stephanie was kneeling beside him, her hair plastered to her head, makeup streaked down her face.

"Thank God you're finally awake." She gave him an appraising look, then picked up his left hand and put two shaking fingers on his wrist. "You stopped breathing. I had to do CPR."

He tried to speak, but his mouth was dry. His ankle throbbed, but the pain was different now—more localized and less fiery.

"Don't try to move." Stephanie gently laid his hand back on his chest and gave it a gentle pat. "I got another look at the snake. I don't need the internet. It wasn't a copperhead, just a water snake. I had to learn the difference in Girl Scouts."

He stared at her, wishing she would make some sense.

"Water snakes are non-venomous," she said slowly as if talking to a child. "You had an awful reaction, though. You hit your head when you fell, too."

He was sitting on the floor at the foot of the staircase to the second floor, with what felt like every pillow in the house shoved behind his back for padding against the steps. His ankle had been neatly bandaged, with a loose compression wrap extending halfway up his calf.

"How did you...?" he began.

"Girl Scouts, again," Stephanie said with a smile. "First aid merit badge was my specialty." She gestured to the open emergency medical kit beside her. "I found that in your bathroom."

Outside, a gust of wind slammed a small branch against one of the hall windows.

"We need to leave," Mac said, attempting to sit up straight.

Stephanie easily pushed him back down. "Okay, but you stay still while I go get the truck and pull it up as close as I can to the front steps."

"I can walk," he insisted, although he had his doubts about that.

"Maybe. But save that energy. You're a big guy, and I can't pick you up again if you fall."

Pick him up *again*?

She stood up, and he saw she had his keys. He wanted to argue, but it didn't matter. She'd come back inside in a minute, complaining about the rain. Maybe by then, he'd only see one of her. He closed his eyes and tried to remember what double vision after a snakebite meant.

He didn't hear Stephanie return, shutting and bolting the door behind her.

They weren't going anywhere.

CHAPTER FORTY-SIX

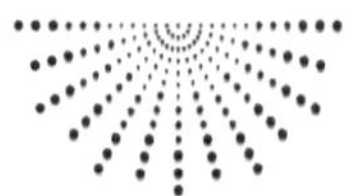

Grace gripped the grab bar in one hand and the dashboard with the other as the F-350 bounced down the road. "I can't believe you don't have a seatbelt in this thing," she snapped.

"Sorry. The driver's side has one—that's usually all we need. We don't joyride around the farm." Lily grinned. "Ever think about getting a vehicle suited to country life? You're ruining that beautiful BMW on these back roads."

"Mac says the same thing. But I'd need to trade it for the down payment, and I can't let it go."

Lily's phone chirped. She gestured for Grace to read the text.

"It's Dove. She wants us to stop and check on Irene first."

"Ask if Irene's still on antibiotics for the UTI they treated at the hospital."

"What? When—"

"The night of the fire. She was dehydrated, scared, and had a raging UTI—common for her age. They gave her fluids and antibiotics." Lily smiled briefly at Grace's quizzical look. "I have hospital contacts. I may also have implied that Irene was a relative when I called to find out why she was released so fast."

Grace didn't want to know about HIPAA violations. She sent the text and got an immediate answer from Dove.

Yes. She's only got another day, though.

Lily swore. Grace swiped to the browser, reading until she lost the signal.

"Dead zone," she told Lily. "Hopefully, the Jensens have a router booster so I can call 911."

"It's that bad? What did you find?"

"An overdose of antihistamine taken with antibiotics can cause hyperactivity, high blood pressure—"

"Delusions?"

"Yes. And paranoia with aggressive behavior."

"Some of that's normal for her," Lily said hopefully. "I can't go any faster, but we should get a signal again up ahead."

They approached the turnaround where Lily had entered the woods to find Josh's campsite.

"I've got a signal!" Grace said and held her phone up. "If we lose it again, one of us can come back here to call for help if we need to. Hopefully, we can get Irene and Dove to the hospital without waiting for an ambulance."

Lily agreed. "I'm sure the emergency crews are swamped. Tremaine said they're jammed this morning with calls, plus a four-car pileup on Route 50 near the outlets."

"North or southbound?"

"Worried about Steph? Don't be. Northbound, and that girl always slips away from trouble."

Grace wanted to argue, but they were reaching the Jensens' house.

Rounding the curve at Twin Corners, Lily said, "Look to your left," as she slowed to pull into Irene's driveway. A dark green car was parked behind the church, partially hidden by overgrown porcelain berry bushes. "Some idiot is hiking in the woods. Probably wants to experience the hurricane in a natural setting. Serves them right if they get blown into the river and wash up on Wye Island." She killed the ignition and checked her phone. "No cell bars, but Irene has a landline. You stay here while I check the back door. Irene won't answer the front when she's alone."

"Wait," Grace protested. "She hates you, remember? Does she have a gun?"

"Shotgun," Lily sighed. "Plus, an old pistol. If she's spooked, she'll have the shotgun out."

"And if she's unconscious, you'll need help moving her."

They jumped down out of the truck into thick, humid air that smelled of damp earth mingled with sharp ozone. Lily yelled Irene's name, waving her arms as they approached the house, but got no response. As they neared the front porch, she said, "She'd be out here already if she'd seen us."

"Are you sure? She didn't answer you the night of the fire."

Before Lily could respond, they heard shouting. A man ran toward them from the church parking lot.

"Get away from the house!" he yelled, stopping at the driveway's edge. "It's full of gas! No one's in there, and I've called 911."

Under her breath, Lily said, "He called 911 with no service and heavy cloud cover? I don't think so."

"Who—"

"Kyle Thatcher." Lily grabbed Grace's arm, pulling her backward. "And I see a bulge under that bomber jacket he's wearing on a ninety-degree day. He's armed."

"So are you. Isn't he a cop?"

"We're supposed to be here. He isn't." Raising her voice, she called, "Kyle, why are you here?"

He looked confused. "I told you about Dove and me. I came to get her and her grandmother and take them to Centreville to her aunt's. But we have to leave—don't you smell the gas leak?"

Grace did smell gas, but Lily wasn't reacting to his question.

She closed the gap between them and said, "I smell it, maybe we should go. We can call for help when we get a signal."

"We'll be fine, Kyle," Lily said as if Grace hadn't spoken. "I think Dove had some workmen out. This is Grace McNamara—my boss. We promised to pick up Irene, too. Looks like she and Dove got their wires crossed, huh?"

Lily's little speech was too chatty, and Thatcher seemed at a loss for a response. Grace checked her phone. Still no service. They needed to quit delaying and check the house. "If you think it's safe, let's go get Irene. We still have to pick up—"

"Get away from the house!" Thatcher yelled. "I checked inside already! No one is in there. Please, we all need to get out of here!"

Then Grace realized why Lily was watching the detective. Thatcher had his hands in his jacket pockets, and he was slowly moving backward.

"Hands where I can see them, Kyle!" Lily's pistol was out. "Stop walking. Let me see your hands!"

Thatcher turned and ran.

CHAPTER FORTY-SEVEN

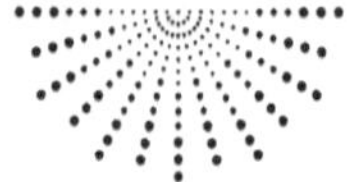

LILY

Lily grabbed Grace and pulled her into a run. They didn't stop until they'd reached the front of the church, with the building between them and the woods.

"Think Thatcher told the truth about the house being empty?" Grace panted. "The gas is bad, but if we open the door—"

Lily shushed her, then whispered, "I don't think Kyle Thatcher has a truthful bone in his body. That house is full of propane gas. If Irene's in there, she's dead."

"You don't know that! We have to try—"

"Why do you think he didn't want us to go inside? He didn't want to blow us up."

Grace was stunned. "Are you saying Kyle was saving us? Why did you draw your gun? Why did he run?"

"Saving us was the last thing on his mind," Lily holstered her pistol. "He didn't want any more murders to deal with, and he wanted to be further away when he set off the explosion. We're going to run for the truck. I'll be yelling—do whatever I tell you. Scream a lot and look scared."

"No problem—"

Grace's words ended in a cry of surprise as Lily grabbed her arm and began running, yelling, "Go, go, go!" When Grace stumbled, Lily yanked her upright, screaming, "Kyle's right! I can smell gas! We have to get away!"

"I can hear you already!" Grace grumbled, scrambling into the truck.

"I wasn't yelling for you." Lily threw the truck into reverse, backed into the road, revved the engine several times, then shot forward as Grace scrambled for the grab bar.

Out of sight of the house and church, Lily slowed and stopped. "Check your phone," she barked, then added a soft 'damn' checking her own.

"Still no service," Grace said. "We're not far from where Dove's waiting, and we know she can call out."

Lily opened her door. "You take the truck and get her. Call for help, but stay there. Tell Mac or whoever you reach the Jensen place may blow anytime. They need to approach with extreme caution. I'm going back and try to get in through a window on the front side of the house. Maybe I can let enough air in to dissipate the gas."

"Do you think Irene's alive?"

Lily hesitated. 'No' was the right answer, but that would only make Grace fight harder to keep her from going back to the house. "It's possible. Hopefully, Kyle thinks we believed him and left. He's probably at a safe distance but watching. I think he's waiting for something—or someone. I'm guessing Dove."

"So? What if he is? You said they had a relationship. He's a police officer. I know you think something's off with him, but if Irene was in the house, he wouldn't leave her there."

"Listen to me. When Kyle pulled his hand out of his jacket, I thought he was drawing a gun. But now I think it was a detonator for the gas fumes. If he tried to trigger it, he was too far away. But, if he gets closer and tries again before I can get fresh air inside, Irene will die."

Grace said, "Hang on, let me try satellite SOS before you go." She pulled out her phone and tried the emergency icon, giving a startled laugh when the signal went through.

"You're a pain sometimes, you know that?" Lily trotted ahead of Grace, who doggedly followed.

"And you're assuming a hell of a lot. What if Kyle only had key fob in his hand? I don't blame him for running—you pointed a gun at him! You didn't tell emergency services that, either. I'm worried. Lily."

Lily, increasingly irritable since Grace refused to let her return alone, shot an exasperated look over her shoulder. Even if she was positive about her suspicions, there was no time to explain them. Grace would ask a million questions, and they'd still be arguing when the hurricane hit. But the conclusions she'd reached not only made sense, they felt right. Right and terrifying.

Kyle's insistence that the sheriff would arrest Irene for Josh's murder. His promise to "stand by" Dove no matter what. But it was his comment that everything Dove had done was for Brooklyn that really stuck with Lily. It all added up to a narrative that Lily knew in her gut was wrong.

But all she said to Grace was, "The junker he's driving is too old for a fob. Now stop distracting me. Do you remember what you're supposed to say?"

Grace didn't give in. "I'm not sure I like this version of you."

They had reached the church. Lily stopped and held her phone skyward. No connection to satellite SOS system this time. "It's high tide," she said quietly. "If the road's underwater at that dip near Ketchum Fork, the bomb squad and whoever else the Sheriff is able to round up will be delayed."

"Bomb? Are you—"

"Explosions, bombs, gas leaks—same team." Lily held up a hand to stop the inevitable next question. "Look, you can see Thatcher's car through those trees. He's still here. I'm going to shut off the gas at the house and get those windows open. This is as far as you go, Grace."

"No way. If it's safe enough for you—"

"It's not safe for anybody!" Lily hissed, rounding on her. "But one of us graduated first in her class on how not to get blown up, and it wasn't you." She stopped, slightly appalled at her rudeness, then decided it was necessary. "Look, boss, you have kids. Kids and a husband who'll never be the same if you die today. Plus, you're distracting, and you'll slow me down. Either one can get us killed." She handed Grace the keys to the truck. "If the house blows, don't try to get me. There could be smaller explosions after the big one, and they may keep coming. Now, run back to the truck, get Dove. Call for help but don't come back here."

Grace's eyes filled with tears, but Lily was already running.

***

She was sure Thatcher was still around somewhere but could only guess at what he could see of the house. Crouching low, Lily darted from the church's cover to the produce stand, then to the overgrown blackberry thicket nearest the driveway, where she paused to wipe rain from her face. She scanned the woods but saw nothing suspicious. Even if Thatcher had removed his blue jacket, he wore a white shirt underneath. She told herself she'd see him if he was near the tree line. The trick was keeping him from seeing her. For once, her preference for darker tones was paying off.

Despite what she'd told Grace, she wasn't positive that there actually was a detonator, or that Thatcher was trying to kill Irene, but either way, someone had to turn off the gas and get Irene out of that house. The one thing she did know for sure was that neither Dove nor Mimi had picked her up and Irene wouldn't have left with anyone else.

She tried remembering her own remote grill lighter's capabilities but drew a blank. It was frustrating to think that even with all her training, she could still get herself killed in an old house full of propane. She reasoned that if Thatcher was deep enough in the woods that she couldn't spot him, he wasn't close enough to trigger the explosion. He'd already tried that once and failed, and he was further away now.

Maybe he hadn't done his homework. He might not know propane gas settled on floors. If he'd placed the igniter on the kitchen table, it would take longer for enough propane to accumulate and catch the spark from the remote-controlled switch. It was a foolish hope, and she was wasting time. If he knew enough to set up the death trap, he knew to leave the igniter on the stove, next to open burners spewing fumes. He was nearby, waiting for his chance to take out Dove and Irene.

Even as the logical part of her brain sorted through that scenario, her stomach flipped at the implications. If this horror story was true, charming, helpful Kyle, the man Dove loved, had killed Josh.

It was a thought for later. She had to act now.

She sprinted across the driveway to the front porch and crouched again, straining to hear over her heartbeat's loud thumps. The wind was picking up. If she could get the doors and a few windows open, a good cross-draft would dissipate the propane quickly.

She moved to the corner window facing the street. Reaching behind an overgrown nandina bush, she pulled out a bucket, flipped it over, and stood on it. This had been Dove's escape hatch in their teenage party years when they'd sneak out after Irene went to sleep. The window slid up so smoothly she wondered if her old friend still used it.

The wave of gas fumes with a strong rotten-egg odor made her gag and jump back. Berating herself for not thinking ahead, she removed her thin cotton jacket, slipped her arms from her tee-shirt sleeves, and pulled the body up over her nose and mouth, tying excess fabric behind her head in a makeshift mask. She grabbed the jacket and tied its arms over the tee-shirt mask. Praying the layers of clothing would be enough of a barrier, she took a deep breath, stepped back on the bucket and pulled herself through the window.

She walked slowly across the carpet, careful to lift her feet as she stepped, and avoiding light switches. Fear of a static spark igniting the propane remained front and center in her thoughts. When she reached the front door, she slowly eased it open and stepped out to gulp air.

Back in the house, she moved counterclockwise through each room, carefully opening every window and door and sucking in a lungful of the humid outside air when she had a chance. She didn't find Irene, but in the last room, the kitchen, broken plates and over-turned chairs told her Dove's Reenie had put up a fight.

Fumes were already lessening as air circulated, but she still had to turn off the propane. She grabbed the burner valve stem, then quickly let go when it seared her fingers. Untying the jacket, she used one sleeve for padding as she turned each burner off. Next, she found the gas shut off in the pantry before making another trip outside to breathe.

Even with the danger of an explosion neutralized, she was reluc-tant to go back inside. Her head pounded and nausea was growing, but she knew Irene would have tried to hide if she were too injured to escape.

Recovering her face with her jacket, she reentered the house and made another round, checking floors and closets as she went. In the small bedroom Irene had once shared with Harvey, an old beach towel and an open metal lockbox lay wedged next to a nightstand. The box was empty, but Lily knew what had once been inside. They'd only been twelve when Dove had shown Lily her grandfather's army-issued Colt .45.

Lily hoped it was Irene who'd retrieved the pistol today. If it had been Thatcher, he would now have two weapons to use on them.

CHAPTER FORTY-EIGHT

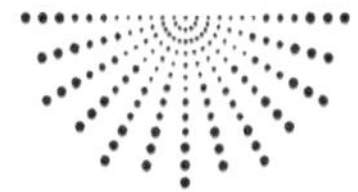

KYLE and IRENE

Kyle Thatcher ran blindly through the woods, slowing only when a thick catbrier vine sent him sprawling face-down into wet muck. As he extracted himself from the vine's vicious hooked thorns, he told himself the tears on his face were from pain, not overwhelming fear.

He was going to die.

Lily and her friend had played him. He'd bought the fake hysterics, yelling, and running. Their wild escape in that beat-up truck had been over the top, but he wanted to believe they were gone. He should have remembered Josh's stories about his little sister. How he had bragged about her rise through the military police ranks and her harrowing combat missions.

A woman like that wouldn't run away.

He'd realized his mistake when he saw the back door of the house inch open, then the windows on either side of it. The wind gained strength, neutralizing his carefully staged explosion, while he pounded frantically on the red button of his useless remote control.

He was too far away. He'd screwed up again.

Now he'd either die in these woods or be shot by the cops who'd eventually show up. Assuming Lily didn't kill him first. Even if he survived this awful day, he wouldn't live long once the crime syndicate got their hands on him. He might be safer in prison, but the thought made him gag.

He was jerked back to real time by new sounds loud enough to be heard over the wind. Someone was crashing through the woods toward him. He looked around frantically. The only protection he saw was the tangle of vegetation he'd just escaped. He crouched down, trying to avoid thorns and poison ivy, and watched through breaks in the foliage. Someone in yellow appeared but moved past with their back to him.

Then a woman with a breathy, hoarse voice—a voice he recognized—began calling someone named Aaron.

Anger flooded through him, erasing his fear. He might die, but he wouldn't hide from an old woman who had made a fool of him.

Irene Jensen turned, taking in each personal landmark in the small clearing. The log bench where she'd sat as her father pronounced her worthless and her child invisible in God's eyes was barely recognizable, its supports long rotted. But there were also reminders of happier times—picnics and Debbie's chatter and Harvey's calm voice telling her they were safe. They were all safe. Even Aaron.

But Harvey couldn't have guessed that a devil would come to this place.

She was so weak, and the burning pain in her abdomen was excruciating. What had the strange man done to her? He hadn't touched her, just shoved that boxy thing at her middle, and she had gone down. She wasn't bleeding, so she hadn't been shot, but she thought she might be dying all the same.

Her gaze settled on a narrow sliver of grass and the big granite chunk. This is where she wanted to be. She blocked out the sound of the storm and unpinned her braid, letting the wind tousle her hair. But her peace was short-lived. Someone was running towards her. Someone real.

And that was when she remembered her plan.

As Kyle Thatcher burst into the clearing, Irene took Harvey's pistol from her skirt pocket, raised it, and pulled the trigger. After that, there was only the wind, and the soft patch of grass, and blessed sleep.

CHAPTER FORTY-NINE

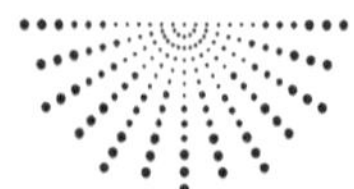

Dove was trying to stand up in the middle of the road, using a thick stick for a crutch. As soon as Grace stopped the truck in front of her, she yelled, "What are you doing here? Where's Lily? Is she with Kyle? I can't reach him."

Ignoring the histrionics, Grace got out and knelt to look at Dove's swollen ankle. "There's been trouble," she said, standing up and offering Dove an arm. "No time to tell you everything. We have to get back to your house. Can you get into the truck if I help?"

"I'm not going anywhere until I know what's happening!"

"Suit yourself." Grace stepped away, took out her phone, nearly crying with relief at the sight of one beautiful signal bar. Her joy was short-lived, though—her call to Mac went straight to voicemail. She left a message with the basics of their situation, watching Dove's face go ashen.

Her next call to Mallard Bay PD was redirected to Kingston County 911, where she learned help wasn't coming—at least not soon. Downed trees and washed-out roads blocked any quick rescue. She listened numbly to instructions to stay at least 500 feet from the house and seek shelter in a sturdy structure, or as a last resort, a vehicle out of range of trees falling from the explosion, a tornado, or hurricane-force winds.

They were surrounded by trees and the only semi-sturdy structure—the church—was too close to the house. Eying the F-350 with dismay, Grace thanked the dispatcher and listened to calm reassurance that help would come as soon as conditions allowed. The "please stay safe" sign-off frightened her more than anything else.

They were on their own.

It wasn't easy boosting Dove onto the running board and into the passenger seat, but she'd stopped complaining and helped as much as possible.

Grace said, "I'm going to have to back up until there's room to turn around. I need you to help guide me." She started the truck. "But first, hold that grab bar and don't let go. You don't have a seatbelt, and the last time I put a manual shift into reverse was 2012."

Shifting was a struggle, and when they were finally rolling backward, Dove seemed to be reconsidering her rescue. "You know you'll have to back up almost all the way to my house, right?"

"Would you rather walk? Turn around and watch out the back. I'll steer by the rearview mirror."

Dove gave a derisive snort. "At your speed, we won't get there until dark."

Grace kept her eyes on the mirror and tried to ignore everything but her view of the road.

Dove didn't ignore anything. "You still haven't told me if Lily and Kyle are together."

Grace slowed to a crawl rounding a curve. The odds of another vehicle coming behind them were slim. The dispatcher at emergency services said the road was blocked in both directions, but she held her breath until they'd made it. After another minute of slow rolling, she backed into a farm road entrance, wrestled the gear shift back to drive, and pulled out.

"Finally!" Dove said irritably. "I need to know—"

Grace's patience snapped. She hit the brakes, bringing the truck to a shuddering halt that nearly bounced Dove onto the floor. "Here's what you need to know. Your house is full of propane, your grandmother is missing, and Lily's risking her life to save her. If you have more complaints, get out and wait for a rescue more to your liking. But know this—your boyfriend tried to kill us, possibly did kill Irene, and is waiting to kill you."

Dove shut up.

They reached the woods' edge next to the church and could see Thatcher's car through the trees. The rain had let up, but the wind was worsening. There was no sign of Lily.

Grace killed the engine. She didn't know what to do next but kept that to herself. Where was Lily? There hadn't been an explosion, but what if she'd been overcome by gas?

You have kids. If not for those words, Grace would be in there, too. She checked her watch. Lily had been in there too long. "Do you recognize that car?" she asked.

Dove looked at the rusting sedan. "That's not Kyle's. He drives—"

"A red Tesla," Grace snapped. "Lily told me. Just what anyone would drive to a murder, right?"

"You don't have to be so nasty! I heard what you said, and I don't believe you. I'm gullible, but I'm not an idiot."

"Sorry." *Not sorry.* Grace hoped Lily's bestie had a whole other side to her personality when she wasn't involved with a killer.

"I told him," Dove said suddenly. "I told Kyle everything about Reenie, how hard it is taking care of her. Once I started, I couldn't stop. I told him she'd started hallucinating about seeing men in the woods."

"How did he react?" Grace tried to sound sympathetic but didn't hit the mark.

"He was so worried about all of us. I wish you and Lily could have heard him. He said Reenie wasn't safe for Brooklyn and me to be around, but that he could help me find a place where she could get care. He said—" Tears drowned out the next words.

Grace gave up fake sympathy and went for the jugular. "Do you want to save your grandmother?"

"Of course!"

"Then stop blubbering and help me. Tell me exactly what Kyle said he'd do with Irene."

"*Do* with her? Nothing. He said he had a psychiatrist friend who'd see her for free and help get her committed for evaluation and treatment. As soon as she was better, she could come home."

"And meanwhile, you and he would do what?"

Dove rubbed her face hard. Her shoulders still trembled, but when she turned to Grace, her tears were gone. "You don't know what it's like! A five-year-old who cries when I go to my crappy job, a vindictive ex who terrifies me, and an eighty-five-year-old grandmother who can't sleep and hallucinates. You think you can do better? Be my guest."

Grace stopped listening. She needed to find Lily. But she also needed to keep Dove out of the way of whatever was happening with Kyle Thatcher. If he was a killer, Dove would make a good hostage.

"I saw him, Josh. Or at least I think I did."

Dove had continued her litany of complaints, and it took a moment for Grace to realize she'd switched topics. "You mean in the woods?"

"Yeah. Once I knew he was the man who died in the church, I made the connection. The first time he looked so scary, I didn't recognize him. I called the sheriff's office and reported him as a stalker. Reenie had been talking about seeing him, but she didn't recognize him either. The second time, I thought there was something familiar about him. The guy made me think of Josh, but he had long, sort of gray hair, and I never saw his face. He was moving through the woods like he'd come from the turnaround clearing up the road from the house."

"Was there a third time?"

Dove nodded. "The guy moved like Josh and was built like him. But I told Reenie we just had more hikers than usual."

"Why didn't you try to talk to him? Or tell Lily?"

The tears started up again. "Kyle had told me what had happened to Josh. About the drugs and how he was living on the streets. I couldn't take care of an addict, too! And if Dom found out Josh was here, he'd use it against me. But I told Kyle, and he said he'd find Josh, or whoever it was, and make sure he was okay. Kyle loves me, and he'll be able to explain what he was doing here today."

Grace noticed that Dove hadn't raised her voice again, and she was looking around furtively. This was Lily's friend—surely, she had *some* redeeming qualities, although it was hard to tell from her recent behavior. The next hours would be so much easier if she cooperated, but there was no time to coddle her.

"Kyle Thatcher might love you, but an hour ago, it looked like he was trying to detonate your gas-filled house while Lily and I were standing next to it, and he has a gun. He may be innocent, but I can't take that chance with Lily and Irene's lives at stake. Can you?" For once, Dove had no response, and Grace pressed her point. "If I'm wrong, I will apologize to him, face to face. But now I have to go help Lily. We'll get Irene, come back here to you and take you both to the hospital."

Dove didn't try to stop her when she left.

The wind was growing stronger, but it was at her back, and Grace quickly reached the edge of the produce stand just in time to see

Lily coming out the front door of the house. She had barely cleared the driveway when they heard gunfire from the woods.

Lily dropped to the ground and belly crawled to Grace. "I'm fine," she panted as Grace reached out and pulled her under the stand. "Irene's not in the house, but there was some kind of struggle in the kitchen. Harvey's old pistol is missing, but I didn't see any blood." She paused, taking deep breaths. "Gas is off, and the house is safe unless there's another booby trap I missed."

Grace filled her in on Dove, ending with, "She's not happy, but she stayed put."

Lily said. "Think Thatcher knows Irene's seen him in the woods? Maybe that's why he's so desperate. If she saw him the night Josh died—"

"Or the night he was stabbed."

"Yep. That's the link."

The words were barely out of her mouth when Dove came around the corner, hop-staggering toward them on her makeshift crutch. Lily darted to her, taking an arm and lifting the weight off her injured ankle. Dove's knees buckled and nearly took them both down.

Lily gave her a rough shake. "Knock it off and keep your voice down."

"But I heard gunfire!" Dove cried. "I thought you or Reenie—"

"I'm fine," Lily said, shushing her again. "But I can't find Irene. Are you sure Mimi didn't come get her?"

"I'm sure." Dove straightened up a bit. "Aunt Mimi was texting me every fifteen minutes until Grace got me."

"Okay," Lily said. "Let's try—" A fierce gust of wind blasted them, and they heard a loud crack. As they watched in shock, an old maple tree toppled toward the Jensens' house.

Dove screamed as half her home disappeared under branches and debris.

CHAPTER FIFTY

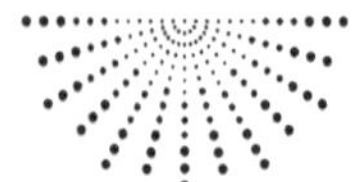

The shock of the crash refocused their attention to the rapidly deteriorating weather. Grace and Lily struggled to half carry Dove up the front steps to the church. Grace took Dove's weight as Lily stripped the crime scene tape from the doors and wrestled them open. They barely cleared the entrance when a tree branch hurtled past, followed by roof shingles from the house.

Once inside with the doors secured, Lily led them to a window-less corner of the vestibule without acknowledging the safer interior closet. It was taped off, and none of them wanted to be in the windowless room where Josh had died.

"Reenie—" Dove started but stopped when Lily shook her head.

"I'm sorry. Wherever she is, she'll hunker down, and I think she has your Grandad's pistol. I found the old shoebox it used to be in. It was empty."

"Oh, my God." Dove rubbed her face wearily. "We've fought more times than I can count about that stupid gun. The big rifle is one thing. I got rid of the ammunition for it ages ago, and Reenie's never liked it. But that pistol. I don't trust her with it, and I can't get it away from her. She still sleeps with it under the bed, so I don't allow Brooklyn to go in her room. I thought I'd found all the ammo for it, too. Reenie promised, she *swore* she didn't have any."

This time when Dove cried, Lily put an arm around her. "You've done the best you can," she said. "You can't control her. As soon as this band of the hurricane passes, I'll find her, I promise."

For the next hour, they huddled together, watching the eerie greenish light that filtered in from the scorched sanctuary. The howling wind made conversation impossible, not that any of them tried to talk. They would make it, or they wouldn't, but there was nowhere else to go.

After what seemed like an eternity, Dove said, "The wind is easing up. Can we call for help again?" Her voice was far from steady, but she sounded like she was pulling herself together.

Lily said, "Good idea. It will be a while before emergency crews can get here, but I should tell them the threat of the gas explosion has been, uhm, neutralized." She gave Dove a level look. "They also need to know Kyle is still here and is armed, and that Reenie might have a gun, too."

"I guess you have to say that, don't you?" Dove said. "I've been thinking, and I know where Reenie might be. I have to get to her. I'm the only one she'll listen to."

"Is she in the woods?" Lily guessed.

"Yeah. There's a clearing where she goes whenever she can. I've followed her, and I know the way. There's a sort of path you can see from the backyard. It twists and turns, but it goes to a small clearing with a big rock and log where she sits and... well, I've told you she hallucinates. She talks to people out there. Grandad, and her mother, and someone named Aaron."

The storm was definitely easing. All three women checked their phones again—no signal.

"According to the last weather report I saw," Lily said, "we've probably got an hour or more before it gets bad again."

"Then let's go." Dove tried to push herself up but gasped and fell back when she moved her foot.

"I think it's broken." Lily said, looking at Grace. "I'll go get the truck and bring it up. You stay with Dove. Get her ankle stabilized so we can move her."

"No way in hell." Dove said. "You go get Reenie now!"

"All right, then." Lily got up and brushed off her wet pants, though nothing short of replacing them would make a difference. "But don't follow me. Hopping around out there is asking to get killed, and then where would Brooklyn be?" She waited until Dove reluctantly agreed, then outlined her plan. "I will get Irene. She couldn't have gotten far. I'll go in making enough noise to wake the dead—maybe I can keep her from shooting me before I can find her."

Grace added, "Promise to stay put and keep quiet and I'll go with her. Two of us will find her faster." Despite her irritation, she gave Dove a quick hug. "This time you have to stay put. We can't carry you and your grandmother."

<hr>

When they had cleared the church, Grace said, "We're not just making noise to alert Irene, are we?"

"Nope," Lily said. "Our ruse worked once, so we talk loudly about the rescue that will be here in minutes and hope Thatcher runs like hell to get away."

"To his car behind the church? What if he finds Dove?"

"He's not stopping for anyone."

The path was hard to find, especially with all the downed tree branches, but they stumbled across it eventually. Following Lily, Grace shouted, "How long have we been out here? That 911 operator said they'd be here in a few minutes—why couldn't we have waited?"

"Anything could have happened to Irene. We have to go in," Lily yelled back over her shoulder. "Keep up! The sheriff's deputies will be here soon. We need to find her and get out of here."

Grace thought that last bit was a stretch, but hopefully Kyle or Irene—whoever was still conscious and had the gun—would believe more help was coming than two soaked, exhausted women.

"Watch where you're stepping." Lily said in her normal voice.

"Why?"

"Patch of poison oak right next to you."

Grace promised herself that her next shopping trip would be for the heavy white waders the watermen wore. "Do you even know where you're going?"

"You try following her directions," Lily snapped. "'Follow the path east until you get there?' If this is a path, I'd hate to see a maze." She pointed to a break in the foliage. "East is that way." They set off again, but Lily stopped abruptly. There was a bright splash of yellow up ahead. "Irene!" she shouted, then picked up a large stick and gave a nearby bush several whacks. "We're coming, and we've got help!"

"Jeez, Louise," Grace nudged her. "If Kyle didn't hear that, he's long gone."

Seconds later, they entered a small clearing and found Irene lying face-down on the ground. Lily reached her first, running her hands gently over Irene's body, then sat back on her heels. "She's alive and nothing's broken that I can see. She could have internal injuries, but we can't leave her like this. Help me turn her onto her side."

Irene whimpered as they moved her onto her side but didn't regain consciousness. A pistol lay beneath her.

"Do you have anything I can put that in?" Lily asked.

Grace produced two dog waste bags from one of her pockets.

"Crime scene techs are going to love this," Lily muttered as she covered her hand with one bag and picked up the pistol. She set the safety before placing it in the second bag with its "Dispose of contents properly!" warning. "It's Harvey's Colt .45. He brought it back from Vietnam." She glanced up at Grace with a sad smile. "I know he'd be proud of his wife."

Lily examined Irene again. "Concussion, I think. But she's breathing okay considering the circumstances."

"Your call," Grace said. "I'll go for help, or we can carry her out." It was raining again, and overhead they heard rumbling. "Is that thunder?"

Just then, both of their cell phones went off.

"No!" A huge grin lit up Lily's face as she scrambled to her feet. "Helicopter!"

CHAPTER FIFTY-ONE

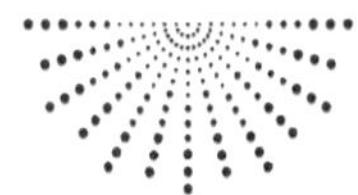

Less than fifteen minutes after lifting off from the Jensens' backyard, the Bell 407 set down safely in front of a stately home across from the University of Maryland Medical Center in Easton. There'd been an anxious moment when escalating winds prevented the pilot from using the hospital's helipad, but all the retired Navy pilot said was, "Piece of cake," as he angled to the left and landed across the street on a wide lawn.

The volunteer EMT who'd flown with them pronounced Irene stable, but that didn't stop Dove's nonstop questions as she was wheeled along behind her grandmother's entourage on their way to the hospital.

When Grace and Lily were alone with the pilot, Ralph Cleever introduced himself as a friend of Mac's before turning his attention to the excited homeowner whose yard they'd commandeered.

"You okay?" Grace looked Lily over. "No snakebites or broken nails?"

"Probably better than you, boss." Lily reached out and pulled several twigs from Grace's windblown hair. "Besides, I told you, these nails are cement." She showed off a remarkably blemish-free manicure. "I may keep them." She tapped her phone to life and called Denise, giving Grace huge smile when her mother answered.

Grace wasn't so lucky. Mac didn't answer, and his mailbox was full.

"Mrs. McNamara?" Ralph Cleever was back and reached out to touch her arm gently. "We need to talk. Let's step away and get some privacy."

Grace glanced up at the sky, wondering if he wanted to tell her he couldn't get them back to Mallard Bay. The cloud cover was getting heavier, and rain wouldn't be far behind. But when Cleever stopped and turned to face her, his expression was grim. This wasn't about transportation or the weather.

"What's happened? Is it the children?"

"I'm sure they're fine, ma'am." He guided her toward a stone bench beneath a maple tree, but Grace ignored his gesture for her to sit. "I'm a friend of Mac's, and I volunteered to come get you. I haven't had an update since I called our coordinates in after we lifted off from Twin Corners." The lanky pilot sank onto the bench.

No longer sure her legs would hold her, Grace joined him. "So, you skipped protocol to come get me because you're Mac's friend?"

"That, and because although the State Police wouldn't have taken much longer to get to you, I knew you'd be needing a second ride once we got here, and I thought I could help. Mac and your sister had a medical emergency at your home. Their 911 call only got through about an hour ago, but they're being airlifted out now."

"Medical emergency? What kind? Are they both hurt?"

Ralph shook his head. "No. Your sister is fine. But based on her statements, the EMTs think Mac may have suffered a heart attack after a non-venomous snakebite. She had to perform CPR at the scene, but he's coherent now and looks good under the circumstances. They'll know more when the docs get him."

His words sounded like gibberish to Grace. CPR? *Mac*?

Cleever touched her arm again to get her attention. "From what

I've heard, your sister is a trooper. She also got him inside the house and stabilized him."

"Stephanie?"

"Is that her name? Well, Mac was lucky she was there. He's being taken to Shock Trauma, but his vitals are good. Your sister did a great job with his initial care, and she insists the snake was an Eastern Water. Like I said, non-venomous, but they can be aggressive, and some people are really allergic to their bites."

"Shock Trauma in Baltimore?" Grace's voice sounded shrill to her own ears. "I need to get there."

"I understand," Cleever said. "And I can take you as soon as we're cleared. The weather's worsening, but we can make if we leave soon."

Lily approached, breaking into a trot when she saw their faces. "What's going on?"

"Mac's been hurt," Grace said numbly, as Cleever stepped away to make flight arrangements. "Snakebite and possibly a heart attack. He's on his way to Shock Trauma."

Lily paled. "Sweet Baby Jesus. How bad is it?"

"Stephanie saved his life with CPR."

"Stephanie?" Lily looked as confused as Grace felt.

"I know, right? What were they even doing at our house?"

Cleever overheard them and returned looking uncomfortable. "Well, all of us feel really bad about that. In his last transmission to emergency operations in Mallard Bay, Mac said he was going to pick up his sister-in-law at your house and would be at the fire department in a half hour. When he didn't show up on time, no one was particularly surprised, given the conditions. There was a lot going on."

Guilt squeezed Grace's heart. Why hadn't she tried harder to stop Stephanie from coming? Instead, she'd been out in a cellphone dead zone while Mac had gone to save her irresponsible sister.

The pilot was still explaining how they'd lost track of the chief of police. "By the time Trey Harper started asking if anyone had seen Mac, well, we all assumed he was in and out doing whatever needed to be done in town. He wasn't answering his phone, and we couldn't reach you. Everything was grounded by that time, and the roads out to your place were flooded. The assumption was that they had lost power at your house and were waiting out the worst of the storm. Trey knew where you were, Ms. Travers, but we couldn't reach you. But again, we weren't worried because we knew cell reception would be spotty out around Twin Corners."

Grace tried calling Mac again and got the full mailbox message. Stephanie's number didn't even connect. "Do you think they've landed at Shock Trauma?" she asked Cleever. "I need to check on them."

He looked relieved to have something to do besides deliver bad news. "Let's load up and get in the air. I'll make some calls and see what I can find out."

Lily put a steadying hand on Grace's arm. "What can I do to help?"

"Find a ride to Mallard Bay and keep everyone at Delaney House calm. I'm betting no one has wanted to break the news to Avril and Cy. Tell them to keep the kids away from any talk about Mac until I have better news." She gave Lily a look that warned her not to argue. "He will be fine, understand? He's in good condition and will be home soon, and that's all you need to say."

"Got it. I'll check with Dove and make sure Irene's stable and scrounge up a ride. Don't worry about anything here."

Grace had just fastened her seat belt when Ralph Cleever said, "Shock Trauma has received Mac. He's stable and responsive. Your sister is with him."

"Responsive? That's good, right?" Grace asked anxiously.

"I reached one of our local guys who was on the flight team. He said Mac said to tell you he's fine."

"Of course he did!" Grace lost her battle against tears. "But how is he, really?"

"All I could get from the EMT was that hypothetically, a person in his condition might have had a mild heart attack or perhaps just an adverse reaction to the snakebite. Sometimes the body can go into shock, even with non-venomous snakebites. He also hit his head when he fell, but apparently that's not much more than a bad bruise. Please don't worry. Your husband is in good enough shape to razz your sister for beating up on him."

The thought of Stephanie performing CPR, of Mac lying unconscious and at her ditzy sister's mercy, still seemed impossible to grasp. So was the image of Mac teasing the sister-in-law who'd driven him crazy.

Her phone buzzed with a text message from an unknown number: *Borrowed this phone. Mac's okay. Really. I'll be with him until you get here-S.* Grace reread the message, trying to reconcile the words with the sister who had upended their lives just days ago.

"Hey! Look at that." Cleever pointed to the sky where anemic rays of sunshine were peeking through the cloud cover. "Let's hop on over to Baltimore, okay?"

His words were too hearty, but Grace appreciated the effort. As they lifted off and gained altitude, she gazed down at the patchwork of flooded roads and fields below. The storm had already left its mark on the landscape, and tonight the last bands of the hurricane would hit. What would this view be like tomorrow?

Apparently still determined to cheer her up during their short ride, Cleever said, "Here's a tidbit you'll probably hear from the EMTs in Mallard Bay. Your sister was cooking when Mac showed up. She not only saved his life, but she also had a whole meal ready when the emergency response team got there, and she sent it all to the station house for the crew. Roast chicken dinner with all the trimmings and a chocolate cake. She'll probably get her name in the paper for that one."

Grace closed her eyes and put her head back, hoping he'd take the hint and stop talking. One more oddball detail and she'd be over the edge. She kept her thoughts on Mac and the children and shut the rest of the world out.

CHAPTER FIFTY-TWO

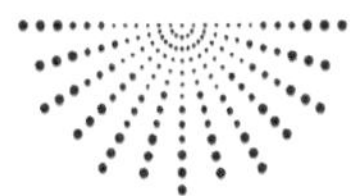

Ralph Cleever was mercifully quiet until near the end of the flight into Baltimore when he insisted Grace eat a candy bar and sip a bottle of water. The short rest and sugar rush helped clear her thoughts, but her hands were still shaking as a hospital administrator greeted her on the helipad at the University of Maryland Shock Trauma Center and escorted her to the sixth floor.

"Your husband is doing remarkably well," the woman assured her as they walked briskly through the corridors. "Preliminary tests indicate the heart issue was caused by a severe reaction to the snakebite, not an actual heart attack. We're still running tests to confirm, but there's no sign of damage to his heart so far." She stopped outside Room 612. "The doctors will be making rounds in about an hour, and they'll have more information for you."

Grace found Mac propped up in bed, looking far better than she had feared. His color was good, and he reached for her as she ran to him. Careful of the monitors and IV line, she got her arms around him, and the strength of his hug told her everything would be all right. "You scared the hell out of me," she whispered against his neck.

"Scared the hell out of myself, too. It's been a one-of-a-kind day, for sure."

Grace eased down on the side of the bed and turned toward the chair where her sister sat, her gaze focused on her tightly clenched hands. "Thank you, Stephanie." Tears choked off everything else she wanted to say, but she'd gotten the important part out, and the relief she saw on Stephanie's face told her it was enough.

"So, what happened? How in the world did you get bitten? I've never seen snakes that close to the house." Grace was giddy with relief at the cardiologist's report. Mac could be released after another twenty-four hours of monitoring for the after-effects of anaphylactic shock and his mild concussion. She bombarded him with questions while she and Stephanie ate the sandwiches Ralph Cleever had brought them before flying back to Easton.

Mac didn't answer but slipped potato chips from Grace's paper plate.

"It was huge," Stephanie said around a mouthful of roast beef and rye. "I'll never wear anything but tall boots at your house again."

Ignoring the obvious opening, Mac said, "It must have gotten washed up into the yard and crawled under the truck for shelter. Usually, the only danger a water snake poses is the heart attack it can cause when people mistake it for a copperhead, unless, of course, you're allergic to the venom."

Grace shuddered and looked at his bandaged calf. "How bad is the bite?"

"Bad," he and Stephanie said in unison.

"I had on my duty boots, but the snake was at least three feet long and must have been coiled. Caught me on the calf. Steph was in sandals, but she ran to save me, anyway."

Stephanie shifted uncomfortably in her chair. "Stop exaggerating. No big deal. Just me, not following instructions as usual. It wasn't that dramatic."

"You performed CPR," Grace said. "You saved his life."

"Everyone's blowing that up. Mac was breathing on his own by the time the paramedics arrived. I only helped him inside when he passed out."

"You restarted my heart, hauled me inside, and kept me alive," Mac said firmly. "Even if you did dump me on the stairs. What was that about? I'll have bruises on my back for a month."

"Then they'll match the ones on your chest." The corners of Stephanie's mouth twitched, and she lost her weepy look. "You were able to help a little getting inside, even if you don't remember, but you passed out again right after. Propping you up on the stairs was the best way to keep you on an incline."

Mac and Grace looked at her blankly.

"First aid? Remember? Well, living where you do, you should read up on it. Your head and heart had to be above the bite wound to slow the movement of the venom up your leg. Plus, that speech of yours about the house flooding worried me. I was afraid I'd have to move you off the floor or sofa if the water started coming in." She got another round of blank looks. "I sure hope you two are sharper than this when you aren't in shock. On the steps, I could get behind you and pull you up to the second floor. Painful for both of us, but doable if necessary."

"More Girl Scout training?" Grace finally managed.

Stephanie shrugged.

"Common sense," Mac said. "But I'm not sure I would have thought of it. I'm so grateful you were there." He cleared his throat and added, "I don't remember much, but I yelled at you—"

"Nothing I haven't heard before." Stephanie cut him off in a tone that said she wasn't doing any more emotional scenes. "You should've heard what I called you while you were unconscious."

The awkward moment was interrupted by the simultaneous chiming of Grace's phone and the arrival of a nurse pushing a cart full of instruments and two wicked-looking syringes. "May we have the room?" she asked. "Unless you want an audience, sir?"

'Sir' did not.

CHAPTER FIFTY-THREE

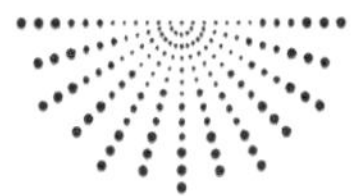

Out in the hall, Stephanie disappeared into the ladies' room while Grace took her call from Tremaine Harper.

"How's Mac?" The sergeant's normally steady baritone held an edge of something that sounded off.

"He's going to be okay," Grace said, giving him a quick update on Mac's condition. "What's happening there? Is the storm still—"

"The storm's behaving better than expected," Tremaine cut in. "Florian's weakening faster than they predicted. But there's something you should be aware of before you get back." He paused, his voice dropping lower. "I'll leave it up to you to decide how much the Chief needs to know right now."

Grace tightened her grip on the phone. "Is everyone okay?"

"Oh, yes—sorry, should have led with that. This is about Detective Thatcher. A search team located his body about a quarter mile from where you and Lily found Irene Jensen."

Grace exhaled, allowing herself a moment of relief that the news wasn't about someone she loved. "Do you know what happened to him?"

"A gunshot wound to the shoulder, but that's not what killed him. He drowned." Tremaine paused, and Grace heard voices in the background, then a door shut, and it was quiet again. "Sorry. This place is packed with volunteers, but I think most of them already know this. The working theory is that Thatcher was shot and fell into Deer Creek or was unconscious at the water's edge and was swept down to the mouth of the river. His body got hung up on some rocks, or we might never have found him."

Grace remembered Lily's description of the small creek that normally meandered peacefully through the woods. "The storm surge…"

"Exactly. The creek was swollen to three times its normal size and moving fast. The medical examiner thinks it's probable Thatcher passed out from blood loss and exertion, then was swept away at high tide."

"Any idea who shot him?" Grace was proud of how calm she sounded, particularly since she was sure she knew who'd fired an old Colt .45 at the Devil.

"A few ideas," Trey said. "But the only thing we know for sure is it wasn't self-inflicted. Angle's wrong. When Mrs. Jensen recovers enough to talk to us, we'll see what she has to say."

"What did the doctors say happened to her?"

Trey's voice dropped again, softening with concern. "I don't have all the details. They talked to Dove, and she called Lily about a half hour ago."

"And Lily called you," Grace finished, anxious to get to the details.

"Miss Irene was tasered. She says Thatcher showed up at her house and attacked her. Hit her in the abdomen, but her denim apron provided some protection, although it must have hurt like hell. No permanent damage. Not from that, anyway. But she's got a couple of cracked ribs, and she had a mild heart attack. The docs say she's doing great for her age and the trauma she's been through."

Grace let out the breath she was holding. "Thank God. What about the pistol we found with her?"

"Recently fired." The words hung between them, weighted with implication. "Ballistics tests won't be done until at least tomorrow."

Tired as she was, adrenaline set Grace's thoughts spinning. She needed to get to Lily and Dove and get Cyrus to sign on as Irene's—

As if reading her mind, Trey said, "Lily got Mr. Mosley to the hospital before they even moved Mrs. Jensen into a room. He was a little shook up after riding in the Traverses' farm truck, but he could still throw a lot of big words around. It was impressive."

"Oh, don't play small-town cop with me, Tremaine Harper." Grace found herself smiling despite everything. "I've seen all those diplomas in your office." It felt odd to laugh after all that had happened, but she felt steadier. This was something she could deal with.

"Oh, I understood Mr. Mosley. But the sheriff might still be looking a few things up."

This time Grace snorted when she laughed at the mental image of Cyrus running verbal circles around Grant Carlisle. "Is there any word about the investigation into Josh Travers's murder?"

"Sheriff Carlisle is backpedaling as fast as those skinny legs of his will go. You be sure to tell the chief that, okay?"

"Of course." Grace laughed again, but then a sobering thought hit her. "Trey, about Grant Carlisle. Should we be worried about him? His motives, I mean. He's been so antagonistic."

Trey didn't answer immediately, but finally sighed and said, "Maybe the Chief can explain it to you when he's up to it. He was on his way back here from a briefing in Easton with Commander Binks this morning when he had to detour to go out to your place. But I don't think you need to worry about the sheriff. He's pretty busy explaining himself right now."

Grace switched topics. "What about the town? How bad is the damage?"

"So far, only the harbor front has flooded. Water's over the bulkhead and halfway up the park. It's slowed, but with tonight's high tide and that last blast from Florian coming through—" he paused, and she could hear the weight of responsibility in his voice. "Well, just say a prayer, Grace. And you and your sister stay put in Baltimore. Check with me before you try to get the Chief back here. I'll let you know when it's safe to come home."

Those were easy promises to make, but they'd be hard to live with. She disconnected, then called Avril. Now that Mac was safe, she wanted to be back in Mallard Bay with her children, but she got a rapid-fire grilling about Mac's condition, then another order to stay in Baltimore.

"We're all fine, and we're going to stay that way." The determination in Avril's voice was both reassuring and infuriating. "Fiona and Sonny are good as gold and are being entertained nonstop. People are stacked up like cordwood around the house, but everyone's pitching in." A roar of laughter drowned out her next words.

"So, basically, you're having a hurricane party?" Grace asked, surprised to find her eyes welling up.

"Margo may pass out from running around trying to stop stains before they happen, but other than that fusspot, everyone here is fine." Avril raised her voice and added, "No, Hallie! No more cookies for the children. Only broccoli and lean chicken, and their vitamins. No sweets."

"Very funny. I wish you could see me roll my eyes. Just remember, Sonny will throw up if he—"

"Got to go!" Avril hung up so quickly Grace wondered if her words had been prophetic.

She called Cyrus next, only to have Marjorie answer his phone. Grace didn't bother to ask why. Mosley's secretary had been answering his phone calls for decades. They were in speaker mode and the connection was scratchy, but both of them immediately demanded news of Mac's condition.

"We're on the second-floor sun porch watching the storm," Marjorie said cheerily when Grace's recital and their rounds of good wishes were finished. "Avril's in charge downstairs, so we're hiding out up here."

"How many people are actually in the house?" Grace asked, hoping Avril's "cordwood" description was an exaggeration.

"Lost count about an hour ago, m'dear," Mosley said. "Ruby Blanchard's family went to Avril's house to stay with the animals, but the space that move freed up was claimed before they got out of the driveway. Things are really buzzing downstairs. This is a happening place."

Grace couldn't remember the last time he'd sounded so happy. When she ran out of answers to Marjorie's endless questions, she turned the tables on them.

"What's the real-time forecast? It sounds like all the emergency preparations are in place." Going straight to The Bat for information would get her more details than relying on Trey. Marjorie wouldn't sugarcoat anything.

"Not as bad as originally predicted," Marjorie said. "But not enough of a shift to the south to keep us out of danger. The ground's so saturated, any significant amount of wind will uproot trees. We've had two tornado sightings in the last four hours, but none closer than ten miles—yet. Irene's house is the worst damage I've heard of so far. Tornadoes and flooding are the main worries over the next twenty-four hours. The timing with the tides is bad, too."

"Anything I can do from here?" She knew there wasn't but had to ask.

"Just take care of Mac," Mosley said.

"We have everything covered, and we'll be fine," The Bat said in a condescending tone. "We don't need you, but Mac does. Stephanie can't do everything, you know."

Grace was still sputtering indignantly when they hung up.

CHAPTER FIFTY-FOUR

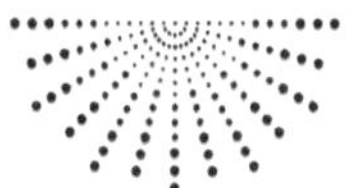

THURSDAY, SEPTEMBER 20

IRENE

Irene woke in the hospital to find a familiar face leaning over her bed. "You?" she croaked. "Are you qualified to be in here?"

"They let me out of the ER once in a while," Dr. Linbow said with a smile. "But only if I'm good. I told them a friend of mine was recovering from a bad experience, and I wanted to see how she was."

Irene studied him for a moment, then said, "Your friend gonna die?"

"Not until she's caused a whole lot more trouble." He patted her hand.

"Can you get a message to my granddaughter?"

"She's right outside—"

"I'll talk to her tomorrow. Maybe the next day. I'll be stronger then. For right now, you tell her I said to ask Lily Travers to come see me when the storm is over. Now, about that, is it as bad as the

TV people said it would be?" The look she gave Linbow squashed any ideas he had of lying.

"Bad enough that I'm here and not at home," he said.

Irene looked interested at that. "Your wife don't mind?"

"I'm sure she would if I had one." He watched her slow smile and wondered how long it would be before he was hearing exaggerated descriptions of her single granddaughter's attributes. "I need to go back to work," he said hastily. "And I'll give Ms. Pontello your message on my way out." Giving Irene his best smile, he picked up her chart. The staff in the telemetry wing was top-notch, but he wasn't taking any chances. He was still smarting over the antibiotic-antihistamine screwup.

"One more thing." Irene was drifting off, but she dredged up one last side-eye glare. "Tell my Dove she's safe now. We all are. The last devil's gone for good. And tell her I ain't havin' no dang hallucination."

CHAPTER FIFTY-FIVE

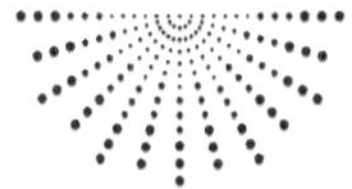

FRIDAY, SEPTEMBER 21

LILY

The early risers among the hurricane refugees gathered for breakfast at Delaney House on Friday morning and peppered Lily with questions about Kyle Thatcher's actions at Twin Corners. She reported what she could, glossed over the rest, then concentrated on her food as the spotlight shifted to Dove. Over the past two days, they had talked more honestly than they had in years, but Lily knew there was more coming. Dove had been at the hospital with her grandmother most of yesterday afternoon.

When Dove had finished giving updates on Irene's improving physical and mental health, she turned to Lily and said, "Reenie wants to see you. Alone."

"She's not still delirious, is she?" Lily asked warily.

When the laughter around the table died down, Dove said, "That's what I thought at first, but she set me straight really quick. Besides, she's being released tomorrow. You'd better go see her today while she's still relatively calm. She wants to apologize to you for the lies she told the sheriff."

"She doesn't need to—" Lily started, but Dove cut her off.

"Yes, she does. She wants to." After taking a deep breath, she looked around the table and added, "You're all going to hear a pretty shocking story about a baby my grandmother had when she was a teenager."

Only Avril and Marjorie showed no surprise.

Dove went on to repeat what had come out in her grandmother's conversations with Sheriff Carlisle. Once Irene's system was flushed clean of antihistamines and she'd gotten some rest, the first thing she talked about was her early pregnancy and the death of her premature baby. Learning that Mac was still out of commission, she had demanded to see the sheriff.

After explaining about Aaron, Irene admitted to taking extra doses of allergy medication when she couldn't sleep. When neither revelation prompted an arrest, she confessed to setting up the barrels to burn down the church and to 'shooting the devil' during the hurricane. Grant Carlisle still refused to charge her, so she insisted he hear a detailed account of everything she'd seen in the woods over the past year.

"I hadn't heard half of that stuff, obviously," Dove said. "Or if she talked about any of it, I wasn't listening. I'm not proud of that, but it does reinforce my decision to get Reenie into long-term care so she'll always have attention. The three of us can't go back to the life we had before, even if we rebuild the house, which we won't. She says she'll give it a go at Aunt Mimi's, but I'm not expecting that to work."

This set off a new round of questioning, and the more Dove revealed about the past few years as her grandmother's caretaker, the better she seemed to feel. She was able to unload her fears and worries on people who not only had her family's best interests at heart, but who were old enough to offer Dove a practical perspective from a senior citizen's viewpoint.

Descriptions of Irene's erratic behavior brought a chorus of

"I've done that!" and "That happened to me, too!" mixed with amateur diagnoses of dehydration, mixing prescription and over-the-counter drugs, and the devastating effects of long-term shame and fear. Eventually the group's conversation wound down to an argument over which local doctors were best suited to oversee Irene's continued recovery.

Lily left them debating medical practices and specialists, her mind already turning to the conversation waiting for her in Easton —and the apology she wasn't sure she was ready to hear.

The hospital room was quiet, with only muted background sounds from the hallways of the telemetry unit. Even in sleep, Irene's expression held a tension that seemed permanently etched into her weathered features. When her eyes fluttered open, she blinked several times, disoriented, before her gaze settled on Lily. Her voice rough with sleep, she said, "You came."

Lily leaned forward in the chair she'd pulled up beside the bed. "You asked for me."

"I did, didn't I? Where's that thingy that makes this bed go up?"

Lily found the remote-control cord while Irene got herself into a semi-sitting position. "Thank you," she said primly when she was settled. "I hear you found me."

"Grace and I both did. Dove told us where to look."

"Thank you for what you've done."

"You're welcome." Lily kept it simple. She sensed Irene was gathering her strength for a harder conversation.

"You know what happened to me? What that policeman tried to do? He hurt me and tried to blow up my house with me in it."

"Yes, ma'am. I know. He can't hurt you anymore," Lily said reassuringly, but Irene stilled frowned.

"That remains to be seen, don't it? More than one way to hurt a person."

"Miss Irene—"

"Oh, I shot him. I've already told that to the sheriff. Used Harvey's old service pistol. I meant to kill the devil, and I know I hit him, 'cause he went down, but then a big pain took me in my chest. A devil can do that, you know. I don't remember anything after that, and Dove won't tell me. What happened?"

Lily decided to bypass the issue of devils. After all, it was a pretty accurate description of Kyle Thatcher. "He made it down to Deer Creek. The medical examiner says he probably drowned."

Irene's fingers plucked restlessly at the thin hospital blanket as she absorbed the information. "Sheriff says he won't charge me for the shootin'. He said that State's Attorney woman won't prosecute me, neither. Seems that getting' blasted in the gut and gassed nearly to death is a good enough excuse to shoot a devil that's tryin' to kill you."

"Sounds reasonable to me," Lily agreed.

"I told the sheriff I set those barrels up to burn, but I can't for the life of me remember setting the fires. He told me the young man they found in Father's church was dead before the fire started, though." She looked away as she finished the last sentence.

"The young man was my brother, Josh."

Irene looked relieved. "So, you know about it."

"Yes, ma'am."

"Josh was your half-brother," Irene corrected. "Being truthful don't make your love for him any less, you know. If I've learned anything, that's it. Don't make things harder than they have to be and don't take on burdens that aren't yours to bear."

Lily didn't know what had sparked that comment, but she didn't think it had much to do with her. "Did you see them? Josh and—"

"The Devil," Irene said firmly. "That Kyle person. I saw 'em both a couple of times in the woods, but I was really confused back then. And real scared."

"I'm sorry," Lily said, knowing the standard response she'd get but unable to stop the words.

"Why?" Irene snapped. "It ain't your fault. That's what I've told the sheriff, too. None of what's happened is your fault, and I was wrong to say it was. But I panicked, so I lied. You were right there and easy to blame, just like when you were a child. I'm…I'm sorry, and *I* got reason to say it."

"Thank you." Lily realized it might be a long time before they were alone again. Irene's color was better, and she seemed to be breathing easily. She was also in a talkative mood, and that didn't happen often.

Lily decided to push a bit more.

CHAPTER FIFTY-SIX

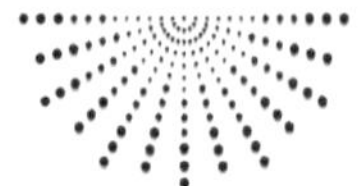

LILY

"What can you tell me about Josh? How long had he been in your woods?"

Irene smiled as if she'd been expecting the question. "I've been seeing Josh off and on since spring, not that I recognized him then, because I only saw him for a second or so each time. I didn't know who he was until I heard his name in the news. I should have recognized him though, even in the state he was in. Josh was always a skinny ringer for your daddy."

Lily managed another "Yes, ma'am," but Irene wasn't paying attention to her.

"I could always see Wayne in Josh's face and the way he moved." Abruptly, she refocused on Lily. "Did you know your daddy used to look out for Dove and me after Harvey died? Your mama did, too. I tried to be gracious, but I didn't have a good heart about it. Jealousy is a terrible thing. Poison. Your mama had a good man and all you good-lookin' kids." Her voice trailed off, and she closed her eyes.

Lily waited, absorbing the words. The math didn't work. Irene was a generation older than her parents. Surely, she hadn't had romantic feelings for a married father of five who had an angry wife and a vengeful girlfriend? Then, other memories popped up. Irene's complaints about the other kids in Dove's class. Her self-imposed isolation and the scowl that was always present unless she was looking at Dove. *Jealousy is a terrible thing.*

No, Lily thought. Irene hadn't had a thing for her father. She'd been jealous of their family. Despite everything that had happened to Wayne and Denise Travers, they'd stayed together, and their children—at least the girls—grew up healthy and reasonably happy.

"Your half-brother," Irene said suddenly. "A couple of days before the fire, I came across him in the woods—course, at the time I couldn't put a name to him, you understand?"

"Yes. When he died, he looked very different from the Josh we knew years ago."

"No, I mean that day in the woods, I only heard him. I was behind a stand of thorn bushes and him and that devil were fightin'. I couldn't have told you who they were, and I didn't understand much of what they were sayin', until one said he was gonna kill the other one. Well, I started yellin' my ownself then, and got back to the house and locked the doors. I tried to tell Dove that night, but she got mad at me for being in the woods."

Irene stopped and licked her lips. Lily held a cup of water for her while she drank. "Did you see either of them again?" she asked when Irene finished and leaned back on her pillows.

"The afternoon before the fire. He was stumbling through the edge of the woods right out where I could see him from the den window. That straightened my brain up right fast. A good scare'll do that, you know?"

She did, but Lily only said, "What did you do?"

"Nothing." Irene's eyes stayed steady on Lily's face. "And I'll never forgive myself. But by the time I was thinkin' right, he was gone. I decided to call the police but stopped myself because Dove had been saying how I was seeing things that aren't there. So, in the end, I let it be."

Lily weighed her options—leave while things were peaceful or get the truth about the night Josh died. In the end, it wasn't a hard choice. "Who set the trash barrels on fire?" she asked quietly.

Irene closed her eyes again and was silent so long that Lily reached over and gently checked her pulse.

To her surprise, Irene placed her free hand on top of Lily's and patted it. "I'm fine. Just tryin' to decide how to put this so you'll know I'm not lyin'."

"Whatever you tell me, Miss Irene. I'll believe you."

"You've got no reason to."

Seconds ticked by, then a minute. A food cart rattled by in the hallway but didn't stop. Lily checked the time and knew they'd soon be interrupted. "Miss Irene? Please tell me what happened. I need to know so I can let it go. You understand how that feels, right?"

When Irene finally answered, her words were clear and firm. "The devil and I both set the church on fire. I doubt he'd have thought of it if I hadn't already put those barrels by the back wall. I planned to go out late that night and set them all on fire. I'd been planning and getting ready for it for weeks. I was going to watch, and when it got going real good, I'd call the fire department and do my hysterical act."

"Why?"

Irene was still contrite, but she hadn't lost her cranky attitude. "Don't interrupt! I'll lose what little train of thought I've got left." She tried to take a deep breath, gasped at the pain it caused. "I wanted to burn that building down so Avril and her friends would go away, and no one would ever live there. The place where my Aaron sleeps is too close to the church's property line. I can't have people traipsing around back there. Over him. What if they brought in bulldozers and one of them went too far onto my side…"

"Of course." Lily took Irene's hand again, holding it gently. She guessed Dove hadn't told her grandmother that Aaron wasn't in the woods anymore. "I can't imagine how much pain that caused you."

"Gettin' the barrels ready wore me out. I only meant to rest a bit, but when I woke, it was way later than I'd planned. I'll never know for sure, but by my reckoning, the devil must have beaten me to the church. The barrels were burnin' good by then, and the church wall was catchin'. It was so different in real life than when I was sitting in my rocker dreamin' it all up. That's when I called you. Dove always said I could trust you, and she left your number by the phone for me. I was so mixed up and fuzzy, I did what she told me without thinking."

Irene's admission of such frailty caught Lily off guard. She opened her mouth to speak, but Irene raised a shaky hand to stop her.

"Your mama and daddy gave you a good life, despite the troubles they had. I tried my best, but I couldn't do that for my children. Aaron, Debbie, Dove—all of 'em deserved so much better than what they got. Little Brooklyn will have it better, though. Her mama will see to that. But poor Josh. Poor boy."

Lily held her hand and said, "A wise woman just told me not to take on burdens that weren't mine to bear. It's very good advice, you know. Josh's death isn't your fault, Irene. You couldn't have helped him, and he wouldn't want you to be sad."

Irene wiped her face with the edge of a bedsheet. "I'll never forget him. Do you know why?" She waited for an answer, never taking her eyes from Lily's face.

"Yes, ma'am," Lily said. "I know why."

"That's good. Dove will tell me in her own time, I suppose, but I want you to know how happy it makes me. You're a good girl, Lily Travers. You always have been."

CHAPTER FIFTY-SEVEN

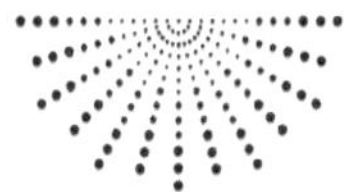

SATURDAY, SEPTEMBER 22

Grace picked her way carefully across the Travers' yard, sidestepping puddles and tree branches. A small birdhouse lay wedged in a shrub by the steps of Denise's front porch, and the twisted remains of what had once been a garden trellis were stacked on top of a nearby pile of debris. It had been two days since the edge of Hurricane Florian had torn across Kingston County and evidence of the storm's fury remained everywhere she looked. Blue tarps covered a section of Denise's roof where shingles had been ripped away, and the steady drone of a generator hummed. Home-owners near the water had fared much worse, but Denise would be making significant repairs in the months to come.

Lily waited on the porch, a smile easing the signs of stress on her tired face. "Thanks for coming out. I didn't want to leave Mom right now."

"No problem. I was glad for an excuse to escape town. Between wrangling the kids and Rocky in a three-room apartment, I'm losing my mind, but I know you have more serious issues."

"We were pretty lucky," Lily said. "It's mostly wind damage and minimal flooding out in the fields. The barn took a huge hit, though. It's a total loss. And we're still on generator power." She gestured toward the utility poles along the driveway, several of which leaned at precarious angles. "Lots of people have it worse. Alexa and Emily made out okay, but Twila's family will be here with Mom for a good while. The roof fell in over their kitchen, and the house is almost a total loss."

"That's terrible," Grace said just as a child's cry of outrage split the air and a screaming match over who ate the last Pop Tart drowned out any chance of further conversation.

"Come on!" Lily trotted down the steps and led her toward what was left of the barn. "Pretend you want to see the damage out here, and we may be able to hear ourselves think."

As they took a slow turn around the half-flattened building, Lily asked about Mac's recovery.

"The swelling is way down, but the bite wound is still painful, and the antibiotics make him nauseous, but all in all, he's good. Except for having to sleep on one of the sofas in the rear parlor. He isn't up to climbing to the third floor with me and the kids yet."

Lily filled her in on Irene as they stood beside the tangled remains of Denise's vegetable garden. When she finished, Grace said, "What about Dove? Have you talked to her?"

Worry lines deepened on Lily's forehead. "At first she seemed to be as eager as I was to know for sure if Brooklyn is Josh's child."

"And how does she seem now?"

"Really nervous. And upset with me, I think. Remember when you asked me if there had been DNA testing? Well, I decided it was time for that. I have a contact at a private lab in Delaware. Dove agreed to let me run DNA tests on a toothbrush of Brooklyn's. My friend called with the preliminary results a couple of hours ago. Brooklyn looks like a biological match with me, which means Josh could be her father. Dove got really upset when I told her."

"Because if those results are confirmed, she'll have to tell her ex-husband he's not Brooklyn's father?"

"I think Dom's the main reason," Lily said. "She's scared of him, and she doesn't want to lose those support checks. I understand, but I'm still hurt, and now I don't know what to tell Mom and the girls."

At a loss for a helpful suggestion, Grace said, "Dove is staying with you, right? What will happen when Brooklyn comes back?"

Lily threw her arms out in a gesture of helplessness. "Dove has known for five years that Brooklyn might be Josh's. She played both sides of the fence on it, deliberately encouraging a relationship between Brooklyn and me—teaching her to call me Auntie Lily. But all the while she let Dom and his rich parents think Brooklyn's theirs."

"Good grief, Lily! You make her sound—"

"Desperate. And even more so now. She's flat broke. Mac told me she gave a lengthy statement detailing how she met Thatcher, and his persistent pursuit of her. She was devastated when she learned he used her and Brooklyn to keep Josh quiet. You know, a 'turn me in and they'll pay the price' kind of deal."

"But how do the police know that? Thatcher and Josh are both dead."

"Let's talk about that later." Lily was looking over Grace's shoulder.

"You girls come on over here for some iced tea." Denise came up behind them and set a tray on a wrought iron garden table. "We've got ice thanks to the generator."

After giving Grace a hug and pouring the tea, Denise said, "I guess Lily's been telling you that Josh's former supervisor with the Baltimore Police Department, Captain Morrow, called me yesterday?" Denise's voice wavered slightly as she looked between them, then sighed. "Fine. You two keep your secrets. He told me about the operation Josh was involved in. How he'd been working undercover for the last two years, infiltrating a crime syndicate."

"Mac told me a little," Grace said. Mac had actually told her a lot, most of which she couldn't repeat.

Denise said, "Josh had an excellent record before his partner was promoted and began to oversee his work. Captain Morrow said the only concern they had at first was that Kyle Thatcher would favor Josh, and for a while that seemed to be what was happening. Josh was making mistakes, and Kyle made excuses for him. Eventually, it was all straightened out, and everyone knows the truth."

Grace looked at Lily, who murmured, "Wait for it."

"Captain Morrow says Josh is a hero. Kyle Thatcher stabbed him and started the fires."

Grace knew that empty gas cans had been found in the trunk of Thatcher's car, but she was surprised that Josh's captain had been so forthcoming.

Denise said, "I believe he's genuinely sorry that they weren't able to uncover the truth sooner and arrest that awful man before he killed poor Josh."

"And I believe it was really lucky for the nice captain that he called you and not me," Lily said.

Denise reached out and rubbed her daughter's shoulder. "Please try to let it go, honey. After all, Josh knew his work was dangerous, and he played an important role in bringing a crime syndicate down."

"I'm sure there will be a lot of other people in line for credit, too, Mom. But what were they doing while Thatcher was sabotaging the task force, feeding information to the syndicate, warning them about raids, and identifying undercover officers?" Lily asked. "It took the brass a year to realize what was going on. A year Josh was on his own with Thatcher's lies turning everyone against him."

Denise rose and smiled at Grace. "Captain Morrow couldn't give me details, but he said that before he died, Josh found a way to communicate without Thatcher knowing. The captain promised that soon everyone will know what a brave man Josh was."

"Some of us have always known," Lily said.

"And some of us needed some help in seeing the truth." Denise leaned down and cupped Lily's chin, turning it gently to look in her eyes. "I love you." Then, with a smile for Grace, she left.

"That woman always gets the better of me." Lily scrounged a crumpled tissue from her jeans pocket and blew her nose.

"I can see that. Want to tell me the rest of the story?"

"There is no 'rest' yet, but Desi Marbury came to see me this morning."

"She was at Delaney House last night bending Mac's ear, too, but he didn't share any details."

Lily looked surprised. "Well, I'm not a cop, and I see no reason to keep any of it secret. Remember how I complained to you about Carlisle's search team not finding Josh's campsite? Well, they must have been right behind me when I searched it—it's a wonder I didn't get caught and arrested. Anyway, most of Josh's stuff, including the box with the notebook, is safe in the Sheriff's Office evidence locker, but they didn't get it cataloged and copied to Baltimore PD and the state police until yesterday. No fingerprints other than Josh's, and there's not much of interest other than the bloodstains and the notebook."

"Have you had time to study the notes you photographed? Was there anything useful in them?"

"Yes." Lily was perking up. Her morose attitude was gone, and she leaned closer to Grace. "The notebook mostly contained surveillance notes on Dove and Brooklyn, plus some recent entries about Kyle. But Desi called me because Josh had written something else—a coded email address in the margin of one of the pages."

"Did you know what it meant?"

"It was the same format as his old Gmail account—family dates and initials. I recognized the pattern because we used to email when I was deployed. I told Desi I thought it was the front half of an email address. I also suggested a password that might work."

"You thought it might work because you'd already tried it?"

"I haven't been sleeping much since I found that notebook, so I've had time to mess around on the computer."

The dark circles under Lily's eyes backed up the insomnia claim but didn't answer Grace's question. "Will anyone be able to tell you've been into the account?"

"Sure. I wasn't trying to hide it. I didn't alter anything, just read the emails that pertained to our family. That's how I know, and now Desi knows, that Thatcher used Dove and Brooklyn to blackmail Josh into keeping quiet."

"Desi knows you read the emails?"

"Yeah. My ears are still ringing. But she told me one of the details from Josh's autopsy that had never been released. The same code was written on the inside of Josh's left arm. They found a pen near his body and think he wrote it after he was in the church but before the fire started. Desi says he probably knew he was dying and was afraid Kyle would find the notebook and destroy it. That email account also has the evidence Josh collected after Kyle started sabotaging him."

Grace thought about that. "So, when Kyle ruined his credibility, Josh recorded what he learned in the emails as he tried to clear himself."

"And in the meantime, he kept watch over Dove and their daughter. One email he wrote said he had named Brooklyn as the beneficiary of his life insurance and pension, including any line of duty death benefits. Maybe that will give Dove the guts—and the money—to get Dom out of their lives for good."

"Josh was a brave man," Grace said. "I think that might be a family trait."

CHAPTER FIFTY-EIGHT

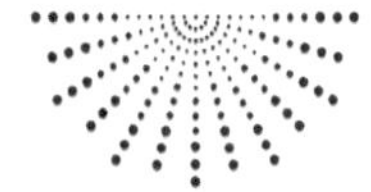

FRIDAY, OCTOBER 24

The attic apartment at Delaney House had low, slanted ceilings and dormer windows that caught the afternoon sun. Grace sat on the tiny love seat in the sitting room, folding laundry and letting her mind wander as the children lay transfixed in front of the small television. *Bluey* was their current favorite show, and she had no heart for enforcing screen time limits on a rainy afternoon.

"Go home, Mama?" Fiona said, sitting up suddenly. It was a common occurrence, and once reassured that they would, indeed, be going home soon, she sank back down on the rug, content with her show.

Grace hoped their contractor would finish the repairs to their septic system by next week. Being back in her once-beloved apartment had quickly lost its charm.

Laughter floated up from downstairs, followed by the sound of several people talking at once. Delaney House had gradually transformed from an elegant country inn to a communal home. With the exception of Grace's family, no one displaced by the hurricane was in a hurry to leave.

Cyrus's contractor estimated it would take at least three more months to complete the remediation from the foot of water that flooded his brick rancher on the south side of Mallard Bay's Harbor. Marjorie's home on Swan Point wouldn't be habitable until next spring. Jeannie and Trey Harper's home was missing half its roof and had suffered extensive water damage. Mother and son were sharing a two-room suite on the second floor of Delaney House for the foreseeable future.

Avril showed no signs of leaving either, even though the minimal wind damage to her property had been repaired weeks ago. Hallie lived alone in the house, but it was temporary. She was leaving for College Park in January. Avril and Grace had made a pact not to discuss the hole the departure of their young friend would leave in their lives. Grace knew Avril was staying at Delaney House to make it easier for Hallie to move on.

She went out into the hallway outside the apartment and listened to snatches of the conversations from the first-floor hall. The late afternoon tea and cocktail hour was well underway. Someone asked for quiet. Stephanie.

Grace smiled. Her sister was really going to do it. After months of scheming and reasoning and grasping at straws, she had decided on a new life—one that didn't include late night drives to New Jersey, or settling for half a life with a man who didn't love her anymore.

After looking over her shoulder to check that the children were still glued to the television screen, Grace moved closer to the railing to listen to Stephanie repeat the announcement she and Mac had heard the night before.

"My new attorney filed our response to Jerry's divorce petition yesterday. My soon-to-be ex-husband can have his mother and his girlfriend. I know my girls will come around to my side before long, and when they do, I'll be able to give them a real home, in a good place with wonderful people. Thanks to all of you, and my sister, of course, I have that now."

Even while she rolled her eyes at Stephanie's over-the-top performance, Grace felt a heady mixture of excitement and relief. Her Mallard Bay family was expanding again, and however that turned out, she was ready for it.

———

"Do you think she'll really do it?" Mac had asked her the night before when the children were finally asleep and they were alone for the first time all day.

"Well, she's giving it a shot." Grace climbed into bed beside him and snuggled down. "I overheard Avril and Marjorie hatching a plan to reinvent Stephanie and fix her life. Avril said she can't rest on her laurels indefinitely and she needs help starting over."

"Stephanie has laurels?"

"She saved you from a six-foot copperhead."

"You mean a three-foot water snake."

Grace laughed. "Depends on who's telling the story, doesn't it?"

Mac gathered her up in a hug. "Are you okay?"

She thought about her children sleeping a few feet away and the people in the rooms below. Then she thought about the wake they would attend the day after tomorrow, and the brave young man who would never come home again.

"Grace?" Mac raised up to peer at her in the darkness. "Are you crying?"

"No," she said, even though she was. "Everything happens for a reason, and where we are right now feels right. For all the damage the hurricane did, some good came of it too."

"You mean Avril finally having the full house she always wanted?"

"I mean all of us settling here together, if only for a little while. I can't wait to go home, but right now, in this minute, I'm so grateful and I wouldn't change a thing."

CHAPTER FIFTY-NINE

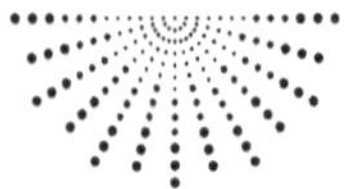

SUNDAY, OCTOBER 26

"It would have been easier to have a funeral," Denise Travers said.

Lily glared at her mother, and Grace quickly backed out of the kitchen to avoid their argument. When she had volunteered to help set up for Josh's wake, she hadn't anticipated having to referee the Travers family's constant bickering.

Rain splattered the windows in the dining room, adding to the tension in the house. They had a number of chores to finish before the guests started arriving at noon. Plans for outdoor dining had been scrapped when a warm front arrived overnight, bringing showers reminiscent of April instead of November. Nature seemed off balance with bare trees outside and window air conditioners running at full blast.

Grace could hear Lily's strident words clearly through the closed kitchen door. "For the last damn time, Mom, we'll have a funeral. All the bells and whistles and honor guards and graveside tributes. Anything you want, but not now."

Josh's death was still being investigated, as was Kyle Thatcher's, and until both were closed, Lily refused to hold a funeral for her brother. As the executor of his will, Josh's remains and his estate were under her control, and she was holding steadfast, but Grace knew it was at a personal cost. When Lily had proposed this gathering of friends and relatives to celebrate Josh's life and remember the good times they'd had, it had seemed to be the ideal interim solution to keep Denise happy. But in the three weeks since the event was announced, Denise had slowly expanded every aspect of the intimate affair Lily had envisioned, and now they were getting ready for more than a hundred people to gather at the Travers farm. In the rain.

The wake had thinned out and settled down to a manageable gathering when Grace found Mac near the drinks table, smiling politely as an elderly neighbor described in excruciating detail the water damage to her basement. Grace interrupted with news of a fresh platter of cold cuts and pastries in the dining room and gave her husband a hug as the space around them cleared.

"How many more times can you hear about the hurricane before your brain liquefies?" she asked.

He took a long pull from a bottle of Natty Boh and said, "My limit was three hours ago, but here we are."

"Well, Lily, Denise, and Dove seem to have made peace, or are putting on a good front."

"Looks like it, but I've picked up some interesting tidbits as I've made the rounds."

"Such as?"

Mac motioned toward the corner, where Father Stephen was now speaking quietly with Irene and Avril. "Irene's doing much better now that her baby's had a real service and is next to Harvey and Debbie in the churchyard at St. Mary's."

"Irene had them moved from the Twin Corners cemetery?"

Mac smiled. "Indeed, she did. And she told the owners of the church property that they could do what they liked with her father and his multigenerational family in their cemetery, as long as they didn't relocate them to St. Mary's."

Grace laughed. "Miss Irene got her spunk back real fast, didn't she?"

"Yep. Think we can scoot out now? I could use some quiet time before we head back to the madhouse."

A familiar squeal came from the back porch and was immediately followed by loud sobbing. Grace sighed and said, "I don't think anyone will mind if we leave as long as we take our kids."

They made their rounds, offering condolences and support, and promising to check in with Denise, Dove, and Irene in the coming days. As they were leaving, they overheard Avril giving Irene what sounded like a sales pitch on a room at Delaney House.

"It's so comfortable there. Cyrus and Marjorie and Jeannie and Trey Harper. Grace's sister is there, too. And even when Grace and Mac take the kids and go home, they'll still be in and out all the time. There's a beautiful bedroom I know you will love. Right across the hall from me. Nice and bright, and it's near the sun porch."

Grace slowed down, but Mac tugged on her hand, pulling her away from the conversation and down the front steps. Fiona and Sonny trotted along beside them, talking nonstop about the desserts they'd eaten.

"Think we'll get out of the attic apartment before Avril hires an entertainment director and starts mandatory exercise periods?" Mac asked, giving her a hopeful look.

"Next week with any luck." She laughed at his theatrical groan of relief.

"That's one problem down, but seriously, Grace, how long can you let your business operate as a hostel for the ancient and eccentric?"

"You forgot my sister," Grace teased.

"Oh, no, I didn't."

He laughed at the look she gave him and repeated his question, but Grace kept her answer to herself. They'd made enough adjustments in the past three weeks, and she would wait a while to tell him they would be the only ones leaving Delaney House.

The old mansion was a home once again, and she didn't see that changing anytime soon.

THE END

Thank you for reading LONG TIME COMING!

Want more Eastern Shore?

I'd love to give you a **FREE** Grace Reagan novella when you sign up for my monthly newsletter on my website: www.Cheril-Thomas.com.

You'll get all the news about new releases, works in progress, and life here on the Eastern Shore. And there's that **free** novella, ***Borrowed Trouble***. I really hope you'll join the newsletter family!

A Note About the "Hurricane Book"

The first draft of *Long Time Coming* was written prior to the horrifying storms and floods in the fall of 2024. I seriously considered shelving it in deference to those who were impacted, but after much internal debate, I rewrote large sections of the story instead.

I lessened the effect of the hurricane on Mallard Bay, moving the point of landfall further south and omitting detailed descriptions of the destruction my fictional storm might have logically caused. Hurricane Florian was never meant to be more than a backdrop to the events transpiring in Mallard Bay and Kingston County. No series set on the Eastern Shore would be complete without at least one hurricane storyline—storm preparation and response are part of the fabric of life here.

Thanks to our wonderful local police and emergency services departments, in most cases we citizens only need to follow weather alerts and local preparedness guidelines. This blessing usually leaves us plenty of time to raid the stores for toilet paper. (Yes, I am guilty. Please don't ask about the Thomas family's emergency stash of cookies and dog treats, or the enormous number of paperback books we assemble for emergency reading.)

I've wanted to be a writer since I read my first book. I treasure the hours when I can escape into a fictional world, and my goal has always been to give that pleasure to my readers. I hope you've enjoyed *Long Time Coming*. And I hope that wherever you are is a safe and happy place with a comfy chair, excellent coffee, and a tall stack of good books.

Happy reading!

Love,

Cheril

ACKNOWLEDGEMENTS

If you have read my notes at the end of earlier books in this series (bless you!) you'll know that I'm perpetually trying to corral my characters into telling the story I want to write. And after much handwringing and angst, I always end up telling their story as they want it told. So this time, I saved myself the battle and let the latest mystery in Mallard Bay unfold naturally. The characters emerged as they wanted, did as they pleased, and solved their own problems.

Well, let me tell you, that was a mess! I had to find the story among all their viewpoints, but when I did, I liked it. (Even if I had to whittle down a *very* long and winding tale to get to the book you've just read.) Fortunately, I have wonderful first readers and a skilled and very patient editor, without whom I'd be lost.

Heartfelt thanks to First Readers Cindy Haddaway, Judith Hohman, Tarah Kleinert, and Roxanne Tury. This book is dedicated to them with love and much appreciation for their eagle-eye editing and kindness. Thanks to them, certain characters don't wander into scenes before their time, and Grace doesn't "yelp."

My sister, Clara Ellingson, is always the *first* First Reader of the rough draft of my books. *In the Absence of Truth* was dedicated to her. God bless her, her first words after reading "The End" are always, "I *loved* it!" Every author needs a support system like mine.

My wonderful editor, Elaine Hyatt, of Clarity Editing Services, has once again worked her magic with my manuscript, and I am, as always, in awe of her talents and skills. She is a treasure.

Another year, another book, and another acknowledgement that

I couldn't produce these stories without the loving support of my wonderful family, especially my sweet husband, Ron. As I write this, he's wrangling Miss Ellie into her harness for a walk so that I can finish the last words of this book without a 40-pound dog drooling on my keyboard. I love you, Sweetie.

Finally, thanks to everyone who reads my stories. I am eternally grateful.

Cheril

I'm so grateful for all of my readers and hope you'll stay in touch.

You can find me on Facebook at CherilThomas.EasternShore-Mysteries

I love getting email, too. Drop me a line at Cheril@Cheril-Thomas.com. Or check out my website and send a message on the link at the bottom of the main page: www.CherilThomas.com.

Want to see the whole Eastern Shore Mysteries series? Check out my Amazon Author Page: www.amazon.com/author/cherilthomas

Until next time, happy reading!
Cheril

ABOUT THE AUTHOR

Cheril Thomas is the author of the Eastern Shore Mysteries series, numerous short stories, and articles. When she's not writing at home in Easton, Maryland, she's traveling with her long-suffering husband, an otherwise brilliant soul who for some reason doesn't mind being married to a woman who researches methods of murder. Their lives are ruled by a bossy little spaniel named Ellie Grace.

Connect with Cheril on her website and sign up to get the latest news from the Eastern Shore Mysteries. You'll receive a FREE short story as a welcome gift!
www.cherilthomas.com